"Would you like to make love with me?"

Cal caught his breath at Elizabeth's question. "I don't think that would be a good idea."

"Because I'd like to make love with you," she added, as if he hadn't spoken.

"You're still upset about last night, Elizabeth. If we made love, you'd regret it later."

"Are you saying you don't want me?"

Cal knew she could feel his arousal. "No. You know better than that."

"Then why won't you?"

"Because you're still on shaky emotional ground and I'd be taking advantage of that. It would be a shabby thing for me to do."

He jumped with surprise when she suddenly touched his chin. "If that's what's stopping you, then let me take advantage of you," she said.

He covered her hand with his. *God, how he wanted her.*

"I need you, Cal," she whispered. "And you need me, too, whether you know it or not."

He did need her. And he knew it. Knew it in his heart . . . in his aching body . . . knew it in his soul.

ABOUT THE AUTHOR

Both Elizabeth Bartlett and Cal Potts—the hero and heroine of *Running on Empty*—were introduced in Kay Wilding's American Romance #340, *Rainbow's End*. Writing the earlier romance, Kay became interested in the couple and decided they deserved a book of their own.

Kay Wilding lives in Atlanta, Georgia, with her husband and their two children. When she's not writing, she's usually reading or working crossword puzzles.

Books by Kay Wilding
HARLEQUIN AMERICAN ROMANCE

340–RAINBOW'S END
390–STAND BY ME

Don't miss any of our special offers. Write to us at the following address for information on our newest releases.

Harlequin Reader Service
P.O. Box 1397, Buffalo, NY 14240
Canadian address: P.O. Box 603,
Fort Erie, Ont. L2A 5X3

KAY
WILDING

RUNNING
ON
EMPTY

Harlequin Books

TORONTO • NEW YORK • LONDON
AMSTERDAM • PARIS • SYDNEY • HAMBURG
STOCKHOLM • ATHENS • TOKYO • MILAN

Published November 1991

ISBN 0-373-16415-7

RUNNING ON EMPTY

Part One

Chapter One

Cal Potts might never have met Elizabeth Bartlett if he hadn't stopped to tie his shoelace. Much later, he wondered what his life might have been like if he hadn't.

It happened on a crystal clear, blue sky morning in early spring of his junior year in high school, after he'd been practicing sprint starts for the better part of an hour. He was hot and sweaty but also fired with enthusiasm, feeling good about himself and life in general. Practice had gone well. His team was a cinch to win the upcoming track meet and he was almost sure that he personally could take at least one first place, probably two, maybe even three if he was lucky.

He grinned, feeling lucky.

He was about to follow his teammates down the tunnel leading from the athletic field to the locker rooms when he saw that one of his cleats had come untied. Stopping to re-tie it, he paused another moment before heading inside. Inhaling the sweet scent of freshly mowed grass and feeling the warmth of the sun on his skin, Cal decided his mother was right—South Georgia was God's chosen place on earth, especially on days like this. Later in the year, even the mornings would be hazy with the combined heat and humidity, but not now in early spring. Today was about as perfect as a day could be. Today was the kind of day you would remember for the rest of your life.

He saw a flicker of movement out of the corner of his eye and turned his head, watching as the freshman girls' phys-ed class trotted onto the field to play soccer. They were all dressed alike in the bright red cotton gym shorts and ridic-ulous orange shirts that everyone in the school hated.

Their school colors were supposed to be maroon and gold, but for the past year all the uniforms had been red and orange. Some people said the mix-up occurred be-cause the school secretary who ordered supplies was color-blind. Others insisted that their normally straitlaced prin-cipal had gone astray and was being blackmailed by a sexy traveling saleslady. Cal personally preferred that idea, but whatever the reason, the uniforms were so bad that all the school teams refused to wear them.

As one of the stars of the track team, Cal was dressed in plain white shorts, no shirt. Feeling superior, he stood at the top of the tunnel and surveyed the new crop of fresh-men girls, planning to report his findings later on to his teammates.

Not bad, he thought, letting his gaze linger on a group of six or eight girls laughing and talking animatedly. Not bad at all.

Then he saw her.

She was tall and slim and had long dark hair tied back from her face with some kind of ribbon. She was standing at the edge of the group of girls, not laughing like the oth-ers, with them but apart from them. He briefly wondered about her, then shifted his eyes to continue the survey. A few moments later something—he wasn't sure what—caused him to look in her direction again. He was sur-prised to find her watching him, too, and all of a sudden he felt a tightening in his groin and an emotion so intense it made him catch his breath.

She hadn't done anything to cause it; she hadn't even moved. She simply stood there straight and tall in her baggy uniform, her long legs glistening in the morning sunshine, staring back at him across the athletic field. Somehow, though, he felt as if he'd just had a huge kick in the mid-section.

At seventeen, Cal was no longer a virgin, but he didn't go chasing everything in skirts like some guys he knew, either. Not that he didn't like girls; it was just that other things were more important. Tops on his list was getting out of this one-horse town, once and for all. The most likely way Cal could see to do that was to win an athletic scholarship to college, maybe even go on to play pro basketball after graduation. That's where the big money was. After that, there'd be plenty of time for girls... all he wanted, and expensive cars and boats, too. Some day he might even come back to Planters' Junction, just for a visit, of course, and show all the snobs and hypocrites what he'd accomplished.

He could see his mother's face when she showed him off to her friends at the mill. "Cal's the first one in our family to go to college!" she'd say with a big, broad smile.

Yeah, that was the kind of future Cal wanted. In the meantime, he needed to concentrate on taking care of his body and improving his athletic skills. Girls were a distraction, and sometimes even dangerous. Hadn't Joey Grove had to drop out of high school last winter because he'd knocked up that girl and her old man came after Joey with a shotgun to make him marry her?

There were plenty of other horror stories like Joey's, too, Cal told himself as he continued looking at the long-legged girl across the field. Plenty. Still...he couldn't seem to tear his gaze away from her. Something in her called out to him. Which was a pretty stupid thing to think, he reminded himself. But it wouldn't hurt if he went over and talked to her for a minute, would it? Just long enough to find out her name. What could be the harm in that?

Casually flinging a towel around his neck, Cal sauntered down the stadium steps and headed for the playing field where the dark-haired girl was standing. Halfway there, he suddenly wondered what the hell he was doing. It was too

late to turn back without looking like an idiot, though, so
he kept going.

OH, DEAR LORD, he's coming over here! Elizabeth Bartlett
thought, feeling her heart start to beat faster. She'd never
dreamed he would do something so daring. It must take a
lot of courage to approach a girl you didn't know and start
talking to her in front of an entire soccer field of onlook-
ers.

Of course, he might be coming over to talk to one of the
other girls, or even the coach, she told herself. But she
didn't believe that, not for a moment. His eyes on her were
too intent. He was coming to *her*. What would he say?
What would she say? What *could* she say? Her mind was a
complete blank, void of everything except the fact that he
was approaching, getting nearer by the moment. He'd soon
be here, standing in front of her, so close she could reach
out and touch him . . . if she dared. She took a couple of
steps away from the girls she'd been standing with and
waited for him.

"Hi," he said. "Nice morning for soccer."

She'd only seen him from a distance before; he was even
more gorgeous close up. "If you like soccer," she replied,
wondering where that remark had come from. She adored
soccer; it was her favorite sport to play. Why had she said
such a stupid thing?

"You don't like it?" he asked.

She shrugged. "It beats archery." He laughed, and she
was starting to relax a little, until she noticed that the other
girls had stopped talking and were now watching them with
undisguised interest. *Well, let them watch!* she thought defiantly.

"My name's Cal Potts," he said.

"I know."

He lifted one black brow. "Oh?"

Oh, dear. She should never had admitted she knew who
he was. Now she'd have to explain it, and she certainly
couldn't tell him she'd secretly been watching him—from

a distance, of course—for months. "I, uh, saw you play on the basketball team last winter."

"Does that mean you like basketball better than archery, too?"

She saw the sparkle of mischief in his gray eyes and was delighted that he had a sense of humor on top of everything else, which included the best-looking body she'd ever seen. "It's no contest," she said, carefully keeping her eyes trained on his face so she wouldn't start drooling over his broad, smooth chest glistening with perspiration.

"What's your name?" he asked.

She felt someone grab her arm before she could reply and turned to see her friend Nora Jane Perkins. "Elizabeth, come on," Nora Jane said with uncharacteristic urgency. "The coach has already blown the whistle for class to start."

"You go ahead," Elizabeth said, disengaging her arm from Nora Jane's grasp. "I'll be along in a minute."

Frowning, Nora Jane looked as if she might say more, but then she shrugged and walked away. Elizabeth turned back to Cal. Neither of them spoke. Then, seeing Cal shift from one foot to the other and adjust the towel around his neck, she knew he was getting ready to leave. Frantically she searched her mind for some meaningful parting remark. "Well..." she finally said, extending her hand, "it was nice meeting you, Cal."

Stupid, stupid, stupid! she thought, even before she saw the look of surprise that crossed his face before he shook hands with her. No girl in her right mind would invite a cute guy to shake hands with her! Cal probably thought she was an awkward, immature freshman...for which she couldn't blame him because that's exactly the way she was acting right now.

"Nice meeting you, too, Elizabeth," he said. "I'll call you sometime and we can talk some more."

How can you call me when you don't even know my last name? she thought. She knew he was just being polite. They *both* knew she'd already blown it with him. "I'd like that," she said. "The phone's listed in my father's name—James Bartlett."

He nodded and turned to leave. Elizabeth stared at his back for a moment before heading across the athletic field to join her phys-ed class, feeling as dejected, rejected, and all-around miserable as she'd ever been in her life. Cal Potts had been interested in her. *Cal Potts!* And she'd spoiled the whole thing by acting silly and immature. How embarrassing! What on earth would he think of her! *Probably nothing,* she was forced to admit. He'd probably already put her out of his mind and she'd never hear from him again.

MAKING HIS WAY DOWN to the locker-room showers, Cal couldn't put Elizabeth Bartlett out of his mind. He tried to think of something wrong with her, but couldn't do that either. She was about as perfect as a girl could get.

For starters, she looked terrific. Her long, slender legs and her small, sharp breasts really turned him on. They were sexier than any other girl's in school. Up close, he'd been able to see that her hair was more auburn than brown, and he liked that, too—a redhead! And her eyes—he'd never seen anything like them. They were deep, deep green, and tilted up at the corners to make her look oriental. Mysterious. Then there was the way she trained those deep green beauties on him, looking him straight in the eye...making him think they were the only two people on earth.

Remembering, he started to sweat all over again. Was it possible to be halfway in love with someone you'd only just met? And she'd as much as told him she liked him, too. She'd watched him play basketball and knew who he was, and said she'd like it if he called her. Most girls he knew would never have admitted such things, but Elizabeth did. And she even shook hands with him. He'd never shaken hands with a girl before, at least as far as he could remember. Only Elizabeth would be open and honest enough to do a thing like that.

"What are you grinning about?"

Cal tried to hide his surprise when he saw his friend and fellow track-team member Quint Richards. He'd been so engrossed in thoughts of Elizabeth that he hadn't even noticed when he entered the locker room. "I was just thinking about practice today," Cal lied. No way was he going to mention his discovery of Elizabeth Bartlett. Even though they were best friends, Cal knew Quint would tease him, and he wanted to keep Elizabeth all to himself, like a secret treasure.

"Yeah," Quint said. "It was great. I think you're a cinch to win two first places against East Central High."

Cal thought so, too, but didn't want to seem immodest so he merely shrugged. "And you have the 220 in the bag," he said, taking the towel from around his neck and using it to swat Quint on the rear end. "Let's hit the showers."

"DO YOU REALIZE WHO you were talking to?" Nora Jane asked.

"Certainly," Elizabeth replied.

"That was Cal Potts!" Nora Jane said in a loud stage whisper, answering her own question as if Elizabeth hadn't spoken.

"So?"

"You shouldn't be talking to *him!*"

"You're just jealous. Isn't he the best-looking guy you've ever seen?"

"I am *not* jealous," Nora Jane said. "And no, he's not the best-looking guy I've ever seen."

"I think he is," Elizabeth stated. "He certainly has the best body."

"Elizabeth!"

"And I'll bet he's at least six two. What do you think?"

"I think you've lost your mind! Don't you know his reputation?"

Elizabeth had heard whispers about Cal Potts always being in some kind of trouble or another, but nothing specific. "What are you talking about?"

"He's a troublemaker."

"What kind of trouble?"

Nora Jane looked around, as if making sure no one could hear the terrible secret she was about to divulge. "They say he spends more time in detention than he does in class."

"Maybe he likes it there. I'd prefer it to some of the classes I have, too."

"And I heard he beat the living daylights out of Billy Parker."

"Good for him! Billy Parker's the biggest jerk I know." Seeing Nora Jane's crestfallen expression as she ran out of ammunition, Elizabeth continued relentlessly. "What other good things have you heard about Cal?"

"Go ahead," Nora Jane said with a pout. "Make a joke of it if you want to, but I'll bet your parents will give you holy hell if they find out you're seeing Cal Potts."

"I'm not *seeing* anybody," Elizabeth said, suddenly angry for no reason she could think of, unless it was the fact that she wouldn't be seeing Cal again because she'd already blown her chance with him. "I talked with him for about two seconds and there's no way my parents could find out about it. Unless some dirty lowlife told them," she added threateningly.

"I wouldn't do that! I never would—"

"I wasn't talking about you, Nora Jane." Elizabeth felt bad for taking her frustration out on her friend. "I know you'd never do a thing like that...not like some other people we know." They both knew that some of the girls resented Elizabeth because her family had money.

Nora Jane nodded knowingly. "Are you going to see him again?"

"I doubt it."

"He is kinda cute...in a dangerous-looking way. Did he say he'd call you?"

"Yes. But he won't."

"What makes you think that?"

"I just know," Elizabeth replied glumly.

AS SOON AS SCHOOL was out Cal pedaled his bicycle across town to Lum Starr's Service Station, where he worked three afternoons a week and all day on Saturdays. Cal loved his job, not the filling-gas-tanks and washing-windshields and checking-air-in-the-tires part of it, but the really good stuff, the mechanical work.

Lum was the best mechanic in town, knew motors inside and out, and everybody in town knew it. Even if they bought their gas someplace else, like the fancy new station or the discount-price station, they still brought their cars to Lum for repairs. And whenever the service-station end of the business was slow, as it often was, Lum let Cal help him work on the motors. Cal was fascinated—the things that man could do with a car engine!

The service station closed at six o'clock, but Lum and Cal often worked in the garage in back of the station much later than that. After they finally called it quits for the night, they'd eat supper together in the garage, where Lum kept an electric hot plate, an enamel pot, and a few reusable plastic bowls and utensils. Their meals—usually soup or stew out of a can, accompanied by saltine crackers and sodas from the Coca Cola machine out front—weren't as good as Cal's mother could cook, but he enjoyed them more because he didn't have to see his mother so tired after working in the mill all day—and then having to come home and clean the house and cook dinner at night—that she practically fell asleep at the table. And he didn't have to see his stepfather—who did practically nothing except drink all day—knee-walking drunk almost every night.

Cal wasn't sure why Lum chose to eat supper at the garage. Some people said Lum's wife was meaner than a junkyard dog—and from the couple of times Cal had met her, he couldn't disagree—so maybe that explained it. Whatever the reason, Cal didn't wish bad luck on Lum but hoped the meals would continue, because he always felt satisfied in both body and spirit after sharing supper with his boss.

Cal took his last bite of beef stew, popped a whole cracker into his mouth, then washed it all down with the last of his soda. "That was great, Lum," he said, burping into his fist the way his mother had taught him. "Delicious."

"Glad you liked it," Lum said, taking credit for Dinty Moore's. "I have some quarters for the machine if you'd like a candy bar for dessert."

Cal held up his hands. "No thanks. I couldn't eat another bite."

"I thought I might open the hood of that Corvette that was towed in this afternoon," Lum said. "Want to stay around and take a look?"

Ordinarily Cal would have jumped at the chance. But he'd told Elizabeth he would call her and he was trying to decide whether to do it tonight. He'd already looked up her address and phone number in the telephone book and written them down, but wasn't sure whether tonight was too soon to call her. "I guess not," he said after debating with himself for a long moment. "The teachers really piled on the homework today. Maybe I could see it tomorrow?"

"Sure," Lum said, reaching across the bench to pick up Cal's bowl along with his before he got off the stool where he was perched.

"Hey," Cal protested. "I'll take care of the dishes."

"Nah. You go along now and take care of all that homework."

Cal felt like a thief, not to mention a traitor, but it was too late to change his story now. "Well . . . guess I'll be going then."

Lum waved a bowl in the air as he headed toward the deep sink to wash their supper dishes. "See you tomorrow."

Cal loved that old man. He swallowed the lump in his throat. "Yeah," he said. "I'll be here early."

Pedaling his bicycle down the street in the dusky twilight scented with the smell of early-blooming jasmine, Cal decided to make a detour on the way home. Jefferson

Street, where Elizabeth lived, was only a couple of blocks out of his way. Why not take a cruise by there and see where she lived? He made a left-hand turn and pedaled a little faster.

The light was growing dimmer by the moment, but he finally spotted the number he'd written down and coasted to a stop by the curb. This was where she lived? It couldn't be. He took out the scrap of paper he'd used to write down her number and looked at it again. The number was right. He looked at the mailbox and saw the name Bartlett. That was right, too.

He was what was wrong—*him*, a nobody from the mill village with a drunk for a stepfather. He'd had the gall to walk up to her, introduce himself, flirt a little, and then casually tell her he'd call her.

And she lived in a mansion!

Damn!

ELIZABETH PICKED UP her salad fork and took a bite of the tomato aspic. She didn't like it very much, but knew it must be good. The other Elizabeth in the house—Elizabeth, the cook—was a genius in the kitchen. Her mother said so. Her father said so. So it must be true.

Two Elizabeths in the house, she thought. If her mother and father had to choose between the two of them, which one would they pick? *No contest.* It would be the cook, hands down.

Elizabeth shifted her gaze from the aspic over to her mother, who was daintily picking at her own aspic. *No wonder she's so thin. She doesn't eat; she only picks. And shuffles the food around on her plate.* She wondered if her father had noticed that his wife ate so little. She shifted her gaze to him at the other end of the table.

He was actually eating his aspic, devouring it, seemingly absorbed in it. *A tisket, a tasket . . . I love my red, red aspic.* Elizabeth sighed, and waited for the other Elizabeth to bring in the next course. Her mother was the one who insisted that their meals be served in courses, even when only the three of them were there to eat—or not eat—them. "It's the only civilized way to dine," Frances Forsythe Bartlett—of *the* Savannah Forsythes—insisted.

So be it. Amen, Elizabeth thought as she watched the other Elizabeth—the talented, self-assured one—bring in the broiled chicken and fresh spring vegetables. And pasta instead of the ubiquitous rice they had nine days out of ten! Elizabeth glanced up in surprise. The other Elizabeth, obviously watching for her reaction, caught her eye and winked. Elizabeth winked back.

Pasta! What a joy in this joyless place!

"Noodles?" Frances Forsythe Bartlett asked when the cook presented the dish to her.

"Pasta," the other Elizabeth corrected her. "I've been told that the British Royal Family has it served regularly."

She's making that up! Elizabeth realized with surprise, noticing the bright sparkle in their cook's brown eyes. Her mother seemed suitably impressed, though, and took an unusually large serving of the pasta. Elizabeth figured it didn't matter how much her mother took; she'd only eat a couple of bites of it at most. Still, she admired Elizabeth . . . the other one.

She made her way through the main course, enjoying the pasta enormously, and waited for dessert, which turned out to be fresh strawberry tarts, another treat. As usual, almost no words were exchanged. When there were dinner parties at the house, conversation was lively, sometimes even spirited, but her parents seemed to have nothing to say to each other when they were alone. And nothing to say to her.

For years, Elizabeth had felt rejected, unloved, until she realized that her parents not only neglected her, they neglected each other. Lately, she wondered if they even did *it* anymore. Glancing at her father now, then at her mother, she doubted that they did. How sad! She hoped that she would never be involved in a relationship like her parents had.

What she wanted in marriage was a wildly passionate affair, one that would continue for years...for forever. They'd make love in the mornings, at noon, at night...and they'd never stop loving each other. Ever.

The phone rang, intruding on Elizabeth's fantasies. "I'll get it," she said, pushing back her chair.

"No," her father said, surprising her. "It's probably for me. I'm expecting a business call," he added over his shoulder as he rushed from the room.

Elizabeth sat down again, prepared to finish her strawberry tart, but happened to glance at her mother before she lifted her fork. Her mother's face was ashen, her eyes twin dark coals, unseeing...

"Mother?" Elizabeth asked in alarm. "Are you—"

"It's for you, Elizabeth," her father said with a touch of impatience in his voice as he came back into the dining room.

"What?" she asked blankly.

"The telephone. It's for you. Some young man who says his name is Cal Potts."

Chapter Two

"Hello, Cal."

Elizabeth's voice over the telephone was so clear she might have been talking to him with her lips touching his ear, which she was doing in a manner of speaking. He gripped the receiver tighter, wondering why he'd called her after telling himself all the way home that he wouldn't. Maybe he'd done it because he was stubborn, just like everyone told him he was, always going after things that were supposed to be beyond his reach.

"Cal, are you there?"

"Yeah, I'm here," he replied finally, wondering again why he'd called her.

"Listen," Elizabeth said, "would you mind hanging on for a minute while I transfer this call to the phone in my bedroom?"

"If you're busy, I could—"

"No! I mean, I'm not busy. We were just finishing dinner."

"Hey, I didn't mean to interrupt—"

"You didn't interrupt. I'd already—"

"Maybe I should call back another time."

"No. Please," Elizabeth said. "It's just that I thought we'd have more privacy if I took the call in my room."

Privacy? "Well..."

"Hold on. I'll be right back."

Cal held on, hearing a brief flurry of sound in the background, then dead silence. Before he had time to consider what the silence meant, Elizabeth was back on the phone, sounding a little breathless.

"Hello. I'm back," she said. "We can talk now."

By then, Cal was feeling more than a little defensive. "What? You didn't want your parents to know who you were talking to?"

"They already *know* who I'm talking to. My father answered the phone, remember?"

"Yeah. But he doesn't know who I am. Neither do you."

"You're Cal, aren't you? The one I talked to on the soccer field today?" Her laugh sounded a little shaky.

"That's right. But what else do you know about me?"

He heard her inhale a deep breath, then let it out again. "Not much," she admitted.

"But you've heard rumors," he persisted, unsure whether he wanted to hurt her or hurt himself by her answer.

"Some," she said.

"Whatever you've heard is probably true. Especially if it's bad."

"What have you done that's so bad?" she asked.

"How much time do you have?"

"I'm serious, Cal."

"So am I. According to the principal at school, I'm nothing but a troublemaker. A rebel."

"And are you?"

Her blunt question surprised him. "Sometimes."

There was a slight pause and then he heard Elizabeth's voice, strong and clear. "I like rebels."

And I'll bet your parents just love rebels, too, he thought. "How old are you?" he asked abruptly, changing the subject.

"What?"

"Freshmen are usually fourteen to sixteen. How old are you?"

"Sixteen. Almost."

"How almost?"

"In three months."

"In other words you're only fifteen, two-and-a-half years younger than I am. A baby."

She didn't say anything for a long time. "Will you tell me something, Cal?" she finally asked, her voice huskier than it had been before.

He was already furious with himself for giving her a hard time they way he had; he couldn't understand why he'd done it. "Sure," he said, bracing himself for whatever she had to say. He deserved it.

"You knew I was a freshman when we met today. If you feel the way you do, why did you call me tonight?"

Damn! Why didn't she simply tear into him the way he'd expected her to, the way any other girl he knew would have done? Then he could have hung up on her without feeling too bad about it afterward. Instead, she'd asked him a straightforward question, one that deserved an answer. He took a deep breath.

"I'm not sure," he said. "I think it was because I liked you today. But then I, uh, happened to ride by your house. After I saw where you lived ... and knew who you really were ..."

"What do you mean you knew who I really was?"

"You live in a damned mansion!"

"It's not a mansion ..."

"A big house, then. Okay? A *really* big house. What does your old man do for a living?"

"My ... father ... is president of Planters' Junction Savings and Loan."

Cal gave a short, harsh laugh. "I should have known."

"Does that matter to you?"

"Yeah. It matters."

"Why?"

Why did she keep asking questions that made him uncomfortable? And why didn't he simply hang up the phone and forget about Elizabeth Bartlett once and for all? "It just does," he mumbled.

"I'm sorry you feel that way, Cal," Elizabeth said after a long silence during which he'd halfway expected her to hang up on him. "I can't help who my parents are. I'm stuck with them, just like you are with yours."

Cal blinked, finding it hard to believe that Elizabeth was only fifteen years old. She sounded a lot more grown-up than he did. "I'm sorry, too, Elizabeth. I shouldn't have said what I did."

"Yes, you should have, if it's what you think. People ought to be honest with each other."

"Yeah, but... well, I'm sorry anyway."

"You're forgiven." She laughed then, and Cal couldn't help smiling in return. "I'm glad you called."

And suddenly, he was glad he'd called, too. They talked about school for a while but all the time they were talking, he kept thinking about what she'd said about people being honest with each other. Gathering his courage, he finally brought up the subject of *his* family and told her about his father being dead, killed in his early twenties when his tractor overturned on him while he was plowing a peanut field. Cal was only a baby at the time, and didn't remember him at all. His mother, Mavis, married a carpenter named Luther Scroggins a couple of years later.

"Mom works at the hosiery mill," Cal said. "She's been working there for as long as I can remember, but she still only makes a little more than minimum wage. And Pop— Luther—does a little carpentry work now and then, whenever he's sober enough. What everybody calls him—and what he really is, I guess—is the town drunk."

"Does that bother you a lot?" Elizabeth asked. "I mean... does it embarrass you?"

Cal wondered how she was able to know what he was thinking, almost before he thought it himself. "Some," he admitted. "But you know a funny thing? I really like Pop when he's sober... except he almost never is. He's usually drunk or well on his way there."

"That's sad," she said. "Why do you suppose he drinks so much?"

Cal blinked again, thinking that he'd never met a girl—a person—like Elizabeth before. He'd been reluctant and embarrassed to tell her about his family, but she'd understood immediately. And she not only sympathized with his own feelings, but even felt sorry for Luther! By the time they finally said goodbye later on that night, Cal had decided that Elizabeth was the easiest person to talk to that he'd ever known. She seemed interested in everything he said, picking up on every little word or inflection, and always saying exactly what she thought, even if you sometimes didn't want to hear it.

It bothered him that she was only a freshman...but then he remembered that his friend Quint's steady girl Sally was just a sophomore. Besides, Elizabeth looked older than almost-sixteen, and acted even older than that.

Her family was a bigger problem. Rich as Croesus. But he'd been honest when he told her about his family, and she hadn't seemed to mind. Besides, he'd probably be rich himself one day. And this was America, wasn't it, where everyone was created equal? *Yeah. Way to go, Potts! Keep telling yourself that, and don't ever forget it.*

ELIZABETH WAS STILL smiling when she hung up the phone after she and Cal had said good-night and he'd told her he'd call again. She hoped he meant it. Talking to him tonight, getting to know him, she knew he wasn't at all the dangerous rebel that her friend Nora Jane had claimed he was. He was so nice...and the easiest person to talk to that she'd ever met. Not that she'd talked to that many people her age, especially in the past year since the private academy she'd gone to all her school life had closed its doors for financial reasons. Her parents had finally agreed to allow her to attend the new consolidated high school that served the entire county, but Elizabeth sometimes wondered if she'd made the wrong choice. She had almost no friends at the new school; some people mistook her reticence for snootiness and others wrote her off simply because her family was wealthy.

It hadn't been easy convincing her parents to allow her to attend public school. Her friend Nora Jane, who lived on the next block and whose father owned the local hardware store, had helped by telling Elizabeth's parents how truly well educated the teachers at the consolidated school were, more than half of them holding advanced degrees. With the help of Nora Jane and her parents—plus Elizabeth's own tearful pleadings—her parents had finally agreed she could attend public school, but with the stipulation that she'd be sent away to boarding school the instant anything amiss occurred.

Elizabeth wasn't quite sure exactly what her parents might consider "amiss"...but felt confident that Cal Potts would fall into the category, and instinctively decided to protect their new friendship by telling them as little as possible about him. With that in mind, she practiced a bland expression in front of the mirror before going downstairs to tell her parents good-night. She found her mother in the library reading a Phyllis Whitney novel, and her father nowhere in sight.

"Where's Daddy?" she asked.

Elizabeth wasn't sure—the changes were that quick—but she thought she saw surprise and anger on her mother's face before the familiar stony, slightly bored look appeared. "He had to go out. A business appointment he *said,* although I can't imagine what kind of business he'd have at this time of..."

Elizabeth saw her mother catch herself, taking a deep breath, and remembered the ashen expression on her face earlier when her father had said he'd answer the telephone because he was expecting a business call. Could it be possible that her father was having some clandestine affair as her mother seemed to think? *Was* it possible...? *No!* she decided. Absolutely, positively not. Never in a million years. He was much too stodgy and straitlaced for that. Besides, he was too old.

"Have you been on the phone all this time?" her mother asked. "Who was it that called you?"

"Just a guy from school. We were talking about home-work," Elizabeth replied easily. It was true. They *had* talked about homework, among many, many, many other things. "I just came down to tell you good-night."

"Yes, well…" her mother said, holding her cheek up for Elizabeth's perfunctory kiss. "Sleep well, dear."

You bet, Elizabeth thought, *but not before I think about Cal and all the things he said tonight.* She wanted to savor them in detail. Then she wanted to plan some way she could arrange to see him again tomorrow.

THEY STARTED going together.

Not that there were many places they could actually *go,* since neither of them had access to a car and since Cal worked at Lum Starr's Service Station three afternoons a week and all day on Saturdays and Elizabeth had piano lessons three days a week, dance lessons another three, and observant parents seven days a week. She solved one of the problems by convincing her parents that she really desper-ately *needed* her own private phone, on which she could discuss difficult homework in detail with fellow students.

She gave her own private number to Cal and to no one else.

They arranged times when he would call, and he always called at the times he said he would. And Elizabeth was al-ways there, awaiting his call.

They saw each other at school, but those encounters weren't very satisfactory as far as Elizabeth was concerned because Cal seemed to have some sort of misguided sense of chivalry regarding her. "I have a bad reputation," he said. "It doesn't bother me, and I deserve it. But I don't want people talking about you."

"What would they say?" she asked. "That Cal Potts and I are going together? It's true, isn't it? Aren't we going to-gether, Cal?"

"Of course we are!"

"Are you ashamed of me?" she goaded.

"Stop it, Elizabeth! You know what I'm talking about."

"And you're talking nonsense. That's the point I was trying to make."

Cal rolled his eyes.

Their late-night conversations on the telephone were much more satisfactory. They talked for hours, telling each other things they'd never told another living soul. Elizabeth told him about her loneliness, about feeling unloved and unwanted in her own home, and about her suspicions that her parents didn't love each other, either.

He told her about his secret dreams, about wanting to make something of his life by becoming the first one in his family to go to college, and of possibly becoming a highly paid basketball star.

They talked. And talked. And the weeks passed—Cal walking on air and Elizabeth living in the most beautiful dream world she'd ever known.

"THE JUNIOR-SENIOR Prom is only a couple of weeks away," Quint Richards said to Cal in the locker room one day. "Are you and Liz planning to go?"

Cal wondered if anything traveled faster than school gossip. People had seen him and Elizabeth talking to each other and knew they were going together almost before they knew it themselves. He resented the intrusion into what had been special and private.

"No. We're not going," Cal said brusquely, hoping Quint would let the matter drop.

He didn't. "Did you ask her?"

Cal hesitated a moment. "No. But I know she doesn't want to go. And neither do I."

"I wish you'd change your mind. My dad's already promised to let me use his new car and I thought we could double-date. You and Liz, and Sally and me."

"Thanks anyway," Cal said.

"At least think about it, will you?" Quint persisted. "The four of us would have a great time. And I'll even loan you one of my suits. I'd loan you a decent pair of shoes, too, but your feet are too big."

Cal swallowed a lump in his throat, touched by his friend's generosity. Quint knew he was saving every cent he could for college, in case the basketball scholarship didn't come through. "I don't know..."

"Sure you do! This is the big dance of the year, man. I'll bet Liz is dying to go."

"Well..." Cal said, thinking about Elizabeth looking pretty as a movie star in her party dress, walking into the country club on his arm. "I guess so. If Elizabeth says it's okay with her."

"She'll jump at the chance," Quint said, punching Cal's arm with his fist. "Girls love things like that."

Cal called Elizabeth that night and brought up the subject of the dance. She surprised him.

"I suppose so," she said, "if you really want to go."

"Me? I thought *you'd* want to go."

He could almost hear her shrug over the telephone line. "I'm not much on that kind of thing," she said.

Suddenly Cal felt acutely disappointed and that surprised him, too. "I think I *do* want to go," he said. "It might be the only chance I'll ever have to see the inside of the country club. Besides, my only expense will be a new pair of shoes and an orchid for you."

"I don't need an orchid."

"Maybe not," he said, "but I want to give you one."

On the night of the dance, both Quint and Sally went to Elizabeth's door with Cal, for which he gave silent thanks, especially when they were met by a uniformed maid who ushered them inside. Cal tried not to gawk, but was keenly aware that this was the plushest house he'd ever stepped into...and it was gigantic, regardless of what Elizabeth said about it not being a mansion.

The maid showed them into the living room where a thin, well-dressed woman and a tall man in a dark suit—obviously Elizabeth's parents—were seated in plush chairs on opposite sides of the fireplace. The woman smiled and came over to take Sally's hand. "How lovely you look, Sally. And, my, how you've grown, Quint! So nice to see you both again. You remember Elizabeth's father, don't you?''

Cal wondered how the woman was able to do all that gushing without even pausing for breath. She finally turned to him. ''And you must be Cal.''

It must be my imagination, he thought. *The room couldn't suddenly have chilled at least twenty degrees.* ''Yes, ma'am,'' he said.

''Potts,'' Mr. Bartlett said, leaning forward in his chair and speaking for the first time since they'd entered the room. ''I can't place the name right offhand. What does your father do?''

Cal took a deep breath. ''He's dead. He, uh…was killed in a farming accident when I was a baby.''

''Oh,'' Mr. Bartlett said. ''That's too bad. What—''

''Hello, everybody,'' Elizabeth said, coming into the room.

Cal couldn't decide whether he was especially glad to see her because she was rescuing him from her father or simply because she looked good enough to eat with a spoon. It was probably a little of both.

THE DANCE WAS okay, but just barely. The country club, which Cal had viewed only from a distance before, was the biggest disappointment. From outside, it had seemed to be a grand mansion, just like the ones he'd seen in *Gone with the Wind*; inside, it not only looked old, but shabby.

There was a live band playing hard rock, which was almost impossible to dance to, but nobody seemed to be much interested in dancing, anyway. They mostly stood around in little groups laughing and talking, the same way they did at school. What Cal couldn't understand was why everybody had made such a fuss about the Junior-Senior Prom. Big deal!

''Let's all go out to the car for some fresh air,'' Quint said when intermission finally rolled around.

"Maybe we should get something to drink first," Cal said, glancing at the punch tables set up along one wall. "We could carry it out with us."

"I have something better in the car," Quint said. "Let's go."

In the parking lot, Cal noticed that there were more people outside the clubhouse than there were inside. He glanced a silent question at Elizabeth, who was walking beside him, her arm looped through his. "I think they all came out for booze," she explained.

A moment later Quint produced his from a cooler in the trunk of his father's new car. He'd brought beer, wine and vodka, with tonic, orange juice and grapefruit juice for mixers.

Quint mixed vodka and orange juice for himself and Sally; Cal chose beer, something he felt comfortable with, and Elizabeth had plain orange juice. Then they all climbed into the car, Quint and Sally in front, and Cal and Elizabeth in the backseat.

As soon as they were inside the car with the doors closed, Quint and Sally sat their drinks on the front dashboard and fell into a torrid embrace. Cal couldn't remember ever feeling more uncomfortable in his life. He finally looked at Elizabeth. She smiled at him, then leaned closer to whisper in his ear. "I guess there's only one thing to do."

He lifted his eyebrows, not understanding what she meant. "You'll have to kiss me," she whispered. He grinned, took the glass of orange juice from her hand and placed it on the floor beside his beer, and proceeded to do just that.

They had kissed before—furtively in hallways and alleyways, and once ducking behind a car in the parking lot at school—but this was different. They were sitting down this time, close together in the semidarkness, with no danger of being discovered and sent to the principal's office for disciplinary action. It was a heady sensation for Cal, and Elizabeth seemed to be aware of it, too. She opened her mouth as soon as his lips touched hers, inviting his tongue inside her. He hesitated a moment, then thrust his tongue deeply, finding wet warmth and softness, and finally her tongue as well. He touched hers with the tip of his, teased it until it came up to meet him, then slowly rolled his over and around hers.

He had done his share of kissing girls before, but never with a girl he cared about the way he cared about Elizabeth. With her, he felt...inspired...not only to please himself but to please her as well. He created things between their coupled mouths that he hadn't even known possible before tonight.

They finally came up for air. Cal took a long swig of his beer and watched Elizabeth drink thirstily from her orange juice. She looked at him and sighed. "Want to trade drinks?"

Cal hesitated, wondering whether she should be drinking beer or not.

"Just a sip," she said, reading his mind. "I want to see how beer tastes."

He handed her the can and she took a sip. She made a face. "It tastes better on your breath than it does from the can."

"You're welcome to taste it on my breath any time you want to," he said with a grin. "Any time at all."

She grinned, too, just before she leaned over to press her lips to his. Then they were kissing again, more passionately than ever. He brought his hand up to touch her small, pointy breast, something he'd never done before, and felt her body tense for a moment. Then she relaxed and tightened her arms around him. He pressed his body against hers, pushing her sideways in the seat until she was almost lying down, with him halfway on top of her. He felt her hands against his chest, pushing him away, and he lifted his head.

"Cal," she whispered breathlessly.

"What is it? What's wrong?"

"My dress," she said, turning her head away in obvious embarrassment. "My parents will be waiting up for me tonight and . . . and . . ." He nodded and moved off her, sitting on the seat beside her while she got up and rearranged her dress.

"Cal, I'm sorry."

"It's okay. I understand," he said. He *did* understand. Although he was on fire with wanting her, he knew she couldn't go home and face her parents looking like she'd just been making out in the backseat of an automobile. "I really do," he added.

He put his arm around her bare shoulders and they kissed some more, less passionately this time. A little later, when it was almost time for the prom to be over, all four of them returned to the dance. Cal was surprised to find the hard rock group already gone. Instead, he heard the soft, seductive voice of Nat King Cole coming over the stereo, singing, "When I Fall in Love."

The lights had been turned down low and a lot of couples were dancing. Without speaking, Cal held out his arms. Elizabeth silently came into them, as if that was where she'd always belonged. She looked up at him and smiled.

Cal blinked, and knew he was a goner. He was in love with Elizabeth Bartlett, totally and forever.

Chapter Three

Elizabeth stared at her reflection in the mirror above her bedroom dresser and wondered why she looked the same as she had yesterday and the day before. She didn't feel the same as she had then. She'd never be the same again. She was in love. Wasn't it supposed to show? A special glow or something?

She turned away from the mirror with a sigh. Then, remembering how anxious she'd been about her parents meeting Cal tonight for the first time—so anxious that she'd been reluctant to go to the dance—decided it was a good thing that her emotions *didn't* show on her face. If they had, her parents would never have let her off so easily when she returned from the prom.

As it was, they'd both still been up, but hadn't been particularly curious. They'd allowed her to escape to her bedroom after only a few queries, which she'd handled easily. "Yes, the prom was nice. Mrs. Chambers was one of the chaperones and she said to tell you hello." "No. We came straight home afterward. Sally and Quint said to tell you it was nice seeing you again." And so on.

If her parents had guessed how she felt about Cal—and if they'd known his background—she dreaded to think what they might have said. Even though they didn't seem to care much one way or the other about *her,* they cared a great deal about the people with whom they allowed her to associate. A very great deal.

She sighed again, this time with relief over what had been averted. Then she rushed to change her clothes and get ready for bed. Cal had promised to call after he got home tonight and she wanted to be prepared to pick up the phone on the first ring, before her parents could possibly hear. Even though she had the bell turned down as low as it would go, there was always the chance they might hear if she didn't answer soon enough.

Besides, she wanted to be in bed when she talked to Cal; it always made him seem closer, so close she could almost imagine him beside her, touching her again the way he'd touched her tonight when they kissed. She brought her hand up to brush her fingers across her lips, then across her nipples... remembering. She closed her eyes.

IT WAS WELL PAST midnight when Quint dropped Cal off after the dance, and he was surprised to find his mother sitting at the kitchen table shelling peas. "What are you doing up?" he asked, dropping a light kiss onto the top of her head. "I thought you'd be in bed hours ago."

"I wanted to hear about the party," she said, giving him a smile that was sweet and sad at the same time. Nobody in the world had a smile like his mother.

"Well..." he said, not knowing where to begin. "It was nice."

"You can do better than that, John Calvin Potts!" she said, pretending to be annoyed.

"It was *very* nice," he said, then threw up his arms as if to ward off a blow. They both laughed.

"Actually," Cal said, taking off the coat he'd borrowed from Quint and carefully draping it over the back of a kitchen chair, "I was surprised at the way the country club looked inside. It was really run-down."

Seeing the obvious disappointment on his mother's face, he realized that wasn't the kind of thing she wanted to hear. She wanted a happy, cheerful report. "But they'd done a terrific job decorating the place," he added quickly. "You should have seen all the lanterns, every color in the rain-bow."

"I'll bet it was beautiful," his mother said, her eyes sparkling in a way he hadn't seen in ages. Years of hard work and disappointment killed something in you, Cal guessed.

"It was," he said. "And there was a live band . . ."

"Oh, my! What songs did they play?"

"All the old favorites. And some new stuff, too." *That could be true,* he figured. The band was so awful—and so loud—they could have been playing anything.

"Did you dance a lot?" she asked.

"Some. Enough. I didn't disgrace you, Mom," he added, teasing.

"I never thought you would," she said seriously. "I'm so proud of you, Cal. Your father would be, too . . . if he were alive."

The sparkle left her eyes suddenly, without warning, and she was once again the woman Cal saw every day—a woman made old before her time by hard work and lost dreams. His throat tightened, and he stuck his hands in his pockets so she wouldn't see him clench his fists. Much as he loved her, he could hardly bear to look at her.

"Well," he said, "I guess I'd better . . ."

"I forgot to ask you about Elizabeth!" his mother exclaimed. "Did she have a good time?"

"I think so," he replied, remembering her face looking up at him so sweetly when she came into his arms. He swallowed. "She said she did."

"I'm glad. Did I tell you about meeting her father after he gave a speech at the Fourth of July barbecue one year?"

Only about a dozen times, Cal thought. She'd told him at least once a day since he'd mentioned that he was taking Elizabeth Bartlett to the prom.

"He shook my hand," his mother continued. "Such a nice man."

Nice? There were a lot of words Cal could think of to describe Elizabeth's father, but nice wasn't one of them.

But if it made his mother feel good to think so, he wasn't going to tell her differently.

CAL COULDN'T BELIEVE it was the last day of school already. The past few weeks had blazed by faster than any he'd ever known. Maybe that's what happened when you were in love. And he *was* in love with Elizabeth, although he hadn't told her yet. He wanted to tell her, but never seemed to find the right opportunity. They saw each other at school, where somebody was always around to interrupt, and he didn't want to be interrupted in the middle of something important like that. Then they talked to each other at night, and telling her over the telephone was out of the question as far as he was concerned.

To make matters worse, Elizabeth was leaving with her mother for Sea Island tomorrow. For a whole month!

That meant he *had* to tell her today.

And he would. This was the perfect opportunity, he thought. What more could he ask than to have her as she was now—sitting on his lap, crunched close together by four other people in the backseat of the convertible Sally Webster had managed to borrow from her brother. He could reach up right now, pull her head down close to his, and whisper the words in her ear.

And she probably wouldn't even hear him.

With the top down and Sally driving at least twenty miles over the speed limit, the wind whistling by made so much noise you couldn't even hear a sonic boom. But that was okay, he still had plenty of time. All day, in fact. They'd all cut school right after homeroom this morning—a longstanding custom at Planters' Junction High—and headed out to Paradise Lake, where everybody would spend the day swimming, sunning and relaxing.

Everybody except him. Cal knew he wouldn't be able to relax until after he'd told Elizabeth he loved her.

He'd do it the first chance he got.

ELIZABETH REMOVED her sunglasses, propped herself up on one elbow and looked at Cal lying on the blanket beside her. He was completely still, with one arm stretched across his face to shade his eyes, but she didn't think he was asleep. "Cal?"

"Hmm?"

"You've been so quiet today. Is something wrong?"

Waiting, listening, she was almost positive there was a moment's hesitation before he replied.

"Nothing's wrong. I'm just relaxing."

"This is the place to do it," she said, pretending to believe him. Something *was* wrong; she couldn't be mistaken about something like that. She was so closely attuned to him—to his thoughts and emotions—that she could almost feel it in her bones.

"Elizabeth, there's something—"

"Hey! No rest for the weary!" Quint said, kicking sand onto their blanket as he came bounding up. "C'mon Cal. We need you for the volleyball game. Pronto!"

Cal was up in an instant, all pretense of *relaxing* as he'd called it, gone, Elizabeth noticed. He was suddenly full of energy, enthusiasm . . . *relief?* And what had he been about to say to her? Something. What something?

Cal and Quint were already several yards away, racing to their precious volleyball game, when Cal turned and called to her, almost as an afterthought, "Come watch the game!"

Sure. Thanks a lot. Nice of you to remember I'm here. Elizabeth sat up and wrapped her arms around her knees, resting her chin on her wrist, thinking. She saw Cal and Quint run up to join the volleyball game that was already in progress farther down the beach, and noticed that several girls were playing, too. Neither Quint nor Cal had asked *her* to play.

Narrowing her eyes against the glare of the sun, she was able to see that none of the girls playing was a dog. Far from it. They were all gorgeous; at least they looked that way from this distance, and all of them were dressed in skimpy bikinis. Elizabeth wore a skimpy bikini, too, but that wasn't the point...or was it? She was nowhere near as well endowed as those volleyball players were, and probably never would be.

A sudden thought struck her—a horrible thought, a thought so painful that it caused her to catch her breath. Had that been the *something* that Cal had started to tell her before Quint came up? Was he interested in someone else?

CAL LEAPED HIGH into the air, hitting the ball as hard as he could and then grimacing with satisfaction when he felt the sting of fist making contact with leather. He'd have been even more satisfied if his fist had been connecting with his own face instead of the volleyball. Damn him, anyway! Why hadn't he told her already? Why had he waited so long this morning...practicing the words over and over in his mind so many times that they'd become meaningless.

And then...when he'd finally gathered his courage to actually tell Elizabeth that he loved her...Quint had suddenly appeared, asking him to join a volleyball game. A stupid volleyball game! The timing couldn't have been worse. But that wasn't even the worst thing. He'd actually felt *relieved* because he was able to postpone telling Elizabeth a little while longer, and had jumped at the chance to prance down the beach and play the jock. The stupid jerk jock.

"Unnh!" Cal grunted, leaping to the left to save a ball and pass it to the front line. Instead of taking his high pass and batting it over the net for a winner, the girl in the red bikini squealed...and batted the ball back to him. He couldn't believe it.

"What the...!" he shouted, then stopped himself. It was only a stupid game; there was no reason to take his anger out on her when it was himself he was really furious with.

"I'm sorry, Cal," the girl said. "But you hit the ball so *hard*... " She really drew out the last word, making it last at least four syllables while she made a cute little pout.

She was definitely coming on to him, and had been during the whole game. "No problem," he said. He turned away, wiping the sweat from his forehead with his arm while he searched the beach for Elizabeth. He saw the blanket where the two of them had been sitting, but it was vacant now. He wondered where she was.

SHE FINALLY DECIDED to go swimming. There was no point in sitting on a blanket alone all day, and Cal seemed to be perfectly happy playing with the nymphets on the beach without her. It didn't seem to bother him at all that she was leaving tomorrow and they wouldn't see each other again for a whole month, but personally she felt like crying and the water seemed a good place to do it.

She waded in until the water was chest-high, then started swimming, as hard and fast as she could. That relieved some of her tension; she didn't think anything could relieve the ache she felt around her heart. When she became tired, she floated on her back for a while, then treaded water while she looked around. There were several floating docks in the lake, most of them occupied. She finally spotted one that was vacant and headed for it. Hoisting herself out of the water, she lay face down on the rough wooden boards, her head cradled in the crook of her arm.

And finally allowed herself to cry.

WHERE WAS SHE?

Cal made a try for a spike and missed, but didn't miss the sound of jeers from his teammates. He didn't care. All he wanted was for this game to be over, so he could go and find Elizabeth. And tell her that he loved her.

She was leaving tomorrow, dammit! For a whole month. She might meet somebody at the beach, somebody from the same kind of background she had, and they'd fall in love and she'd forget that Cal Potts ever existed. It could happen. Everybody knew how romantic ocean beaches were. Or were supposed to be; he didn't know because he'd never seen one.

Of course, the same thing could happen even if he told her he loved her before she left. But that way, at least she'd *know*. And he would know that he'd tried. As it was...
Damn! Would this game ever be over?

Finally it was.

But Cal still couldn't find Elizabeth anywhere.

"I saw her swimming a little while ago," Sally said when he asked her. Cal walked down to the water's edge, scanning the lake, then the various floating docks. He saw several couples who, feeling that they were alone in the middle of the lake, were making out to the amusement of everyone on shore. He grinned.

Then his eyes focused on another float and his grin disappeared. He couldn't believe it. He recognized Rodney Adams immediately. Rodney was the top star on the basketball team, and one of the biggest jocks. According to Rodney, the list of mares in his stable was at least a mile long, and still growing. Cal saw some other team members he recognized, too. They were all laughing—showing off their stuff—while they crowded around the only female on the float. Around Elizabeth. *His* Elizabeth.

Feeling sick to his stomach, Cal turned and walked away from the beach. He heard someone call his name, and didn't pause to see who it was. He heard a distant rumble of thunder, and it echoed his feelings. Exactly.

Reaching the snack bar, he clinched and unclinched his fists a couple of times before walking to the counter to order a drink. Taking a deep breath, he told himself to calm down, that it was no big deal. But it was.

He felt someone touch his arm and closed his eyes for a moment of silent prayer before he turned around.

It wasn't Elizabeth. It was the girl in the red bikini from the volleyball game.

"Hi," she said breathlessly. "I called out to you on the beach, but I guess you didn't hear me."

"I guess," he said, forcing a smile.

"That was some game, wasn't it?"

"Yeah. Some game." The waiter brought his drink and Cal reached into the back pocket of his swim trunks for money to pay him.

"So..." the girl said. "What are you drinking?"

"Gatorade." Cal hesitated. "Would you like something?"

"Are you asking me to join you?"

Was he? He hadn't thought he was, but maybe it had seemed that way to her. And why shouldn't he? With Elizabeth out there...

There was another long rumble of thunder, punctuated this time by a sharp shriek of lightning. And Elizabeth was out there!

"No!" Cal said. "I mean...I have to go find someone." He left his drink on the counter, left the girl in the red bikini, and raced outside. Rain was already beginning to fall in fat wet dollops; by the time he reached the beach, it was coming down in a steady sheet. He spotted Elizabeth; she was frantically trying to gather up their clothes and personal belongings from the blanket where they'd left them...how long ago? Minutes? Hours? A lifetime.

Cal ran toward her, feeling the rain beating against his skin like a million tiny pinpricks. Then something heavier, harder, hit his forehead and he realized that hail was coming down along with the rain. He saw Elizabeth suddenly stop and touch the top of her head—where a hailstone must have hit her—and he could almost feel her pain.

Reaching her, he grabbed her arm. "Are you okay?" he shouted above the roar of the rainstorm.

She turned to look at him—only for a brief moment before she quickly turned away and jerked her arm from his grasp—but the expression on her face, in her beautiful green eyes, was one he'd never forget. He saw pain, anger and pure animal fury that burned straight through to his soul.

Stunned by her fierceness, he watched helplessly while she resumed the task of trying to pack their belongings. Then, feeling the hail coming down harder, he realized it was strong enough to hurt them, to possibly do bodily injury, and that galvanized him into action.

"Forget that!" he shouted, grabbing the tote bag from her hand and flinging it onto the beach. He picked up the blanket, flung it over his head, then pulled Elizabeth underneath it alongside him. She opened her mouth to protest, but he plopped down to the wet sand—pulling her with him—before she could speak. Then he lifted his arms, holding the blanket as a shield over both their heads.

He was breathing hard; so was she, but he couldn't tell whether hers was from exertion or anger. It was probably both, he decided... but why should *she* be angry? He saw her rub her upper arm, on the spot where he'd grabbed her so roughly. "I'm sorry if I hurt you...." he said.

She didn't look at him, merely kept rubbing her arm. "Which time?"

Come again? "Just now. The hail was coming down so hard, I knew we had to get out of it some way...." As if to punctuate his remark, a sudden brief flurry of hailstones hit the blanket, then bounced onto the beach beyond their feet. Cal shifted and crossed his legs. His right knee brushed against Elizabeth's thigh while he was moving, and she promptly drew her legs up to her chest, wrapping her arms around them. *Talk about body language!* And *he* was the one who had a right to be hurt and angry.

"What were you doing out on the float with Rodney Adams today?" he asked.

"What?"

"I think you heard me," he said. The blanket muffled most of the noise of the storm raging outside; underneath, it was like a cozy cocoon.

"I heard you, all right," Elizabeth said, her voice tight with what sounded like suppressed fury. "What I meant was what gives you the right to ask me a question like that?"

"I thought we were going together."

"I thought so, too, until today."

"And what's *that* supposed to mean?"

"You tell me. What's your definition of going together, Cal? Bringing me out to a picnic and then running off and leaving me all day while you flirt with a bunch of bimbos on a volleyball team?"

"I never—"

"Is that what you call going together, Cal? Is it?"

"No, dammit! And going together also means that *you* don't swim out to a float with the biggest jocks in school... with everybody watching!"

Elizabeth narrowed her eyes until they were twin slits. "What are you trying to say?"

"I'm not trying. I'm saying it. I saw you carrying on out there with Rodney Adams and—"

"Carrying on?"

"Yes. I—"

"Get this straight, Cal. The dock was empty when I swam out to it. Rodney came out a long time later and started talking to me from the water. He said he played on the basketball team with you, and he'd noticed I was all by myself.... Then he *asked* me if it was all right for him to come up on the dock, too."

"Rodney?" Cal asked, finding that image of Rodney hard to picture.

"Yes, Rodney. He couldn't have been nicer. A perfect gentleman."

Cal knew Elizabeth wouldn't lie about something like that, so it must be true. And if it was, that meant Rodney must have been telling some lies himself... or at least, exaggerating the truth all along.

"The others came out later on," Elizabeth said, "one or two at a time after they spotted Rodney on the float. They started horsing around some... the way you and Quint do...but there was no 'carrying on,' as you call it. None at all. And all I did...was have a little fun for the first time today." Cal's arms were starting to ache from holding the blanket over their heads, but the pain was nothing compared to the pain around his heart. He thought back to this morning, when he'd started out with such high hopes and great expectations. How had things gone so wrong?

"I'm sorry for what I said, Elizabeth," he said. "And also for the way I've acted today. I've been a total jerk."

He waited for her to say something, but she didn't. Which meant she agreed with him. And he didn't blame her; he'd feel the same way if he were in her place. "The thing is..." he began, then stopped. He didn't know where to go from there.

He took a deep breath and started again. "The thing is, that I'd planned this whole day...in my mind. I stayed awake all last night thinking about it. I knew you were going to leave tomorrow, so time was running out and I had to make my move, now or never. And today was the perfect chance—Paradise Lake, a beautiful day, lots of sunshine like we had this morning. What more could you ask? I decided that the first time we were alone, I'd tell you right off the bat that I loved you. And then—"

"What?"

"Then things started going wrong. I don't know—"

"*No!* What you said before that!"

"That I was going to tell you I love you?"

"Not that either. I mean...*do* you?"

"Love you?"

"Yes."

"Of course I do. I was just telling you..."

"Cal," she said, shaking her head, tears welling up in her beautiful green eyes. "Oh, Cal."

He watched with alarm—his arms outstretched above their heads to hold the blanket in place—while she lowered her head to her knees and started crying in earnest, not making loud sounds, but breaking his heart with her muffled sobs, with the tremors he saw shake her thin shoulders. When he couldn't bear it any longer, he dropped the blanket, letting it fall around them, and gathered her into his arms, holding her close, trying to comfort her, loving her with all his being.

And knowing that he'd lost her.

The tremors stopped, then the sobs, and finally the tears. She sniffed.

"Feeling better?" Cal asked hesitantly, continuing the gentle, circular motion he was making around her shoulder with the tips of his fingers. She nodded.

"I'm sorry I upset you." He cleared his throat. "I know how you must feel. But don't worry."

She lifted her head, revealing wide green eyes still shining with the last of her tears. "What are you talking about, Cal?"

"I mean...just because I love you doesn't mean you have to feel the same way. So I don't want you to—"

She stopped him by placing her entire hand over his mouth. "You think I was crying because I don't love you?"

Unable to speak, he nodded his head.

She took her hand away from his mouth...and then she laughed! "Cal. Oh, Cal! I wasn't crying because I don't love you. I was crying because I *do!*"

He wasn't sure he'd heard her right, but tightened his arms around her all the same.

"That's why I was so unhappy today," she continued. "Knowing how much I loved you and was going to miss you...for a whole month! And I thought you liked me, too...but you never said anything..."

"I was too scared. I kept trying to get up the nerve to tell you today...and then I got into that stupid volleyball game and..."

"And it hurt my feelings when you seemed to be enjoying yourself so much..."

"And all the time I was playing, I kept thinking about how much I'd rather be with you and..."

"Oh, Cal!"

"Elizabeth," he murmured, closing his mouth over hers. Firmly. Surely. Reaffirming his love. Branding her as his. Forever.

Chapter Four

Lum Starr removed a faded baseball cap from his head and scratched his scalp while he studied the big Harley-Davidson motorcycle. "I'm not sure it's a good buy, Cal," he said after several minutes.

"But you know how great Harleys are," Cal protested. "And the price is dirt-cheap!"

"So you told me. The thing is . . . this particular Harley might be worth even less than they're asking for it." Lum replaced his cap and leaned closer to the bike, squinting his eyes. "It's seen a lot of rough wear."

"Well . . . yeah."

"The tires are completely bald . . ."

"I can get a barely used set off a wrecked bike down in Albany. . . ."

"Sounds like you've already made up your mind," Lum said.

"No-o . . ."

"I thought you were saving your money for college."

"I was! I mean . . . I still am. But Coach says the basket-ball scholarship is looking pretty good."

"Pretty good don't count. You ought to know that by now."

Cal nodded. "I do. But if I don't get the scholarship, the money I've saved will only last me through a couple of se-mesters at the most. So I thought . . ." He looked at the Harley again. He couldn't tell Lum what he'd really been thinking—that the bike represented freedom as well as transportation. With it, he'd be able to drive Elizabeth someplace where they could be alone when she finally returned home this weekend after being gone for so long.

Cal might have spent a more miserable month in his life, but if so, he couldn't remember when it was. The time while Elizabeth was away at the beach had creeped by as slowly as the summer sun moving across the sky, each day like the one before—hot and dry, as arid as his heart.

Now she was coming home at last, but how could he arrange to see her? School wouldn't start again for another couple of months, so he wouldn't be able to meet her there. And the idea of the Bartletts' reaction if he suddenly showed up at their door—coming to call on their only daughter—was enough to make him laugh. Except he didn't feel like laughing.

The only other alternatives he could think of were an automobile, which was out of the question price-wise...and this broken-down piece of junk, which he'd hoped that Lum would help him put into working order. But now that hope was dead. He sighed.

"You really want it, don't you?" Lum asked, interrupting Cal's thoughts.

"Wel-l..."

"I can't remember how long it's been since I worked on a big ole Harley."

Cal caught his breath. "You mean..."

"It'll be a challenge," Lum said, chuckling as he scratched his head again. "Hand me that wrench over there and let's take a look inside."

Cal suppressed the urge to give a wild whoop, and rushed to get the wrench Lum had requested instead.

ELIZABETH ARRIVED BACK in Planters' Junction a little after noon on Saturday, tanned to a golden bronze, sick to death of all her mother's boring relatives and desperate to see Cal. After an entire month away from him—a month where she thought about him dozens of times a day and kissed her pillow at night, pretending it was him—she couldn't wait a second longer to see Cal. As soon as she was alone in her room—not even bothering to unpack—she dialed the number for Starr's Service Station, something she'd never done before.

She was relieved to hear Cal himself answer the phone. "It's me," she said. "Eliza—"

"I know who it is," he interrupted. "When did you get back? When can I see you? What—"

"One question at a time," she said, laughing. "We arrived a few minutes ago... and I called you first thing."

"I'm glad you did. You don't know how much I've missed you."

"I missed you, too, Cal. Every day..."

"How about every night?"

"Especially every night," she said with feeling, wanting him to know it was true. She had no patience with girls who deliberately tried to make their boyfriends jealous; it was cruel and sadistic.

She heard him take a deep breath. "I'd really like to see you," he said.

"I would you, too. But my parents are having some friends in tonight for an informal welcome-home party and I'll have to be here."

"How about later this afternoon, then?" he asked. "I have a surprise for you."

"I thought you had to work."

"I can take off a little early and meet you someplace downtown around five. Can you manage that?"

"Sure," she said, thinking. She could get her friend Nora Jane, who was now old enough to drive without an adult in the car, to take her. And if Nora Jane wasn't available, she'd walk. "How about Ellerbee's Drugstore?"

"Perfect. See you there at five."

CAL PULLED UP IN FRONT of the drugstore and accelerated the engine one last time before he killed the motor, crossing his fingers as he sent up a hope that it would start without too much trouble next time he tried it. Lum had worked miracles on the Harley-Davidson in a few short days, but there was still a lot more that needed to be done. At times, the big, black machine seemed to have a mind of its own, purring smooth as a kitten one minute, and coughing and sputtering as if it were on its last breath the next.

The Harley was temperamental, all right... and Cal already was in love with it. He removed his helmet and slung it over the handlebars. "Be a good girl," he said, patting the chrome.

He'd rushed home from the station to shower and scrub himself at breakneck speed, not wanting to be late for his appointment with Elizabeth, and was surprised when he glanced at his watch and discovered he was a few minutes early. Looking up into the blazing glare of the afternoon sun, he decided to wait for her inside the air-conditioned drugstore. He pushed open the door, and she was the first thing he saw.

She was sitting at the soda fountain talking with Doc Ellerbee, her elbow propped on the counter and her chin resting in the palm of her hand, her long, tanned legs curled around the bar stool. She was even prettier than he remembered. She was everything he could want in a girl... and more. And she was waiting for him... him and nobody else. Elizabeth. Waiting for Cal. How had he been so lucky?

He took a deep breath and walked over to the counter, gradually picking up snatches of the story she was telling Doc Ellerbee, something about a shark washing up on the beach.

Cal slid onto the stool beside her and she abruptly broke off her story, whirling around to face him. The look that leaped into her eyes was one of such pleasure, such pure joy, that he had to fight against the urge to pull her into his arms and kiss her right on the spot, right in front of Doc Ellerbee and anybody else who happened to be in the store.

"Cal."

That was all she said. But the way she said it—and the
look she gave him when she did...

"Hi, Elizabeth." He leaned closer, still wanting to kiss
her but again remembering Doc Ellerbee standing there
watching them, listening to every word they said. "I'll have
the same thing she's drinking," Cal said to the elderly
druggist.

"That'll be limeade."

"Great." As soon as Doc Ellerbee moved away to make
his drink, Cal turned back to Elizabeth, wanting to say
something meaningful, something that would express all
the things he felt. "It seems like forever."

Not too original, he thought, wishing he could have come
up with something better. Elizabeth deserved better.

Yet, somehow, she seemed to understand what he was
trying to say... all the things he really meant.

"Yes," she said, placing her hand over his on the
counter. She immediately snatched her hand back and
looked around guiltily.

"It's okay," Cal said. "Nobody saw us. Besides, all you
did was touch my hand."

"It felt like more than that."

"I know," he said. And he did. Whenever he was close
to Elizabeth—not only today when he was seeing her for the
first time in a month, but *any time*—he was acutely aware
of her. He'd find himself watching the way the sun brought
out golden highlights in her auburn hair, or the way her
fingers curled around a glass, or he'd lean closer to inhale
the sweet, fresh scent of her. He'd read somewhere that
each person on earth had a distinct aroma all their own, but
he had never noticed it until he met Elizabeth and fell in
love with the way she smelled, along with everything else.

And he found himself wanting to touch her—not in a
sexy, intimate way—but something as simple as brushing
his arm against hers...or even giving her a high five.
Something to touch base.

Doc Ellerbee returned with Cal's limeade and wanted to
hear the rest of Elizabeth's story about the dead shark that

washed ashore with a beer can crushed between its sharp teeth. Cal only half listened to the story; he was more interested in the sound of her voice, and the short golden hairs on her tanned forearm, and the way she'd turn to him every few seconds to make sure he wasn't feeling left out. He knew he probably had a silly grin on his face, but he didn't care. It was just so damned good to *be* with her again.

Elizabeth finally came to the punch line of the story, which she promised was true. Some fraternity boys, at a house party at nearby St. Simons, had come over to Sea Island one night and found the shark washed ashore. They'd prized its gigantic mouth open with a crowbar, inserted the beer can, and sneaked away into the night. "Nobody would have ever known the truth if one of the boys hadn't had too much to drink a couple of days later and started bragging about it," Elizabeth said.

Cal laughed along with the others, wondering at the same time how soon he could manage to get Elizabeth outside to see the Harley.

"Shouldn't we be leaving now, Cal?" she asked, solving the problem herself.

Breathing a sigh of relief, Cal nodded and paid for their drinks, then followed her out to the sidewalk, where they were met with a blast of hot air. She turned to him expectantly. "What was the surprise you wanted to show me?"

"There," he said, pointing to the Harley-Davidson, gleaming like a sleek, well-fed cat in the parking space directly in front of the drugstore. "That's it."

He watched her intently. No reaction at all. He felt his heart take a deep plunge, all the way to the bottom of his toes. He should have known she'd feel the way she did. A girl like her, born to wealth and to a fine, proper, upstanding family...how else would she feel? Motorcycles—even expensive, finely tuned Harley-Davidsons like this one had been at one time in its life—were ridden by rough gangs wearing black leather jackets, not by people such as Elizabeth and her parents. He knew the stereotype wasn't true, but was sure that must be what she was thinking.

Cal had been so proud of the Harley, but now he wished there was a convenient hole nearby so he could slither down into it, taking the bike along with him. He held his breath when Elizabeth finally trained her deep green eyes on him again.

"Oh, Cal," she said in a voice that was barely above a whisper.

Why wasn't there a hole around for him to crawl into?

"Cal," she said again. Then, before he knew what was happening, she hurtled herself at him, grabbing him around the neck and saying over and over again, "Cal. Cal. Cal."

"What?" he finally managed to ask.

"Is it yours?"

"Yes."

"Oh!" she exclaimed, hugging him tighter. "Can we go for a ride on it? Now? Right now? Right this very minute?"

At first, Cal found it hard to believe his ears, and that she actually meant what she was saying. But then he remembered that she was no ordinary girl; she was Elizabeth, *his* Elizabeth, so naturally she would love the motorcycle as much as he did.

"Sure," he said, struggling to lessen the death grip she had around his neck. "If you're positive you want to."

"Want to? *Want to?* I've always thought I'd be willing to kill for a chance to ride on a real Harley-Davidson."

Cal grinned, pulling out the shiny new helmet he'd bought her. "Then put this on while I crank the motor...Killer."

For the first time since he'd bought it, the Harley caught on Cal's first attempt to start it—a good omen, he thought. He waited while Elizabeth settled into the passenger seat behind him, her arms wound tightly around his waist. He looked down to make sure her legs were properly placed on the side stirrups. "Ready?" he asked.

"Let's go!"

Cal revved the engine a last time and then took off down Main Street. He slowed down almost immediately though, remembering how hard he'd heard Sheriff Maxwell could be on speeders. When they reached the city limits, he looked back at Elizabeth. "I'm going to speed up a little now," he shouted.

She nodded her head in agreement.

Cal debated with himself for a moment and decided not to go full-throttle. Elizabeth seemed to be enjoying herself so far, and he didn't want to run the risk of scaring her. He eased the bike into a relatively safe, moderate speed and tried to content himself with that, although he was itching to go full tilt. He leaned his head back, savoring the sight and smell of the tall pines lining the macadam road on both sides. And the feel of Elizabeth behind him, her arms wound around his waist. How happy could one person be?

She pinched his waist. Hard. He dipped his head in her direction, still keeping his eyes on the road, and heard her say something he was unable to make out. "What?" he shouted over his shoulder.

"Will...it...go...any...faster?" she shouted back.

He turned all the way around. "You sure you want to?" he shouted.

She nodded vigorously.

Okay!

Cal turned up the power and felt the Harley respond immediately, just the way it was supposed to do but never had done before. Maybe it knew how important this ride was, too. He gave the machine a little more gas, and still more, and felt the satisfying roar of the powerful engine beneath him, the burst of speed.... He felt and heard the wind whishing by his ears...felt the solid warmth of Elizabeth behind him...saw the orange glow of the South Georgia sun sinking behind tall pine trees.... *How good could it get?*

They roared together down the straight road where you could see for miles ahead, then careened around a curve where you had no idea what was in front of you. Cal could feel Elizabeth leaning into the curve with him, her body exactly in tune with his. When they came out of the curve and onto a straightaway again, he turned around to look at her, and the sight of her made him catch his breath.

She was totally alive, exhilarated...with her arms wound tightly around his waist and her long auburn hair flying wildly around her helmet...laughing into the face of the wind.

If we live to be a hundred, I'll always remember her this way, he thought. If he hadn't been in love with her already, he would have fallen in love with her at that moment.

ELIZABETH FELT A KEEN disappointment when Cal guided the bike to a stop under a shade tree beside a small pond. Then, remembering they still had the ride back home to look forward to, she perked up.

"I've never had so much fun in my entire life," she said, taking off her helmet after they'd dismounted.

"Really?" Cal said, removing his own helmet. "I thought you were hating every minute of the ride."

Seeing the mischief in his gray eyes, she made a fist and lightly hit his arm. "You," she said, shaking her head.

He captured her fist in his much larger hand, pulling her up flush against him, his expression changing from teasing to serious. "I missed you so much."

"And I missed you," she said, lifting her arms to cup his dear face between her hands. "I love you."

"Ah, Elizabeth." Then he kissed her. Once, twice, again and again.

And she kissed him back, loving him with all her heart, wanting to show him her love the way her parents never did show theirs...if they had any to begin with. He touched her breast and she raised her arm higher—winding it around his neck—to give him easier access. He slid his hand up underneath her T-shirt and she liked the warm feeling of his big hand cupping her. She was only sorry that there wasn't more of her for him to cup.

She felt his other hand on her buttocks, pulling her closer, until they were as close together as two people could stand... And then she felt *it*...felt *him,* rock hard and hot. She could feel the heat of him even through his jeans and her own clothes. She moved slightly, shifting her hips to the left and then to the right, and heard a muffled sound coming from Cal's mouth pressed against hers. She repeated the movement. *Good Lord, he was so big!*

She suddenly felt weak.

She'd always expected they would make love sooner or later, but now she wondered—as big as he was, could he possibly fit inside her? She remembered seeing a movie once where the woman cried out in terrible pain when a man climbed on top of her.

Then she remembered something else—the woman hadn't liked that man; she was in love with someone else and he'd forced himself on her. It wouldn't be that way with Cal and her. They were in love with each other. He wouldn't hurt her, the same way she'd never deliberately hurt him.

Relaxing a little, she rubbed her hand across the broad expanse of his back, loving the feel of him. She felt him move his hand from her buttocks to her waist, and then he was slowly pulling her down to the mossy grass beneath the shade tree. *Were* they going to do it? Now?

It was beginning to seem that way. And she was beginning to feel weak again...but not with fear this time. With excitement. Anticipation. He lifted his head for a moment to gaze into her eyes, as if asking a question. She put all the love she had into the look she gave him back, and then pulled his mouth down to hers again, answering his silent question.

His body was half covering hers, his hands roaming all over her, and she loved it, feeling a sweet yearning building between her thighs. She heard the sound of a zipper. His jeans. The yearning became an aching need. She felt his hand at the waistband of her shorts and lifted her hips, helping him guide the shorts down her legs. Then he kissed her again, pressing his hot, satiny manhood against her stomach, and she moaned. She wanted him inside her... had to have him inside her. They'd find a way to fit, somehow.

She felt his fingers coaxing her legs to part, and eagerly complied. Then his fingers were touching the tenderest part of her, and she felt his hand tremble. She'd never loved him more than she did at that moment. And soon...

Suddenly, abruptly, Cal moaned, then cursed, then flung himself away from her. She opened her eyes and saw him lying on the grass beside her, one arm across his face, covering his eyes. A horrible fear gripped her, leaving her body cold and her heart constricted.

"Cal, what's wrong?"

"We can't do this."

She didn't want to ask, but had to know. "Why not? I know you want to. And I do, too."

He took a deep breath, then let it out slowly. "I didn't bring anything to keep you from getting pregnant. We can't take the chance."

She closed her eyes as a thousand emotions rushed through her—regret, relief... and above all, an overwhelming love for Cal, who had stopped short of making love because of concern for her! She didn't think that many boys—maybe not any—would have been as noble. She reached out her hand to touch his shoulder. He jumped. "I'm sorry," she said. "I didn't mean to startle you."

"It's not that. It's just... I'll be okay in a minute." For the first time, she let her gaze drift below his waist. Feeling herself grow warm all over again, she also understood why he'd jumped when she touched him. He still wanted her... very much, judging by appearances. She loved him even more for his sacrifice. Forcing herself to look elsewhere, she spotted her discarded shorts and started getting dressed.

Cal dressed a little while later, and they climbed aboard the Harley for the trip back to town... except the motorcycle wouldn't cooperate. It took Cal more than half an hour to get it started, and Elizabeth was starting to get nervous because she was due back home and her parents would be wondering where she was. Finally, the motor coughed loudly...and caught.

"At last!" she said with relief.

"Don't be too sure about that," Cal warned. "When the Harley starts acting up like this, there's no telling what it'll do."

What it did was sputter and stall half a dozen times on the way back to town. By the time they finally reached Elizabeth's house, it was already completely dark outside and she'd been gone for hours.

"I'm sorry—" Cal began.

"Don't be," Elizabeth said, removing her helmet and handing it to him, then giving him a quick kiss on the cheek. "I loved the afternoon...love the Harley..." She kissed him again. "Love *you!*"

"Still..."

"Don't worry, it'll be okay," she assured him, starting up the walkway to her house. "Call me later?"

"Sure."

Elizabeth walked faster, wondering what she was going to tell her parents—and their guests—about where she'd been. In spite of what she'd told Cal, she couldn't imagine any possible way her absence would be "okay." She'd gone for a walk this afternoon and hadn't returned until hours later. Maybe they'd even called the police to report her missing! She raced the last few steps to the front door and stepped inside, then blinked in the sudden brightness.

She heard the sound of voices and laughter coming from the living room, but couldn't see anybody from the foyer...which meant they couldn't see her either. Maybe she could sneak upstairs and...

"Elizabeth! Come here this instant!"

With a sinking, sick-to-the-stomach feeling, Elizabeth turned and saw her mother standing in the doorway to the living room, almost livid with rage, and knew with certainty that things were going to be bad, very bad. She walked over to her mother.

''Where have you *been* for almost five hours?'' her mother said, her voice rising steadily until it was almost a shriek.

Elizabeth saw the dinner guests over her mother's shoulder—saw them stop talking and turn around to stare at the two of them.

''Mother, please—'' she said, feeling her face grow hot, blazing with embarrassment.

''Don't 'Mother, please!' me! I asked you a simple question—where ... have ... you ... been?''

''I ... walked downtown ...''

''For five hours?''

''And then I went for a ride with Cal Potts,'' Elizabeth said quickly. ''We had engine trouble on the way home.''

She sought her mother's eyes with hers—imploring her to believe her, begging her to have mercy and not continue making this scene, with all those people standing horrified, watching and hearing everything they said....

Her mother slapped her.

Elizabeth felt the sting of it on her cheek, and felt the sting of tears in her eyes. She blinked rapidly, clenching her fists. *Please don't let me cry. Not now. Not yet.*

''Go to your room,'' her mother ordered.

Elizabeth went gladly, gratefully, without another word.

And by the time both her parents came to her room much later, after the guests had finally left, her mind was made up and her heart was steeled against them. She listened quietly as they laid down their orders, number one of which was that she wouldn't see Cal Potts again, not only because of tonight but also because her father had investigated his background and found it completely unsuitable.

She didn't cry; her tears had already been shed in private. And she didn't protest; she had no intention of following her parents' orders, especially those that concerned not seeing Cal. He was the one person she loved above all others, including her cold, uncaring parents. And Cal loved her, too. He'd proven that today in the most dramatic way possible—by denying himself, and her, of the pleasure of fulfillment because of his concern for her!

If that wasn't love, she didn't know what was! And she didn't intend to take it lightly. She would be as strong as Cal, protecting him and the love they shared anyway she could, for as long as they lived.

She made it a vow.

Chapter Five

Maybe it was because it was his last year in high school, but to Cal, time seemed to be flying by faster than it ever had in his life... fall semester had barely begun when it was already over and everybody was getting ready for Christmas. After much indecision, he wound up giving Elizabeth a silver necklace with a heart-shaped locket that had their initials engraved inside it. Up to the last minute he wondered if it was too corny, but she cried and hugged him and said it was the best gift anyone had ever given her and that she'd treasure it always.

She gave him a blanket—which she insisted on calling a car robe—for the Harley-Davidson. The blanket/car robe was really nice. It even came in its own waterproof pack that fit neatly behind the backseat, yet was big enough to hold a small picnic, so they were able to travel farther, and stay away longer.

They started venturing beyond the boundaries of Planters' Junction on the bike, beyond the county line, even as far away as Albany a couple of times. Cal was delighted that Elizabeth loved the Harley as much as he did, and that she never seemed to be afraid. No matter how fast he drove, or what fool stunt he might try to do, she was with him all the way, urging him on.

He sometimes wondered what she told her parents about where she was and what she was doing, and finally figured out that maybe she didn't tell them anything, because she never had him pick her up at her house. They usually left from school or from the homes of her friends, or they met downtown. He didn't want to spoil a good thing, so he never questioned her about the arrangement.

With the big motorcycle to take them almost anywhere they wanted to go, and a blanket to relax on when they got there, their petting sessions were long and serious, with much heavy breathing coming from both of them. Cal always stopped things short of making love, although everybody in school thought that they were doing it.

Some of the jocks on the basketball team tried to get Cal to talk about it, to tell them how good Elizabeth was in bed. "I don't know," he always said, knowing at the same time that they didn't believe him. "And don't any of you jerks try to find out either. If you try anything with her, I'll make you into eunuchs. Count on it." The trouble with his teammates, Cal knew, was that they didn't understand what love—real love—was all about.

Elizabeth herself brought up the subject, too, one starry night when they were lying on the blanket stretched out over a mound of soft, fragrant grass beside Miss Maudie Brewster's fish pond. Cal had just rolled away from her...again...short of penetration.

"Why do you always *stop?*" she asked, sounding frustrated. "Why don't we go on and make love, the way we both want to do? Everybody in school thinks we're doing it anyway."

"I can't help what everybody in school thinks. I'm thinking about you and me, and what would happen if you got pregnant."

"It wouldn't be the end of the world if I did get pregnant," she said. "We were planning to get married anyway."

"Yes," he agreed. "But after we finish college. We're still in high school, remember?"

"You could go on and finish...and I'm sure I could pass that graduate-equivalency exam or whatever they call it.

Then after the baby was born, we could enroll at the university together."

Cal was surprised that she seemed to like the idea of their having a baby. It was the most frightening thing he could think of that could happen, but instinctively he knew he shouldn't say that to her. "I don't have the basketball scholarship for certain, Elizabeth. And your parents have already made plans for you to go to school up north."

"They'd change their minds once they learned about the baby," she said blithely. "And if the scholarship doesn't come through, you could take a part-time job. I could get one, too."

"And who'd take care of the baby?"

"We'd work something out."

Cal closed his eyes. For the first time, he realized how much older he was than Elizabeth. He knew that he'd have to be responsible for both of them, and vowed that when they did make love, he'd be the most protected man alive.

He also knew they *would* make love eventually; it was only a question of when and where. And once they crossed that bridge, there'd be no turning back. He already dreamed about her every night, and lived for the time they spent together. Once they made love, he'd want her even more than he already did; he'd want to touch her, taste her, bury himself inside her again and again. He wouldn't be able to get enough of her.

And he knew one last thing—it was better for everybody concerned if they postponed their lovemaking as long as possible. Regardless of how much Elizabeth thought her parents would welcome a new baby into the family, Cal was certain that her father would want to kill him if he made the Bartlett's only daughter pregnant.

OKAY. *So having a baby wasn't such a good idea*, Elizabeth thought, only half listening to her teacher in last period. It was the only thing she'd been able to come up with, though, and she was getting desperate. Cal would be graduating in only a short while, and then . . .

She tried not to be selfish about it. She knew how important it was to Cal to go to college—to be the first person in his entire *family* to go to college—and she admired his determination, respected his ambition. Even so, she dreaded the idea of having to suffer through two more years of high school without him. *Two whole years!*

She had a sudden thought. Maybe it didn't have to be *two* years. Her grades were good—excellent—so maybe she could take some kind of test and graduate a year early. Of course, there was the matter of her parents, who were already making plans to send her to her mother's alma mater up north, but she had no intention of going there, and hadn't had since she fell in love with Cal. She was going to attend the same college as he did, wherever it was.

A year's separation would be bad enough but not unbearable, the way two years would be. Besides, Cal would be home for summer vacation, plus all the holidays. And while he was away, she'd just have to be strong…the same way he was. She *would* be strong, for as long as it took until they could be together again.

The bell rang. With a sigh of relief, Elizabeth gathered up her books and hurried outside to meet Cal.

She found the Harley-Davidson in its usual spot in the parking lot, and wasn't surprised that she'd arrived before Cal. He had chemistry last period, and cleaning up after lab experiments sometimes made him late. She perched herself on the bike to wait for him.

Everybody seemed to leave the school in one huge exodus, and the parking lot was almost deserted in a matter of minutes. Elizabeth took out her American Literature book to read tomorrow's assignment, a short story by Truman Capote.

Finishing the story, she sighed with satisfaction and closed the book. Then, glancing at her watch, she frowned. Cal was really late today, later than he'd ever been before. They must have made a terrific mess in chemistry lab. She yawned, stretched, and then resettled herself on the bike to wait for him.

Twenty minutes later, when he still hadn't shown up, she started to wonder what could be keeping him this late. He might be in detention, but that seemed unlikely. Since they'd started going together, he said he'd cleaned up his act, preferring to spend time with her rather than in detention. Besides, even if he *had* had a relapse, he'd have been out long before now.

Where could he be?

She started getting worried. Maybe somebody had made a *real* mess in chemistry lab today. Maybe there had been an explosion and Cal was hurt.... But news about something like that got around school fast, and surely she'd have heard about it....

Then she saw him. Walking down the school steps and across the parking lot toward her.

And seeing him, she knew immediately that something was wrong. Terribly wrong.

She ran over to meet him. "Cal! What is it?"

"I'm okay," he said, looking down at the asphalt rather than at her. She knew he was lying. He *wasn't* okay, nowhere near it, but she didn't know what to do, so she fell in step beside him, heading back to the Harley.

When they reached it, Cal seemed not to know what to do next. "What happened?" she asked.

He didn't answer, merely shook his head, looking like he wanted to cry.

She took a firm grip on his forearm. "Cal, this is me. Elizabeth. You can tell me what happened."

He shook his head again. "No."

"Tell me what happened!"

"I..." He finally lifted his head. He wasn't crying, but there was such grief—such deep agony in his eyes—that Elizabeth felt tears spring into her own eyes in response to his pain. "I didn't get the scholarship. The basketball scholarship," he added, as if she wouldn't automatically know which scholarship, after they'd talked about it so many times.

"Oh, Cal."

He closed his eyes, and she could feel his pain as if it were her own. It *was* her own. "Oh, Cal," she said again, wrapping her arms around him and pulling his head down to her shoulder. "Cal. Cal," she said, holding him fiercely, trying to absorb some of his pain so it wouldn't hurt him so much.

She held him for a long, long time, neither of them speaking. Finally Elizabeth removed her arms from around Cal's neck and took his head between her hands, looking him squarely in the eye. "I think what you need...what we both need...is to take a long ride on the Harley. It'll help clear our heads. What do you say?"

He shook his head. "The mood I'm in... It could be dangerous for you."

"No more than it would be for you. And we're in this together, aren't we?"

He took a deep breath and let it out slowly. "Yes, I guess we are."

"Then let's go."

He nodded, and Elizabeth settled herself onto the passenger seat behind him, winding her arms tightly around his waist, holding onto him for dear life...both hers and his.

He took off with a roar.

GONE. *Gone. All gone. His hopes, his dreams... gone forever.* And what about all the practice? Years of it—hours he could have spent working at Lum's saving his money to pay for college instead of hoping it would be handed to him on a silver platter. *Nothing in life is free,* Lum had told him time and time again. Why hadn't he listened?

Cal gritted his teeth, giving the Harley more gas and feeling it surge forward underneath him. Faster. Faster. Maybe if he could get the machine to go fast enough, he could outrace all the terrible demons screaming inside his head. He grinned, not with pleasure but with pain, and hunched forward, urging the bike to go faster.

He roared down a lonely stretch of highway outside town, not noticing the scenery as he usually did, intent only

on the road stretching out in front of him...and on speed.
He spotted a logging truck several hundred yards ahead, so
overloaded that it was lumbering along at a snail's pace.
The road ahead was clear, so Cal pulled over into the left
lane. He was about halfway past the truck when he saw its
twin—another flatbed loaded to the gills with tall, sagging
pines—pulling onto the highway from a dirt road at the
left.

Oh, dear Lord.

He had three choices, but quickly discarded one of
them—if he tried to put on the brakes too fast and pull in
behind the logging truck beside him, there was a good
chance he'd lose control of the bike, especially at the speed
he was going, so that was out.

He could take off into the field on the left side of the
road. It seemed to be fairly level from this angle...but Cal
knew that standing water was often lying immediately beneath the surface, just out of sight, and if they happened
to hit some, they'd flip over for sure. In his mind's eye, he
could see Elizabeth flying up into the air...and landing, her
body twisted and broken....

So that left one choice...their only one. He had to
maintain his speed, and hope they'd be able to sneak between the two logging trucks before they met. He leaned
forward, urging the Harley to go faster....

The oncoming truck was already on the road; Cal could
hear the change of pitch as its driver shifted into another
gear, picking up speed. They weren't going to make it! *Oh,
Elizabeth, I'm so sorry,* he thought. *Forgive me....*

At the last possible moment, just before they smashed
into the oncoming truck, Cal saw the front end of the truck
beside him and angled the Harley to the right, barely
clearing both sets of front bumpers. He felt a gigantic
shudder of relief go through him, then another one. He
swiveled around to look at Elizabeth, but couldn't see her
face because it was hidden behind her helmet.

"Are you okay?" he shouted.

"Yes!" she shouted back. "And so are you! It wasn't the end of the world, after all!"

He gave her a thumbs-up sign, and turned his attention back to the road. He wanted to find a place to pull off as soon as possible...a place where he could stop and tell Elizabeth how much he loved her.

CAL GRADUATED FROM high school, worked full-time at the service station during the summer, and enrolled at the nearby community college for fall semester. He turned in his resignation at the station, and was surprised when Lum wouldn't accept it.

"You think I'm going to let you get away now, after I've spent years training you and you're finally starting to be worth something to me?" Lum said. "Hell, I'll hire a new kid to pump gas. I need you to help me repair engines! You can work as many hours as you have free, and I'll pay you by the hour."

Cal accepted the offer gratefully, swallowing the lump in his throat.

Cal started commuting to and from the community college on the Harley, putting on a big front with Elizabeth and telling her he had the best of both worlds—being able to attend college, and still being able to see her as often as he had while they were still in high school. That's what he told Elizabeth...but secretly he was scared to death.

For one thing, he'd only saved enough money for a few semesters at college...tops. In addition to that, he didn't know how long the Harley-Davidson could hold up under the pressure of a long commute twice a day. When it finally collapsed—as he was sure it would do eventually—he didn't know what he'd do. Maybe the best thing would be to drop out of school for a while and work full-time. He could save his money and... And then what?

Elizabeth would probably be in some fancy college up north by then, safely ensconced someplace far away from him, out of his reach. She wouldn't want to go; he was certain of that. But how much choice would she have? He tried to push depressing thoughts of the future out of his mind, and they kept crowding their way back in relentlessly.

ELIZABETH WAS ALL EXCITED when he met her at Sally's house after work one night. He waited to quiz her about it until they were alone outside. "What's going on?" he asked. He could see her struggling to suppress her elation.

"How would you like to spend the weekend at my house?" she blurted.

"What?"

"My parents are going to a convention down in Ponte Vedra. They won't be back until Tuesday."

He swallowed, refusing to let himself think about the ramifications of what she was suggesting. "So?"

"I just thought it would be nice to spend some time together in a real house for a change... instead of outdoors on a blanket," she said. It was one of the few times he'd ever seen her angry. "We don't have to *do* anything, if you don't want to."

"You know I want to!" he said, growing angry himself. Didn't she know how many miles he ran, how many hours he spent under cold showers, trying to control his desire to make love to her? She had to know. "I've been trying to protect you—"

"Protect *me*...or yourself? If it's really me, then I don't want your protection!"

"Elizabeth—"

"Don't *Elizabeth* me! A simple answer will do—yes or no."

"Yes, dammit! But I want one thing understood. This is your idea."

"That's great, Cal! Just great! And if something goes wrong, it'll all be my fault, I suppose."

Her voice broke, and he looked at her more closely under the glare of the streetlight, suddenly seeing her in a different way. She was already seventeen, he realized with surprise. In no time at all she'd be eighteen, an adult in the eyes of the law. Wasn't it strange that he'd still been thinking of her as she was when they first met—an appealing and attractive fifteen-year-old who needed his protection.

Now here she was almost an adult...and almost in tears, tears *he* had caused...and for what? He'd always told himself he was holding off making love mainly for Elizabeth's sake, but maybe that wasn't true. Maybe he was merely trying to protect himself, as she had said, and if that was the case... Hadn't almost everything that could go wrong *already* gone wrong for him? Why continue to deny both of them something they both wanted?

He pulled Elizabeth into his arms, holding her against his chest. "No it won't be your fault. I want this more than you do, Elizabeth, probably much more. And you know it. Thank you for making it possible."

WHEN CAL FINISHED work the following Saturday, he rolled the Harley-Davidson inside the garage, planning to leave it there and walk to Elizabeth's house. A big black motorcycle parked at the Bartlett's would be sure to attract attention—and talk—from the neighbors.

"Is it okay if I leave this here tonight?" he asked Lum, who was trying to wipe grease from his hands with a rag already saturated with grease.

"Sure. Something wrong with the Harley?"

"Something's *always* wrong with the Harley," Cal said with a rueful grin. "I thought I'd take a look at it tomorrow."

"Want me to come down and help?"

"Nah, thanks anyway. I don't think it's too serious this time. Besides, aren't you and your wife supposed to go to that family reunion tomorrow?"

"Hell, yes. Why do you think I offered to come down and help you?"

They both laughed. Then Cal went over and washed his hands in the deep sink, using special soap to remove the worst of the grease. He wished he had time to go home and scrub before heading for Elizabeth's, but he didn't. Reaching for a towel beside the sink, he was surprised to see

Lum watching him, a thoughtful expression on his lined face. "Something wrong?" Cal asked.

"No!" Lum said quickly. "I mean... Well, there's something I've been meaning to talk to you about."

"Okay."

"Well..." Lum said again. "The thing is...I know how much trouble you have with the Harley...."

"It's nothing serious this time," Cal said, breaking in.

"Maybe not, but something or other is wrong with it almost all the time, like you said before. And I was thinking...you need dependable transportation to and from school."

Cal wondered what Lum was getting at...and also why he seemed so ill at ease. "So here," Lum said, pulling out what looked like a small notebook from the pocket of his coveralls and handing it to Cal.

Cal looked at it, then opened it up. It wasn't a notebook. It was a savings-account passbook from the local bank. The account had been opened in the name of John Calvin Potts...and a deposit had been made, as well. The deposit...

Cal opened his mouth to speak, but nothing came out. He cleared his throat and tried again. "Fi-...fi-...*fifteen thousand dollars?*"

"It's for college," Lum said, "and transportation to get you there and back if you want to commute. If it was me, I'd go ahead and enroll at the university and forget about that little community college. It's only a two-year school anyway, and everybody knows it takes four years to get a real degree."

Cal shook his head, finding it hard to breathe. "I..."

"I know that probably won't be enough to cover four years, but it'll get you started...and we can deposit some more money later on."

"Lum," Cal said, still shaking his head, feeling his throat tighten so much it hurt when the full impact of what his friend was trying to do finally sank in. "Lum...I can't..."

"Course you can! I don't have any kids...but if I did, I'd want them to be like you...so who better to give my money to?"

"I'll never forget the offer, Lum," Cal said. "But I can't take the money."

"But I told you..."

"No."

Lum took a deep breath, then let it out slowly. "I had a feeling you'd feel that way. I wish you'd listen to reason, but if you won't...then we'll make it a loan instead of a gift."

"A loan? How would I ever be able to repay a loan like that?"

"I thought of that, too," Lum said, cackling with obvious delight. "You'll pay me back right off the bat...just as soon as you make your first million!"

A SHORT TIME LATER, Cal reviewed his conversation with Lum while he walked the eight blocks to Elizabeth's house, carrying his small athletic equipment bag with a change of clothes inside. He still couldn't get over Lum's offer. Even though they cared deeply for each other—more like father and son than employer and employee—an offer like that was...unbelievable.

When they said good-night, they were still arguing about it, Cal refusing to accept the money and Lum saying he was a damned fool if he didn't accept it. And maybe Lum was right. Suppose he did use part of the money—as little of it as possible, and strictly as a loan—to finish college. He could start repaying Lum as soon as he graduated and got a job...couldn't he?

Cal decided to think about it some more...but tomorrow or the next day, not now. Now he had more immediate things to worry about—and be nervous about—because he was getting close to Elizabeth's house. He decided not to tell her about Lum's offer, which he probably wouldn't accept.

Squaring his shoulders, Cal marched up Elizabeth's front steps, and reached out to ring the bell. She opened the door before his hand was halfway there. "Hi," she said, looking as nervous as he felt.

He returned her greeting and stepped inside, watching her close the door quickly before she turned and gave him a smile that seemed forced. She took a step toward him, but he held up his hand to stop her.

"You don't want to touch me. I'm filthy." He was embarrassed for her to see him as he was after a day of working in and around car engines. He'd always made it a point to scrub himself before meeting her, but hadn't been able to tonight. "Is there someplace I can wash up?"

She led him upstairs to her bedroom, which had an adjoining bath and was almost as big as his entire house. The furnishings in the room—the thick, plush carpeting, elaborate drapes and expensive-looking furniture—probably cost more than everything in his house had. "I put out clean towels," she said. "If there's anything else you need . . ."

"I'll be fine. Thanks."

"Well . . ." She seemed about to say something, but then changed her mind. "I'll wait for you in the kitchen. Is pizza okay for dinner?"

"Great!" he said, trying to sound enthusiastic. As soon as she left he looked around the room again, knowing he didn't belong there. Elizabeth knew it, too, but now they both were trapped into this silly idea of hers—the idea of playing house while her folks were away. He headed for the shower.

After he finally finished scrubbing himself, he felt better. He put on the clean clothes he'd brought and reached for his sneakers, then noticed they had grease on them. They'd already made a spot on the bathroom carpet, and he hadn't brought extra shoes. He went downstairs barefoot, feeling more out-of-place than ever.

Elizabeth was seated at the kitchen table. As soon as she saw him, she jumped up so fast that she almost overturned her chair. Cal suddenly remembered how nervous she'd been when she let him in, and felt some of his own discomfort vanish, replaced by a great tenderness. He walked over and took her hand in his. "You can touch me now," he said. "I'm clean."

She smiled, and everything was okay again. Elizabeth put frozen pizzas in the oven to cook, and offered him a beer from a six-pack she'd managed to get somewhere, even though she was underage. After they ate, they went upstairs to her room and watched TV in bed, lying on top of the covers, carefully not touching each other at first, but gradually moving closer together.

Cal finally reached for her hand and simply held it between them on the bed. When the movie they were watching came to an end, she leaned over and kissed his cheek. Feeling his heart start to hammer faster, he pulled her back to him and kissed her on the lips. He felt a little embarrassed when he excused himself later to get the protection he'd brought with him... but not so embarrassed that he didn't get it. Then they made love for the first time.

When it was over, after his first euphoric joy and wonder had subsided, Cal started to worry. Elizabeth had held him and welcomed him, but she hadn't said a word during the entire lovemaking. He knew he'd been too fast—not at first, when he'd kissed her all over her entire body, time and again—but later, when he was finally inside her. He'd tried to hold back, but hadn't been able to. Maybe he'd hurt her. Damn him!

"Look," he whispered against her hair. "I'm sorry if that wasn't very pleasant for you, but—"

"But it was!" she contradicted. "It was... very nice."

Nice? "It'll be better next time," he said. "I promise. Wait and see."

Cal wasn't as confident as he tried to sound, but when they made love again later that night it *was* better. It was better for him because he wasn't as nervous this time, and he could tell it was much better for her. She cried out with pleasure several times, and was trembling and sweating when it was over.

"Oh, Cal," she whispered. "I've never felt anything like that before in my entire life. It was wonderful!".

He felt pretty wonderful himself. Cradling Elizabeth in his arms in her soft bed while she drifted off to sleep, he couldn't remember when he'd ever been as happy and content. And maybe... just maybe... he *would* take Lum up on his loan offer after his own money ran out. Cal decided to tell Elizabeth about it tomorrow and see what she thought.

CAL OPENED ONE EYE, saw bright daylight and quickly closed the eye, trying to orient himself. Judging by the sunshine, it must be late morning. But it was Sunday and he didn't have to rush, if he remembered correctly.

Also if he remembered correctly... the warm, soft feminine form lying underneath his outstretched arm belonged to Elizabeth. He opened both eyes, and smiled when he saw her face on the pillow beside him ... saw her rosy cheeks, her pink lips, her long, dark lashes. He felt the steady rhythm of her heart beating against his arm... and his smile broadened. He could be perfectly happy... lying just like this in bed beside Elizabeth...for the rest of his life.

He sighed.

Then he frowned, sensing that something was wrong, although he had no idea why he would feel that way. What could possibly be wrong on such a beautiful morning, with Elizabeth sleeping peacefully in his arms? In a little while, he might start kissing her until she woke up. And then...

He still couldn't shake the feeling that something was wrong, and finally turned over. He looked toward the door... and stopped breathing.

A woman was standing in the open doorway leading from the hall. Well dressed. Immaculately groomed. Painfully thin. Mrs. Bartlett.

She was watching Cal and Elizabeth.

Neither Cal nor Mrs. Bartlett moved or spoke for what seemed an eternity. He felt paralyzed, and she merely stood there, an expression of disbelief on her face. "Oh, my God!" she finally said, lifting one bony hand to clutch her throat.

Then she screamed, her voice reverberating through the room.

"Oh, my God!"

Part Two

Chapter Six

Seventeen Years Later

The afternoon sun was ferocious, blistering the concrete sidewalk and causing heat to rise up in waves. The weather was no hotter than she was, Elizabeth Bartlett decided, the only difference being that she was steamed because she was mad as hell.

She could believe such a thing happening in a big city, but not here. Her car had actually been stolen on Main Street in Planters' Junction *in broad daylight!* It boggled the mind.

Elizabeth strode with determination toward her destination, a weathered cinder-block building that had seen better days. Reaching it, she hesitated, studying the faded sign that said Sheriff's Office, and dreading the confrontation ahead.

She didn't want to talk to the sheriff anymore than he wanted to talk to her. *Damn this for happening,* she thought. But it had happened . . . and to her. Her car had been stolen, and the sheriff was the only law in town, so . . . She flung open the door and stepped into a large room that was silent except for the drone of a window air-conditioning unit fighting a losing battle against the heat.

The room was dimly lit, contrasting sharply with the glaring sunlight she'd just left, so that she could barely see. Pushing her sunglasses to the top of her head, she blinked several times and at last was able to make out a solitary figure in uniform seated at a desk behind a waist-high wooden railing.

Closing the door behind her, she walked over to him, her high heels making a staccato sound on the tiled floor. The man, a deputy according to the badge on his uniform shirt, seemed to be absorbed in reading something lying on his cluttered desk. "I'm here to report a crime," Elizabeth announced.

The deputy didn't bother looking up. "I'll be with you in a minute."

Trying to control her impatience, Elizabeth waited silently, fidgeting from one foot to the other as the moments ticked by. She took another look at the deputy. He was young, probably in his early twenties, judging by his smooth pink face that still had traces of baby fat. His forearms, stretching out from the short sleeves of his uniform shirt, were tanned, with a sprinkling of freckles and blond hair of the same shade as that on his close-cropped head. She wondered what he was reading that was so important he couldn't take time to hear her complaint. What if she'd just witnessed a murder?

She cleared her throat in order to remind the deputy that she was still waiting. He merely held up one hand to signal silence. Heaving an exaggerated sigh, Elizabeth stood on tiptoe and craned her neck to get a better look at what he was reading.

It was some kind of report...a very long one. She sighed again, trying to be patient but getting madder by the moment. She was a taxpayer, a person who paid the deputy's salary, yet he placed more importance on a stupid report than on the crime that had been committed against her. "Listen—" she muttered.

"Just a minute."

Elizabeth clenched her teeth. *"No."*

The man must have heard the controlled fury in her voice because he immediately lifted his head and stared at her with startled blue eyes. "Not in a *minute,*" she said. "Not in a second. *Now.* This is important. A crime has been committed."

She watched with mounting rage while the deputy deliberately rearranged a stack of papers before returning his attention to her. "I'm Deputy Siddons," he said officiously. "What can I do for you?"

"I'm Elizabeth Bartlett, and I'm here to report a theft," she said slowly, trying to keep a tight rein on her temper. She almost lost the battle when she saw the deputy suppress a yawn as he reached for a pad and pencil.

"What was stolen?"

"My automobile."

Deputy Siddons looked up at her and blinked, then blinked again. Elizabeth would almost swear she saw his face grow pale beneath his tan.

"Your... your car was stolen?" he said haltingly.

What was wrong with the man? Judging by his tone, you'd think she'd just told him the country had been invaded by aliens from Mars. "That's right," she said.

"When did it happen? And where?"

"Just a short while ago, on Main Street."

"I...I think the sheriff himself needs to handle this," Siddons said, jumping up from his chair and heading for a door at the back of the room. "I'll tell him," he said over his shoulder. "You wait right here."

Where else would she go? she wondered, and also wondered whether Deputy Siddons might be "not quite right in the head," as her grandmother used to say. His behavior was strange to the point of being bizarre—rude and aloof one moment, abnormally upset the next. She heard the muted sounds of men's voices coming from inside the sheriff's office and promptly forgot about the deputy, bracing herself instead to confront his boss.

Deputy Siddons was back in a matter of moments, his formerly pink face now beet red. Elizabeth wondered what he and the sheriff had said to each other. "He'd like to see you in his office," Siddons said.

"Thank you, Deputy," she said with exaggerated politeness. She approached the office slowly, deliberately pacing herself, then stepped inside. She vaguely heard the sound of Siddons closing the door behind her...but her eyes, her attention, her entire being...were focused on the man seated behind the desk only a few steps away.

The sheriff. Cal Potts.

This was the moment she'd dreaded, and one of the first things she'd thought about as soon as her car was stolen— meeting Cal again face-to-face. The two of them hadn't spoken in seventeen years, not since her parents had found them in bed together and then immediately shipped her away to school in Europe.

She'd seen him from a distance...several times, in fact, after she'd moved back to Planters' Junction following her divorce two years ago. But she'd also noticed him going to great lengths to steer clear of her. A couple of times she'd even seen him cross the street in order to avoid meeting her on the sidewalk.

That suited her just fine. Dandy. It was what she wanted, too. *But now, Mr. Sheriff Potts, you're going to have to talk to me, even if it's the last thing either one of us wants to do.*

She took the last few steps and stood in front of his desk, staring directly into his cool gray eyes. "Hello, Cal," she said, and marveled at the fact her voice sounded so calm when she was anything but calm inside.

John Calvin Potts slowly got up from his chair and stood facing her, all six feet two inches of him, all long, lean, muscular body of him. He didn't respond to her greeting immediately, but that didn't surprise her; Cal always did things at his own pace, in his own sweet time. Finally he inclined his head in a brief nod. "Elizabeth."

She'd expected him to be cold, but that response must have come directly down from the Arctic Circle. She didn't know why his reaction caught her off guard. What had happened between them had been a long time ago, a lifetime ago. There was no logical reason for her to feel a sudden, overwhelming need to penetrate his icy reserve. Still...

"You can relax," she said. "This isn't a personal call. I'm here on business."

His expression didn't change, but she was almost certain she saw a subtle tightening around his lips, enough to convince her that she'd succeeded in getting through to him.

"Deputy Siddons already told me you said your car was stolen. Otherwise I wouldn't have agreed to talk to you."

Elizabeth caught her breath. She knew she should have expected a biting response from him, and actually it was no more than she deserved after her remark to him . . . but still it stung. "You've turned into quite the charmer, haven't you?" she said.

"I'm merely being honest. Didn't you used to say that people should always express what they feel?"

She knew he was being as sarcastic as she'd been, but suddenly felt a tightening in her throat and an incredible sense of loss—of something infinitely precious being gone forever. "I may have said something like that...a very long time ago."

"But now you've changed your mind?"

Why wouldn't he let it drop? "Let's just say...I try to be more discreet."

"You mean devious, don't you? Is that a trait you learned in your law practice in Atlanta?"

She flinched, feeling as if he'd just slapped her. "You're determined to make this as difficult as possible for me, aren't you?"

He didn't say anything for a long time. Finally he took a deep breath and let it out in a rush. "Have a seat and let's get this over with."

Feeling both frustrated and relieved, she sank into the chair across from him while he seated himself behind his desk. "Are you sure your car was stolen?" he said without preamble.

"Sure?" she repeated, thrown off guard by the abruptness of his question. "How could I *not* be sure about something like that?"

"Maybe you forgot where you parked it? That could happen."

"It might happen to little old ladies with short memories, but it didn't happen to me. I know exactly where I parked—directly in front of Ellerbee's Drugstore at one forty-five."

"How can you be so sure? And so sure of the time?"

"Because I *am!*" Elizabeth replied impatiently. "I had an important appointment with Peyton Shipp for two o'clock at Planters' Junction Savings and Loan." Peyton was the president of the savings and loan, the man her father had handpicked to carry on in his place when he retired six years ago.

"I couldn't find a parking space in front of PJS&L, so I settled for a spot across the street in front of the drugstore," Elizabeth continued. "Then, because I was early, I went inside the drugstore to talk with Doc Ellerbee until it was time to walk across the street for my appointment. Understand?"

"Spell it out for me. For instance, what was so important about your meeting with Peyton?"

"I don't believe this! I came in here to report a crime— an automobile theft, with the criminal probably still somewhere in the neighborhood—and you're questioning me about my personal business!"

"It's my business to ask personal questions."

Elizabeth rolled her eyes. "My mother still owns a sizable amount of savings-and-loan stock. I merely wanted to talk to Peyton about her investment."

"I repeat," Cal said. "What was so important about this meeting?"

"It wasn't all that important!"

"You said it was. You said you had an 'important appointment' with Peyton Shipp."

Did Cal know about the sorry mess that Planters' Junction Savings and Loan had gotten itself into since her father's retirement and subsequent death? She could only hope he was guessing and didn't really know anything. "I'd have said that about any appointment I had. I consider all of them important."

"Cut the garbage, Elizabeth. What you mean is you won't tell me."

"I'll tell you anything you want to know about the reason I came here—the theft of my car! Doesn't that concern you at all... *Sheriff?*"

Her deliberate use of his official title didn't seem to intimidate him; he acted as if he hadn't even noticed. "It concerns me," he said. "Just as everything in this town concerns me... including the proper operation and functioning of our financial institutions."

So he *did* suspect that something was wrong at the savings and loan! And he was correct—something *was* wrong, terribly wrong, although Peyton had assured her that he had everything under control and that things would be looking up soon. She couldn't let Cal know that, though, any of it. Peyton had cautioned her about the need for secrecy. It wouldn't do for townspeople to lose trust in the savings and loan; that would almost certainly lead to disaster.

"I'm sure we'll all sleep better knowing you're concerned about us, Sheriff. And if you're that much concerned," she added, trying to steer the conversation in a different direction, "you might consider doing something about your deputy's behavior."

Cal narrowed his eyes. "What do you mean?"

"He's rude and unprofessional."

"What? Because he didn't bow when you came into the station?"

Elizabeth felt her cheeks grow hot. "Because I came in to tell you my car had been stolen, and he kept me waiting while he read a report."

"Maybe the report was important."

"More important than a crime that's just been committed? What if I'd just witnessed a murder? Would you let
him get away with ignoring that, too?"

Cal shrugged his shoulders. "Well . . . he *is* Mayor Buck
Maxwell's son-in-law."

Elizabeth stared at him, finding it hard to believe that
this was Cal Potts speaking. The fiery young man she used
to know would have fired such a rude, incompetent deputy
in two seconds flat . . . and probably beaten him up to
boot . . . even if he'd been the king's son. What was going
on?

She kept staring at him and finally managed to capture
his gaze with her own. She felt a flash of intuition, almost
like a jolt of electricity, like the old karma they used to have
between them . . . and suddenly she knew, with certainty. *Cal
was playing some kind of cat-and-mouse game with Siddons.* She didn't know what it was . . . but Cal knew. And
she knew it was serious.

He suddenly blinked, breaking the eye contact and the
bond between them, then blinked again as if to reinforce the
break. "I'll need to get some information from you for a
stolen-vehicle report," he said, pulling a printed form from
his desk drawer and reaching for a pencil and notepad.

She could almost hear the sound of the door being closed
between them. "Very well," she said. She leaned back in
her chair across the desk from him and watched surrepti-
tiously while he scribbled on a yellow legal pad. He was
how old now? Thirty-six? *Looking good.* Except for
broader shoulders and chest, and a couple of lines that
hadn't been there on his forehead before, he looked much
the same as he always had. There was no thickening at his
waist, and no gray visible in his straight brown hair.

He was more rugged than handsome, but there was
something about him that caught and held a woman's attention—many more women's than hers, or so she'd heard
since she moved back to Planters' Junction after her divorce. If what she'd heard was correct, he had been hotly
pursued by almost every eligible woman in town, al-

though—again going by hearsay—none of them had managed to "snare" him so far. What a dreadful expression that was! Still, she could understand what all those women found attractive about Cal. Even as antagonistic as he was toward her now, he still managed to emanate a powerful physical appeal that was both sensual and sexual, and dangerous at the same time.

"What name is on the title registration?" he asked abruptly, interrupting her thoughts.

"Beg pardon?"

"I'm not being personal," he said, obviously misinterpreting her reaction. "This is essential information. Is the car registered in your name or your ex-husband's name?"

"Mine. Bartlett."

"I *know* what your name is, Elizabeth."

"I thought you might not know I'd taken back my maiden name after the divorce . . . *Sheriff.*"

He opened his mouth to speak but didn't. Instead, he wrote something on the pad. "Make of vehicle?" he asked without looking up. She told him. "Year model?" he said, scribbling again.

"It's two years old."

"Oh. Part of the divorce settlement?"

She clenched her fists in her lap. "I bought the car myself—with money I earned myself—not that it's any of your business."

"I like to be thorough."

"Is that what you call it?"

"What do you call it?" he asked.

"I'd rather not say. You might arrest me for indecent language."

"You have a point," he said, nodding his head. "Let's call a truce while I take down the rest of the information."

When they'd finished, Cal got up from his chair. "We're hooked up to a nationwide computer system," he said. "I'll feed this information in right away."

Elizabeth got up, too. "What do you think the chances are of recovering my car?"

He shrugged. "I have no idea."

Her temper, which had been building for some time, finally exploded. "*Damn you!* Aren't you even going to *try* to recover it?"

He stepped back, looking as if she'd physically struck him instead of verbally assaulted him. She saw him take a deep breath. "Of course we'll try to recover it. But you asked me what the chances were and I honestly told you I don't know. This is the first car theft we've had in Planters' Junction in the three years I've been sheriff."

She took a deep breath herself, feeling like the awkward teenager she'd been the first time they met, instead of the supposedly mature woman she was today. She swallowed. "I...I'm sorry, Cal. Really sorry I said that. My only excuse is...I was on edge today."

"It's okay. I'd be upset, too, if somebody stole my car."

"It wasn't just that!" she said before she could stop herself. She debated with herself for a moment, then plunged ahead. "I was nervous about talking with you again, too. You know, after all this time..."

He started to say something but stopped. She tried to read his expression but couldn't.

"There's no need to apologize," he said finally. "I, uh, we'll do the best we can to find your car."

She was almost sure that wasn't what he'd intended to say; it certainly wasn't what she wanted to hear from him. But then... what *did* she want to hear?

"I'll have Siddons drive you home now," Cal said after another long, awkward pause. "Unless you'd rather wait and have me drive you after I've finished up here."

She shook her head. "No. You go ahead with what you need to do. I'm sure Siddons and I will manage fine...if he can tear himself away from his reports long enough to drive me, that is," she couldn't help adding.

"Siddons will do what I tell him to do. The department will be in touch with you as soon as we have anything to report."

There was no doubt that he'd said exactly what he intended to say to her that time, she thought. And there was no mistaking the look of disdain that accompanied his words.

CAL FINISHED FEEDING the data on the stolen car into the computer and settled back in his chair, thinking. When Deputy Siddons had told him that Elizabeth Bartlett was in the outer office today, he'd been dumbstruck. And his first rational thought had been: *Why is she here?*

He'd studiously avoided her for the entire time she'd been back in Planters' Junction since her divorce, and she must have known it. *Of course she'd known it!* So why...? And then, for one wild, insane moment, he'd thought, imagined...

As it turned out, she had a completely valid reason for showing up at the station, on his turf. Her car had been stolen. And instead of acting like the calm, professional law officer he was supposed to be, he'd found himself trying to needle her, trying to make *her* feel uncomfortable. He shouldn't have done that.

He closed his eyes, taking a deep breath. He shouldn't have done a lot of things where Elizabeth was concerned. Above all, he should never have fallen in love with her in the first place. He frowned, remembering things he'd sworn to himself that he'd never think about again: the time they met...how they fell in love...and later on, when they were torn apart after her parents came home unexpectedly and caught them in Elizabeth's bed together....

STANDING IN THE DOORWAY, watching them, Elizabeth's mother had started screaming, "Oh, my God!"

All hell broke loose then, everything happening at the same time. Mrs. Bartlett started weeping hysterically; Elizabeth woke up and immediately burst into tears, too, and Cal was torn between trying to comfort her and wondering whether he shouldn't get out of bed and run for his own life. He might have done that cowardly thing, if it hadn't been for another problem—he wasn't wearing a stitch of clothes; both he and Elizabeth were completely naked. His problem was solved, in a manner of speaking, when Mr. Bartlett rushed into the room and grabbed a handful of Cal's hair, literally yanking him out of bed.

"You...you..." Mr. Bartlett sputtered, so furious he wasn't able to speak coherently. He pointed to Cal's clothes, strewn on the floor where he'd left them the night before, then pointed to the bathroom. *"Get dressed!"* the man finally thundered.

Cal swiftly scooped up his clothes and ran for the relative safety of the bathroom. While he was pulling on his clothes, not bothering with buttons or shoes or stuffing the shirt into his jeans, he clearly heard the war raging in Elizabeth's bedroom. He heard first Mr. Bartlett, then Mrs. Bartlett ranting at her, calling her all sorts of terrible names. He heard Elizabeth crying heartbrokenly. He rushed back into the bedroom. "I'm sorry, sir," he said to Mr. Bartlett. "It was all my fault...."

"You're damned right it was. And now you're going to pay for it," the older man said, grabbing Cal's arm and pulling him toward the door.

"Daddy, no!" Elizabeth screamed.

"I'll deal with you later," Mr. Bartlett said. Then he turned to his wife and added, "Keep her in this room. Lock her in, if necessary, and don't let her out of your sight."

Mr. Bartlett pulled, pushed and shoved Cal down the stairs, out of the house and into his car parked in the driveway. Cal thought about telling him there was no need to be so violent, that he had no plans of trying to escape, and then thought better of it. He kept silent, and wondered where Elizabeth's father planned to take him. He found out only a few minutes later when they stopped in front of the county jail. Cal swallowed.

Mr. Bartlett opened his door and got out, so Cal did the same. The older man looked at him across the top of the car. "If you try to run, I'll have the sheriff shoot you down like a dog."

Cal nodded, and tried to fight back his rising fear. They went into the jail house, where Sheriff Maxwell himself was on duty. "James!" the sheriff said, getting up from his chair. "What are you doing here? I thought you were on a convention down in Ponte Vedra."

"Hello, Buck. I *was* on a convention but my wife got sick and we had to come home early. It turned out to be a blessing."

"That right?" the sheriff said, glancing at Cal for the first time.

"Look, Buck," Mr. Bartlett said. "I need your help on this, and I need everything to be kept confidential, just between us."

"Why sure, James. You know you can count on me. Any time."

"Thank you. The thing is..." James Bartlett paused a moment and straightened his shoulders. "When we got home...we found our daughter Elizabeth in...in bed with this *animal!*"

The sheriff's mouth dropped open. "Good Lord!"

"I want him put away...someplace where he can never touch her again."

"I don't blame you." The sheriff shot a brief venomous glance toward Cal. "Was he attacking her, right in your own home?"

"Not exactly," Mr. Bartlett said. "We don't know all the details yet, but we found them both in her bed, without a stitch of clothes between the two of them."

Cal was watching the sheriff, and felt a glimmer of hope when he saw the lawman's eyes narrow. The sheriff understood exactly what had happened; he *knew* that Cal hadn't attacked Elizabeth.

"I *want* him put away, Buck," Mr. Bartlett repeated. "For a long, long time."

Cal's hopes died a quick death when he saw the sheriff nod. "We'll have to decide on the charges first," Buck Maxwell said. "How old is Elizabeth now?"

"Only seventeen. Could we get him for statutory rape?"

Rape! Cal clenched his eyes together tightly, feeling sick to his stomach.

"The age of consent in Georgia is fourteen, so that wouldn't hold up," the sheriff said, shaking his head. "But we can sure as hell nail him on something else . . . like contributing to the delinquency of a minor—or sexual exploitation of children."

"How much prison time are we talking about?" James Bartlett asked matter-of-factly.

"It's hard to say. Back in the old days we could count on life, for sure. But you know how lenient the judges are these days." The sheriff turned to Cal. "You have a prior record, boy?"

Cal shook his head. "No, sir," he said, then watched the two men exchange a significant look.

"There'd have to be a trial, too," the sheriff said. "We could have it moved to another county, but word might leak back here."

"Any other suggestions?" James Bartlett asked.

Cal saw the sheriff think for a moment and then grin wickedly. "I hear the army rangers are still looking for a few good men. They send 'em up to North Carolina first for survival training . . . you know, teach 'em how to get along with snakes and bears and such. Then, after they've finished that, they ship 'em down to Fort Benning to learn how to be paratroopers."

"What's the minimum enlistment?"

"Two years, but the army will gladly sign a recruit up for four. And if some guy gets the idea of maybe trying to weasel his way out during that time, he can be thrown into an army prison for no telling how long."

"Sounds good to me," Mr. Bartlett said. "Do you think this young man will go along with it?"

"I'll have a heart-to-heart talk with him personally. I'm sure he'll agree it's the perfect opportunity for him."

Cal watched the two men with horror and amazement. They were discussing his life, deciding his future, and neither of them even bothered to look at him! He was sure the sheriff didn't even know his name.

By Monday, though—after a day and night in jail—Cal knew the sheriff very well. Bruised, hurting all over, and bleeding from a gash over his blackened eye, Cal—accompanied by Sheriff Maxwell—hobbled to the recruiting office and asked to join the United States Army Rangers.

Cal didn't know how they arranged it, but between the two of them, Mr. Bartlett and Sheriff Maxwell managed to have him shipped off to North Carolina almost immediately. He tried frantically to call Elizabeth before he left. Her father answered the first time he called, and hung up the phone the instant he heard Cal's voice. Her mother answered when he called again later and was a little kinder. "Elizabeth is well, as well as can be expected, but she doesn't want to talk to you."

"That can't be!" he shouted, knowing the woman was lying.

"I'm sorry," Mrs. Bartlett said. The phone went dead, and Cal stared at the receiver he still held clutched in his hand.

Cal called Quint as soon as he could after arriving in North Carolina, and asked his friend to get in touch with Elizabeth for him, at least to tell her where he was. Quint called back a short while later. "They said she's sick in bed with the flu and can't come to the phone."

Two days later, Cal called Sally, Quint's girlfriend, who also was a friend of Elizabeth's. "She's gone, Cal," Sally said sadly, and for a horrifying moment he thought she meant Elizabeth was dead. Then Sally continued, "They've sent her away to school in Europe. Switzerland, I think, but they won't give anybody the name or address of the school. I'm sorry, Cal. So sorry."

Cal nodded and tried to replace the receiver, but was unable to see because of the tears in his eyes, and unable to talk because of the terrible aching in his throat.

He despaired for several days, but then had a flash of inspiration. He might not be able to contact Elizabeth, but

she could write *him* ... and *would!* He called his mother
immediately. After a couple of perfunctory words of
greeting, he brought up the subject closest to his heart.
"Have there been any messages for me since I left?" he
asked. "Any letters?"

He thought she hesitated for a fraction of a second, but
then her voice came in loud and clear. "No. Why do you
ask? Were you expecting something important?"

"No. Well...I was sort of expecting a letter. Will you do
me a favor, Mom? Will you forward any mail I get?" He
gave her his address and waited while she wrote it down,
then had her read it back to him to make sure she had it
correct. "I'd really appreciate it, Mom, and I'll pay you for
the postage and all."

His mother didn't forward any letters to him. And when
he called her the next time, and the next and the next, she
told him that no mail had come for him. She sounded
apologetic.

He never heard from Elizabeth, and never saw her again
until many years later...until after she'd been married and
divorced, and he'd been to hell and back in a jungle in
Central America.

CAL HEARD A SOUND and looked down at the broken pencil in his hands. He'd been clenching it so hard that he'd
snapped it. He dropped the two ends onto his desk, thinking it was a pity that he couldn't break the ties that still
bound him to Elizabeth as easily as he'd broken the pencil.
For a time, he'd thought he *had* broken them.

When she'd come back to Planters' Junction to lick her
wounds after her scandalous divorce two years ago, he'd
steeled himself against her. He'd refused to feel sorry for
her, refused to talk to her, refused to even think about her.
And it had worked...or so he'd thought, until today.
Damn! The first car theft they'd had in town since he'd
become sheriff, and it had to be *her* car!

He sighed. Well, he'd just have to deal with it—and with her—until the case was resolved. What had happened between him and Elizabeth was long over and done...and he was going to make sure it stayed that way.

Chapter Seven

"I tell you, Cal, the country's going to hell in a basket," Lum Starr said. "Can't even balance a budget anymore. Why, if I'd run my business the way they run the country, I'd be in debtor's prison by now."

Cal kept his smile to himself, and tried to keep a serious expression on his face for his old-friend-and-ex-boss's benefit. Since his wife had died and he'd sold his service station for a tidy profit—later making even more money on stock investments—Lum had started fancying himself as a homespun philosopher and local financial wizard. Cal was glad that Lum was well fixed financially, but sorry that the old man was so lonely since he'd retired. That was the main reason Cal had built a garage behind his own cabin and occasionally bought an old clunker for the two of them to work on. They rarely made a profit on the cars they restored, but it made Cal happy to see Lum happy working on engines again.

"How about another cup of coffee?" Cal asked, getting up from behind the desk in the outer office of the station, where he was the only one on duty on this hot, slow afternoon.

"Believe I will," Lum said. "But just half a cup this time...and don't put in any cream to cool it down."

Cal nodded, still keeping his grin to himself. No matter how hot the weather was, his old friend still wanted his coffee even hotter. He was in the process of getting Lum's coffee when he heard the sound of the outside door being opened and closed. He waited until he'd finished pouring to look around and see who'd come into the station... then stopped dead in his tracks, sloshing hot coffee on his hand because he thought he was seeing a ghost from the past.

It wasn't a ghost; it was Elizabeth... a vision in crisp white slacks and a silky green blouse coming across the room in that long-legged stride of hers he'd know anywhere, looking much the same as she had years ago. As she drew closer, though, he could see the changes, the earlier promise of great beauty now fulfilled in her face, her fuller breasts, her riper body.

She wore her hair shorter than she had seventeen years ago, but it was still the same rich auburn shade, and her deep green eyes seemed even greener now that she accented them with eye shadow. Aside from the eye shadow, she appeared to be wearing no other makeup except lipstick, but he could be wrong about that. Hadn't he read somewhere that women could apply makeup so skillfully that they appeared to be wearing none? It didn't matter whether she was or wasn't, he decided. She looked terrific, and he could feel his body responding to her the same way it always had. He hated his body for betraying him... and hated her for still having such physical appeal to him... and loved Lum for *being* here and perhaps keeping him from making a fool of himself.

Cal walked over and handed Lum his coffee, then looked at her again. "Hello, Elizabeth. I assume you're here to make your daily inquiry about your stolen car."

He was vaguely disappointed when she refused to rise to his bait. "That's right," she said cheerfully. "I assume there's nothing new to report."

"You assume correctly." He heard Lum clear his throat and shifted his gaze to his ex-boss. Lum was frowning, and made a motion in Elizabeth's direction with his head. Cal didn't understand. "What?" he asked.

"You going to introduce us or not?" Lum asked with exasperation.

"Oh. Sorry." Cal made the introductions.

"I'm really pleased to meet you," Elizabeth said, shaking Lum's hand. "I've heard about you for years and years."

"That right?" Lum asked warily.

"Don't worry," she said with a laugh. "It was all good. People said you knew more about car engines than anybody alive."

"Well... I wouldn't say that...."

"You don't have to say it...as long as everybody else says it," Elizabeth pointed out, and the two of them laughed.

Just like old friends, Cal thought, wondering how Lum could allow himself to be taken in by a little flattery. He was positively beaming!

"So how come you never brought your car into my station?" Lum asked.

"I, uh, left Planters' Junction years ago... before I was old enough to have a car. And by the time I moved back, you'd already sold your station."

Lum nodded, and patted the chair beside his. "Have a seat."

Cal hoped Elizabeth wouldn't follow Lum's suggestion, but after a moment's hesitation she did.

"You want me to have Cal bring you some coffee, Elizabeth?"

"Thanks anyway, Lum," she said, patting the old man's hand. "But I never drink hot coffee unless the temperature outside is below ninety-five degrees."

Lum cackled with delight. "We got us a live one here, Cal. And when are you going to do something about finding her car?"

"We're doing the best we can—" Cal began.

"Appears to me, that's not good enough," Lum said.

"That's what I keep telling him," Elizabeth agreed.

"So do *better*, you hear?" Lum said.

Cal nodded, seething with righteous indignation and...and what? Something. After all, Lum was *his* friend, the best friend he had. Who did Elizabeth think she was, coming in here and trying to charm her way into Lum's life? And doing a damned good job of it. She had no right doing that! And as soon as that thought crossed his mind, another one came right behind it—*he was jealous!* He was immediately ashamed of allowing himself to fall prey to such a base juvenile emotion. He mentally chastised himself...but the emotion didn't go away. Then another thought—an even more disturbing one—crossed his mind. Was he jealous of Elizabeth?...or of Lum?

"How do you find retirement, Lum, after working at the service station all those years?" she asked.

"It was pretty boring at first," he admitted. "Damn boring. But then Cal came back home and he keeps me busy. We keep each other busy."

"Oh? How so?"

"Working on car engines," Lum said, as if she should have automatically understood that. "Cal went and built this dang garage behind his house...and on top of that, he bought all kinds of fancy tools. He must have spent a fortune!"

"Really?" Elizabeth asked, looking at Cal instead of Lum.

Cal saw a smile playing around the corners of her mouth, and an expression in her eyes that bordered on friendliness...if not outright admiration. He shook his head vehemently. He didn't want her friendship, and certainly didn't want her admiration. He wanted her healthy disregard—her disgust, her hatred, her repulsion. And he wished with all his heart that Elizabeth and Lum would stop talking about him as if he weren't in the damned room!

"Of course you have to understand something else, Elizabeth," Lum said, continuing to ignore Cal's presence. "Since my wife died, and since Cal's mama was killed in that terrible fire, the two of *us* have been almost like family. We're all each other has."

Elizabeth looked at Cal again, frowning, seemingly distressed. "Your mother died? Oh, Cal. I'm so sorry, so very sorry. I . . . I didn't know. . . ."

How could you know? he thought. *You wrote me off even before she died . . . about the same time your father had me shipped off to that stinking jungle.* "It happened a long time ago," he said.

"*How* long ago?" she persisted.

He shrugged. "Ten or twelve years."

"Sixteen years," Lum said, correcting him.

"Right after . . . ?" Elizabeth said, a horrified expression on her face. "Oh, Cal. What happened?"

Cal fought desperately against a rapidly rising panic inside him. He didn't want to be discussing this—any of it—and certainly not with Elizabeth Bartlett. "A house fire," he muttered.

"A holocaust is what it was," Lum said. "The whole house and everything and everybody inside it burned to the ground. And all because of that drunken idiot Luther Scroggins!"

"Why . . . ?" Elizabeth said, her eyes still fixed on Cal's. "I mean . . . how . . . ?"

This time, Cal was grateful when Lum answered her questions. "All the fire department was able to piece together—and there wasn't much left to go on—was that the fire started in the bedroom. Luther must have been drunk again, as usual, and must have been smoking in bed when he passed out. According to the neighbors, the whole house was up in flames in a matter of minutes."

Cal swallowed, feeling the familiar helplessness when he heard the story again for the umpteenth time. He tried to focus on the farthest wall in the station room—tried to distance himself from what he was hearing, as well as from Elizabeth, who was hearing the story for the first time—but found his gaze drawn back to her. She had one hand over her mouth, and was staring at him with tears in her eyes. Either she was a damned good actress or . . .

Damn it! He didn't want her pity! He didn't want anything from her, except to be left alone. The past was dead, so why couldn't she let it rest in peace? *And why couldn't he?*

"Now don't you fret, Elizabeth," Lum said, awkwardly touching her shoulder. "Like Cal said, it all happened a long time ago."

She nodded, still looking at Cal. He turned away. "Did you know Cal's mama?" he heard Lum ask.

"No!" Cal exclaimed, wheeling back to face them. "She didn't know my mother at all. She never even met her. Isn't that right, Elizabeth?"

"Yes, that's right," she said quietly, looking directly at him, tears still glistening in her eyes. "But I know how much you loved her."

Cal clenched his fists. He'd forgotten how much of himself he'd revealed to Elizabeth in their late-night conversations years ago. She knew more about him—him as he'd been back then—than anybody on earth, including Lum. He tried to hate her for that, too, but couldn't. He had only himself to blame.

A short while later Elizabeth left. As soon as she was out the door, Lum turned to Cal. "She's a pretty little thing."

"She's not so little," Cal said, thinking about her long legs that seemed to go on forever.

"Littler than you," Lum argued. "And me," he added, patting his stomach. "You going to disagree with me that she's pretty, too?"

"No," Cal said with a sigh. "I agree with you on that."

"It's about time you agreed with me on something. Why were you so rough on her?"

"I wasn't—"

"C'mon Cal. You might be able to fool some people, but don't try it with me."

"Okay," he said, sighing again. "Maybe I was a little rough on her, but she can take it. And she had it coming."

"What'd she do?"

"I really don't want to talk about it, Lum."

Lum removed his baseball cap and scratched his head, the way he always did when he had serious thinking to do. "Wait a minute..." he finally said, and Cal dreaded what was probably coming next. "You two knew each other years ago and... Is she the one whose daddy—"

"Yes." Cal said. "Now let's drop it, will you? Please?"

"Hell, no, I won't drop it! If her old man was mean enough to do what he did to you, there's no telling what he did to *her!*"

"All he did was send her away to a fancy boarding school in Europe. What's so bad about that?"

"And you blame her for everything that happened."

"No, I don't."

"It ever occur to you that she might not even know what her daddy did to you?"

"Of course it did. And it doesn't matter whether she knew or not. The point is, she didn't care enough to try to find out what happened to me. I never heard a single word from her."

"Still—"

"And I don't want to talk about it anymore! Not now... and not ever."

ELIZABETH REACHED FOR the telephone book to look up the number for the sheriff's office, but then realized she already knew it. She'd called it so many times that she'd memorized it without knowing she had. She hadn't been back in person to inquire about her stolen car, though, not since the day when she'd made such a fool of herself by crying when she learned that Cal's mother was dead. Her tears had seemed to make Cal even angrier with her than he already was, like pouring salt into an open wound, almost as if he hated her for intruding on his personal and private grief.

She wondered—not for the first time—why Cal seemed to actively dislike her so much. She could understand hurt, regret, even some anger... all the things she felt. But his animosity was stronger than that, bordering on all-out hatred. And not knowing what had caused it, she didn't know how to combat it . . . even if she'd wanted to combat it, she reminded herself as she punched the numbers for the sheriff's office.

A man answered after two short rings. "Sheriff's office, Deputy Lovejoy speaking."

"Hello, Travis," she said. "This is Elizabeth Bart—"

"Hello, Miz Bartlett," the deputy said, interrupting her. "We still don't have anything on your stolen car, but we'll keep working on it."

How many times had she heard that before, either from Cal or one of his deputies? She sighed. "If you find any—"

"Yes, ma'am," he said, interrupting her again. "We'll let you know, first thing."

She compressed her lips and hung up the phone. It wasn't as if she suddenly expected her car to be recovered after almost a month, but Lovejoy could have at least let her finish a sentence. She sighed again, then went out to the sun porch, where she found her mother just finishing breakfast, touching the corners of her mouth with a linen napkin that appeared to be as delicate as she did.

Appearances can be deceiving, Elizabeth thought, knowing how resilient her mother really was. Still slender and attractive in her early sixties, Frances Forsythe Bartlett had the look of a fragile, bruised flower—a look that made men fall all over themselves trying to protect her. But when Elizabeth's father had died five years ago, her mother—who had lived for years in the shadow of her rich and powerful husband—had changed almost overnight, blossoming fully grown into her own person.

Now, Frances Bartlett was free to wield her own power and exert the will she'd always had—a will as strong as tempered steel. Elizabeth knew that will of her mother's, knew it from years past; she'd battered herself against the strength of it several times, and had come up a loser every one of them.

"Any news?" Frances Bartlett asked, looking up expectantly.

Elizabeth shook her head, helping herself to another cup of coffee before she sat down opposite her mother. "I suppose I should give up and buy another car. I can't keep using yours forever."

Frances nodded. "That's what the insurance man suggested weeks ago...not that I mind sharing the Cadillac with you."

"It's just that I *hate* the idea of giving up!" Elizabeth said. "Of letting someone get away with such a blatant theft, in broad daylight. You'd think that someone out of the entire population of Planters' Junction would have noticed *something!*"

"I'm sure that Cal Potts and his deputies have done everything they could."

Elizabeth caught her breath, and quickly put down her coffee cup before her hand had a chance to shake. What had prompted her mother to say that, when she'd never had a complimentary thing to say about Cal before? Was she deliberately testing the waters to see what her daughter's reaction would be?

"Everybody in town talks about what a fine job Cal has done since he's been sheriff," Frances said.

She *was* doing it deliberately, Elizabeth thought, determined to hide her emotions from Frances. She wouldn't give her the satisfaction, not to mention the advantage. Any ammunition she supplied could upset the uneasy truce that had existed between her mother and her since Elizabeth had returned home after her divorce two years ago. It could throw the balance of power in Frances's favor, and make it impossible for her to live in this house any longer.

"What do you think, Elizabeth?"

Lifting her eyes to meet her mother's steady stare, Elizabeth shrugged. "I wouldn't know. He certainly hasn't had any notable success with my case," she said, hoping her mother would drop the matter.

She didn't. "Are you suggesting that he carries a grudge against our family from that matter years ago... and that he's not doing a proper job because of it?"

"I'm not suggesting anything, Mother." Cal *did* carry a grudge, Elizabeth knew, but her mother was the last person to whom she'd admit it. "I merely stated a fact."

"Still..."

"I don't want to talk about it anymore, okay?" Elizabeth said, losing control for a moment and regretting it immediately afterward. *And forever after that,* she thought, wondering how she had allowed herself to be drawn so easily into the trap her mother had set for her. Whenever they got into an argument—or a discussion, as Frances called it—Elizabeth always lost. Wouldn't she ever learn to refuse the challenge of still another confrontation? Taking a deep breath, she tried to do so this time. "What happened back then is long over and dead. Let's let it rest in peace, shall we?"

"I can let it rest," Frances said slowly, "but I'm not so sure you're able to do the same."

Underneath the table, out of sight of her mother, Elizabeth clenched her fists. *Here we go again.* "I can do whatever is necessary. After all, I survived seven years of marriage with Tate Northrup, didn't I?"

"I knew you'd get around to bringing that up sooner or later," Frances said. "I suppose you consider me responsible for that, as well."

"No," Elizabeth said, shaking her head. "I consider myself solely responsible for that stupid mistake." *You've made your point, Elizabeth, so stop now while you're ahead,* she told herself. But she didn't stop. She couldn't. "You and your friend Callie Northrup threw Tate and me at each other, but I was over twenty-one by then, so you couldn't force me into marriage the way you forced me to go to that school in Switzerland."

"If you had ever had a child," Frances Bartlett said in icy tones, "you'd understand that your father and I had no other choice. We *had* to send you to Switzerland. We couldn't let you throw your life away because of—"

"Because of Cal?" Elizabeth interrupted. "Only a minute ago, you said the whole town was talking about what a great job he's doing."

"Don't deliberately misinterpret what I say, Elizabeth. If you'd let me finish, I started to say because of some silly, schoolgirlish notion. That, and confusing rebellion with simple teenage lust."

Elizabeth felt her cheeks grow hot. *Let it go,* she told herself, but knew she wouldn't. In that respect, she was very much like her mother. "It was more than that!" she said, hearing herself shouting now and still unable to call a halt to the conflicting emotions crowding her senses. "You know it was!"

"You were only a teenager, for heaven's sake!"

"I was almost eighteen... and in love."

"You didn't know what love was at that age!"

Reality, and an overwhelming sense of defeat, finally caught up with her. Elizabeth suddenly felt tired, very tired. "You're probably right," she said. "But the thing is... I still don't know what love is, even now, after all these years."

Frances sat up straight in her chair, completely still. "And you blame me for that, don't you? You hate me."

Elizabeth closed her eyes for a moment. Her mother had triumphed again. "No, Mother," she said with a sigh. "I think it's myself I hate."

Hearing a faint sound, Elizabeth opened her eyes, then blinked. Her mother was no longer sitting straight as a ramrod in her chair; she was leaning toward the table, her head in her hands. *Crying?* Elizabeth frowned. *It couldn't be true. Could it?* She'd never seen her mother cry before, not once in her entire life, and the most emotion she'd ever seen her show was the time Frances had discovered Cal and her in bed together.

Elizabeth was suddenly as confused as she'd ever been in her life. Was it possible she'd been *that* wrong about her mother all these years? No. And yet... Wasn't it possible for people, including Frances Forsythe Bartlett, to change? Pushing back her chair, Elizabeth got up and walked around the table to her mother. After a moment's hesitation, she tentatively reached out her hand to touch the older woman's shoulder. And after another moment, Frances reached up and clutched Elizabeth's hand with her own bony fingers.

Elizabeth blinked back the unexpected tears that sprang to her eyes. But why shouldn't she cry? Her mother was offering her affection—a small amount of it, to be sure—but real, honest affection...for the first time in Elizabeth's life, for as far back as she could remember.

Frances removed her hand after another long moment, and Elizabeth withdrew her own hand from her mother's shoulder but remained where she was...completely still, silent, waiting...for what, she didn't know. Frances finally lifted her head and Elizabeth saw that there *were* tears in her eyes. She swallowed.

"You seem surprised to see me cry," Frances said.

"I am...a bit."

"I'm not a complete monster, you know."

"I never thought you were," Elizabeth said, lying a little.

"It's just that...living with James all those years..."

Elizabeth caught her breath and held it.

"Under his command, so to speak," Frances continued. "And putting up with his endless affairs..."

So what she'd always halfway suspected was really true! Elizabeth thought, trying but unable to suppress her gasp.

"I'm sorry to shock you, but it's true," Frances said. "The first one...the first time I found him out...happened only a few months after your little brother died at birth. You were too young to remember, but I was so distraught that the doctors had put me on sedatives around the clock."

Elizabeth wondered why her mother had still been taking sedatives *months* after her child's death.

"James had taken to sleeping in his study so he wouldn't disturb me, or so he said. And then one day when I was

feeling better, I decided to go downstairs for the first time
and surprise him.''

Elizabeth saw her mother take a deep breath, drawing
herself up to sit ramrod straight in her chair again, as if that
posture would protect her.

''I surprised him,'' Frances said, ''...and your pretty
little nursemaid, as well. Right there on the sofa in his
study...in *my* house. Our house. I dismissed her on the
spot, of course. And James...''

Elizabeth waited as long as she could, and when her
mother still didn't continue, she prompted her. ''What did
he do?''

''He reacted like the sneaking, sniveling coward he was.
He actually started crying, swearing that he loved me and
no one else...''

''And...and you didn't believe him?''

''After what I'd seen with my own eyes? I told him that
his vile, tainted hands would never touch me again! I meant
it. And I stuck by it, to the day he died. And his later ac-
tions proved I'd made the right decision.''

Oh, dear Lord, Elizabeth thought, finding it hard to
breathe. *Like mother, like daughter.* Except she'd never
denied Tate sex the way her mother had denied her father.
And Tate had never cried and sworn he loved her and no
one else. He'd laughed and dared her to take him to
court.... But she didn't want to think about that now, not
after her mother had finally revealed herself to her, after all
those years...those sad, wasted years...years of desolation and loneliness for both of them, for everybody in this
household. She finally felt a small measure of forgiveness
for her father, too, after all this time.

''Mother,'' she said, placing her hand on Frances's
shoulder and giving it a gentle squeeze.

Frances didn't say anything, and didn't cover Elizabeth's hand with hers this time, but she nodded in ac-
knowledgement of the proffered sympathy. It was a
beginning.

ELIZABETH BORROWED her mother's car again—for the last time she hoped—and went shopping for a new automobile for herself. She was shocked at how much prices had risen since she'd bought her last car. And she hadn't actually bought it, she suddenly remembered; Tate had picked it out and told her it was the car she should have. She'd merely paid for it.

Thinking about it some more, Elizabeth realized that she'd never picked out her own car, on her own, in her life. Always before, some man had made the major decision for her... first her father, then her husband. Ex-husband, she corrected herself. And deceased father. And her mother knew even less about buying cars than Elizabeth did... so she really was on her own this time. It gave her a heady sensation, a sense of power.

For such a small town, Planters' Junction had a surprisingly large number of automobile dealerships. She visited every one of them, including one that specialized in used foreign imports. "Pre-owned," the salesman corrected her, "so you know what you're getting." Elizabeth wondered about that. If the previous owners had thought so little of the cars that they'd traded them in or sold them out-right... what *would* she be getting?

After several hours of shopping, Elizabeth was tired and everything was beginning to look the same. She was thinking about calling it a day and coming back again tomorrow, when she spotted... it. She stopped in her tracks and stared at it for a long moment...several long moments. The salesman accompanying her must have noticed, but didn't comment for some time. "You like the Jeep Cherokee?" he finally said.

"Is that what it is?"

"Yeah. Sweetest little four-wheel drive on the market today... sporty, sassy. You can drive that baby *anywhere*, in any kind of rugged weather."

Elizabeth didn't plan to drive anywhere except on paved highways, and the weather in this part of the country was anything but rugged, but she adored the car. She wasn't about to admit that to the salesman, though, having heard all the old jokes about women shopping for automobiles. "Tell me some more about it," she said, walking closer to the object of her affection. "What about gas mileage, city and highway...and safety features?"

With one part of her mind, she heard the salesman rattle off facts and figures, but she wasn't really listening. She'd already made up her mind; she had to have this car. She was in love with it. She touched it—touched the gleaming white exterior paint job that wasn't really practical. It would probably be a muddy brown mess the first time it got caught in a South Georgia rainstorm. No matter. She would wash it herself, giving it the care it deserved.

She bought the Jeep, and insisted on driving it home that very afternoon. The salesman volunteered to follow her in her mother's car, with a second salesman following him to drive them both back to the dealership. Elizabeth enthusiastically accepted his offer.

She was feeling very pleased with herself as she turned into the circular driveway in front of her mother's home and motioned the entourage of salesmen to follow her. Another car was already parked there, but the drive was wide enough that the salesmen would have no trouble getting past it. After thanking the men, Elizabeth started up the walkway to the front door, but stopped after only a few steps and turned back to look at the visitor's car. At first she'd assumed it belonged to one of her mother's friends, but now she remembered that Thea Richards also drove a car like that.

She quickened her steps, hoping it *was* Thea who was visiting, because she really liked Quint Richards's new wife. Then she grinned when she realized she was still thinking of Thea as Quint's *new* wife, even though the two of them had been married for more than a year. The reason Elizabeth continued to make the error was because she remembered Quint's first wife, Sally, who had died young, leaving Quint a widower with two children.

Quint had had a terrible time of it and Elizabeth, who had just gone through a traumatic divorce herself, had tried to console him. For a short time, she had imagined that something might develop between the two of them, but it hadn't. And if there had ever been a chance of romance between Elizabeth and Quint, that chance had died a quick death as soon as Thea came to Planters' Junction. Almost from the moment Quint met Thea, other women had ceased to exist for him. The spark—the excitement, the sexual awareness—between the two of them was so strong you could almost feel it when you were in the same room.

Elizabeth had recognized it, and known it for what it was, the first time she'd seen Thea and Quint together, although it had taken those two longer to realize the obvious...that they were meant for each other. Quint had leftover guilt feelings about Sally, and Thea had troubles of her own—two young sons and an ex-husband who was a dangerous drug addict.

But Thea and Quint had gotten together finally and now were happily awaiting the birth of their first child in only a few months. Elizabeth sighed. She loved happy endings. Then she sighed again, with a little envy and regret this time. *But enough of that,* she told herself, going into the house to look for Thea.

She found both her friend and her mother having iced tea in the sitting room. "Thea," Elizabeth said, rushing over to kiss her cheek. "It's so good to see you! And don't you look great."

"You mean great as in 'great with child?'" Thea asked with an exaggerated grimace.

Elizabeth laughed. "No, I mean great as in 'terrific.'"

"Liar. But thanks anyway."

"No. I really mean it."

"Would you care for tea, Elizabeth?" her mother asked.

"Yes, please. I'm about to perish from thirst."

"Your mother told me you were out shopping for a car," Thea said. "Did you have any luck?"

"You bet I did. Thanks, Mother," Elizabeth said, taking the glass of tea Frances handed her and drinking thirstily. "You are now looking at the proud owner of a brand spanking new Jeep Cherokee."

"Really? That's—" Thea began.

"A *jeep?*" Frances asked with a frown, making "jeep" sound like a dirty word.

Elizabeth refused to let her mother dampen her spirits. "That's right. Four-wheel drive and all."

"But... a *jeep,*" Frances repeated.

"It's not the same kind of jeep the army uses, Mother. This one is fully enclosed and has more doors than I'll ever use. And it's solid white, just like your Cadillac."

"Maybe you should give it some more thought...." Frances said.

"Too late. It's already bought and paid for. Fait accompli." Elizabeth smiled to herself, thankful that she'd anticipated the possibility of just such a reaction from her mother and had gone ahead and bought the car today. "It's parked in our driveway, even as we speak."

"Where's *my* car?" Frances asked.

"It's in the driveway, too. I had the salesman follow me home." Elizabeth drank the rest of her tea. "Want to come outside and see my new toy, Thea?"

"Sure," Thea said, finishing her own tea.

"How about you, Mother?"

"No," Frances said. "I, uh, have some other things to do. I'll see you girls later."

Thea waited until they were outside, walking toward the new car. *"Girls?"*

Elizabeth rolled her eyes. "There's no hope. Her own friends are still *girls,* too." They both laughed.

Elizabeth was delighted that Thea seemed to like the Cherokee as much as she did, making "Oooh's" and "Aah's" at all the right times. She even wanted to go for a short ride, a request to which Elizabeth happily complied. "You really, really, really like it?" Elizabeth asked when they pulled to a stop in the driveway after the ride.

"Yes," Thea said. "Really." She looked at her watch. "In fact, I like it so much that it's already time for me to go home and I still haven't mentioned the reason I came by."

"You mean you didn't come to see the new car, after all?"

"No," Thea said, laughing. "I didn't know you had it. I came to see you . . . and also to ask a favor."

"Name it," Elizabeth said, feeling expansive.

"You'd better wait until you've heard what the favor is first."

"Okay."

"I don't know where to begin," Thea said, frowning.

"Just jump in anywhere."

"Well . . . there's a young man. His name is Lance Strickland, and he's Jacinda's boyfriend. . . ."

"You've lost me already. Who is Jacinda?"

"Jacinda Phillips, a young woman who works for my Aunt Maudie . . . you may have seen her driving Aunt Maudie around town."

"Thin . . . long hair . . . pretty in a waifish way?"

"That's the one. Jacinda is sort of a combination chauffeur and companion. Aunt Maudie thinks the world of her. And Jacinda, in turn, thinks the world of Lance. She's in love with him."

"And . . . ?" Elizabeth prompted.

Thea took a deep breath. "Cal Potts has arrested Lance. For car theft. We want you to defend him."

Chapter Eight

"What?" Elizabeth asked. "You're asking *me* to defend someone accused of stealing a car... after what happened to me less than a month ago?"

"I know it's asking a lot but..."

"I'm the last person who should be defending someone accused of car theft," Elizabeth pointed out. "I'm still mad as hell about my own car being stolen. There has to be a conflict of interest here somewhere."

"I asked Quint about it, and he said there's no conflict unless Lance was the one who stole your car... and he wasn't."

"How do you know he wasn't?"

"He's not even *accused* of stealing your car. Cal arrested him for a completely different theft."

"Even so..." Elizabeth began.

"Please, Liz. You have to help us. Jacinda goes around crying all the time, upsetting Aunt Maudie, who in turn upsets the kids and everybody else.... The whole house is in turmoil."

"I'm sorry, but you'll have to find someone else."

"There *is* no one else. The only other lawyer in town is George Pulliam, and he's so old and forgetful that he can't even remember his own name half the time."

Elizabeth thought for a moment. "If the case against this young man... Lance...?"

Thea nodded.

"If the case against Lance should go to trial, will Quint prosecute it?" Elizabeth asked. Quint had recently been reelected district attorney for a second term.

"No. He's so close to Aunt Maudie, and she's so close to Jacinda, that he feels there'd be a conflict of interest if he did it. He'd bring in a prosecutor from another county."

"So bring in a defense attorney from another county, too."

"We want *you*."

A sudden thought occurred to Elizabeth. "Why are you so set on having me defend Lance?"

"Because you're the best..." Thea said, obviously hedging, and confirming Elizabeth's suspicions.

"Who says so?" she asked.

Thea looked decidedly uncomfortable. "Quint."

"And what else does Quint say, Thea?"

"What do you mean?"

"I mean, my dear," Elizabeth said, not unkindly, "that you're a terrible liar. You and Quint have cooked up this little scheme to bring me out of my shell, so to speak... to force me into practicing law again."

Thea blushed furiously. "We didn't..."

"Quint must have told you what happened to me in Atlanta—how my ex-husband and law partner was caught not only having an affair with one of our firm's clients... but also of grossly mismanaging her financial interests, as well. He must have told you that my ex-husband was disbarred... and that I escaped actual disbarment, but was severely censured."

"Quint also told me you were innocent!" Thea exclaimed. "How could they do that to you?"

"That's the question I asked. I was told that the bar association felt it had to set a precedent... it had to tell the world that we could be watchdogs over our own profession."

"It wasn't fair!" Thea said.

"That's what I said, too." Elizabeth shrugged and attempted a smile that didn't quite come off because the wounds and the terrible hurt still hadn't healed. Then, noticing Thea's obvious distress, Elizabeth took her hand and squeezed it. "Look, I appreciate what you and Quint tried to do. I'm very touched. Truly. But I still can't accept the case."

"I wasn't making up the story about Lance," Thea said, hanging on to Elizabeth's hand. "He *was* arrested for car theft and he's still in jail and needs a lawyer. Won't you at least talk to him? If not for yourself, then as a favor to us . . . to me?"

Elizabeth debated with herself for a moment. "Is that all you're asking? That I talk with him?"

"That's all . . . for the moment."

Elizabeth sighed. "I think you should have been a lawyer yourself."

"Is that a yes?"

"I suppose so . . . but only to talk with him. I'm not promising anything else."

"Thanks, Liz. You won't be sorry."

Elizabeth wasn't so sure about that. Talking with Lance would entail visiting the county jail, where there was a good chance she'd encounter Cal Potts again. It wasn't a prospect that filled her with girlish delight.

CAL BLINKED WITH SURPRISE when he saw Elizabeth walk into the station. The last time she'd come in person to inquire about her car, Lum had been visiting him. Cal remembered how she'd cried on hearing that his mother was dead, and how he'd reacted by throwing her sympathy back in her face. He was sorry he'd done that . . . and sorrier still that she still had the power to raise unwanted emotions in him. Her sudden appearance this time, though, seemed almost as if she had read his mind.

"Elizabeth," he said, hanging up the phone and getting up from the chair behind the desk in the outer office. "I was just trying to call you."

"Oh?"

"Yes. I was in the process of dialing your number when you came in."

"You must have heard from Thea or Quint, then."

"What?"

"They asked me to come by and talk with Lance Strickland, the young man you arrested for car theft."

It took a moment for what she was saying to register. "You mean they want you to represent him?"

He saw her eyes narrow before she spoke. "I am still a lawyer—and qualified to practice in the State of Georgia—in spite of what you might have heard."

"I didn't mean that the way it sounded, Elizabeth," he said, determined to keep peace between them this time. "All I meant was ... you caught me by surprise because I was calling you about something else entirely." He saw her relax a little, but not completely. She was still wary of him ... and with just cause, he had to admit, after the pressures he'd put on her the last times they'd met.

"And what were you calling me about?" she asked.

"There's a possibility that we may have located your stolen car."

Her eyes widened this time. "No kidding?"

He nodded. "We think it probably *is* your car."

She shook her head and suddenly, to his surprise, she laughed. "You're a lucky man, Potts," she said.

"I don't understand."

"I was about to hit you with both barrels. I was going to say, 'How is it that you're able to resolve other theft cases, even those that occurred after mine ... and to arrest innocent young men to boot ... and still not do a darned thing about finding *my* car?' And then I'd go on from there ... but you get the picture."

Cal had to grin. "Lucky me."

"Yeah."

"But don't get your hopes up too much, Elizabeth," he said, sobering quickly. "I haven't had a chance to look at the car yet, but it was found in an automobile graveyard, which doesn't sound too good."

"Why not?"

"Well...it might be in pretty bad shape...I mean, don't expect it to look the way it did when it was stolen. Very often..."

"Cal."

"What?"

"You sound as if you're a doctor, trying to prepare me for the worst, when a relative of mine is gravely ill."

"I guess I am, in a way. I know how upset you were when your car was missing. So naturally I thought..."

"I *hated* that car. And always had. The only reason I was upset was because someone had stolen my property... something that was *mine.*"

"And that's it?"

"I'm afraid so."

Cal might have laughed then, if he hadn't remembered something. *I was yours at one time, too, Elizabeth, body and soul. How did you react when your father stole me away from you?* He remembered how he had felt—violated, beaten, shaken to the core... and hopelessly outraged because he'd not only lost Elizabeth, but also lost every hope and dream he'd had for the future.

What he couldn't understand was why the memory was still as vivid as if it had happened yesterday. Maybe it was because the thing between them had never been *resolved.* He and Elizabeth had been torn apart and then...nothing. They'd never even had the chance to talk about what happened. And perhaps—after all these years—they *should* talk about it. Maybe if they did, he could finally get it, and her, out of his system once and for all.

That's a fine plan, Potts, he thought. *Excellent.* Except for one flaw. How could he bring up the subject without looking and sounding like either an idiot or a self-serving coward... or both?

He couldn't.

"Deputy Siddons comes on duty in about ten minutes," he said. "Would you like to drive out with me and take a look at the car after that?"

Elizabeth looked at her wristwatch, one that Cal recognized as expensive. *Just like she is.*

"Fine," she said. "I'll be ready to go as soon as I've finished talking to Lance Strickland."

Cal hesitated. "Elizabeth," he said, then cleared his throat. "I...uh, know how important it is for you to get back into the swing of things again...."

"What do you mean?"

"You know...to start practicing law again..."

"Has Quint been talking to you, too?"

"About what?"

"Don't play innocent with me, Cal. I know how close you and Quint are."

"So?"

"So Quint has taken it upon himself to try to rehabilitate me by having me get involved in Lance Strickland's case. And now you come along, repeating the things Quint must have told you...."

"Quint told me nothing. What I said to you was something I already knew myself."

"Of course!" Elizabeth said, slapping her forehead with the palm of her hand. "How stupid of me. The whole town knows. Planters' Junction—where everybody knows everything there is to know about everybody else. How could I have forgotten that?"

He could understand why she was defensive with him, trying to protect herself by hiding her feelings from him. After their recent encounters, her attitude made complete sense and it was justified. But this was something else, something that went deeper. And unexpectedly he felt anger at the people who'd hurt her so much—enough to make her sarcastic and brittle, when she'd once been open and honest.

"The point I wanted to make was..." he began. He made the mistake of looking into her eyes then, and stopped when he saw the mingled hurt, anger and distrust in their green depths. "I'm not sure this is the case you should take on now...at this time...." he finished lamely.

"And what's *your* suggestion about the cases I should attempt at this time... *Sheriff?* Jaywalkers, perhaps? Parking-meter violations? That sort of thing?"

"You know that's not what I—"

"No, I don't! And that's the point *I* wanted to make... *Sheriff.*"

It was a good point. And even though he wasn't guilty of what she was accusing him, he could see how she would feel the way she did. He shrugged, pretending indifference because he didn't know what else to do. "Would you like me to take you in to see Strickland now?"

She hesitated, as if she were unsure he was really capitulating so easily. "Yes. Please."

Cal led Elizabeth to Lance Strickland's jail cell, expecting her to stop him any moment and quiz him on the evidence they had against the young man. She didn't. Which meant she must *really* be upset, even more than he'd suspected. "Just call out when you're finished," he told her. "I'll leave the door open so I can hear you." She nodded.

Walking back to the station room Cal frowned, his mind racing furiously, and finally made a decision. He and Elizabeth *did* have to talk about what had happened between them seventeen years ago... and not only for his personal peace of mind. She needed the catharsis as much as—perhaps more than—he did. He didn't delude himself that their talking would solve all her problems, just as it wouldn't solve all of his, but it could at least get that particular part of the past out of the way, leaving each of them free to deal with their other problems and get on with the rest of their lives.

His HAIR WAS GORGEOUS. It was a beautiful shade of honey blond, sparkling clean as if he'd just washed it, and long enough to pull into a ponytail that would reach halfway down his back if he'd chosen to bind it into a ponytail instead of allowing it to spread out in soft curls around his shoulders.

And she was in more trouble than even she had imagined, if all she could think about was Lance Strickland's hair. For the second or third...or was it the fifth time?...Elizabeth chastised herself for being so upset that she'd neglected to ask Cal what evidence they had against the young man. True, she hadn't practiced law in more than two years...and hadn't practiced criminal law in more years than she could remember...but those weren't proper excuses; they were desperate crutches, and lame ones at that.

She saw Lance watching her warily from pale blue eyes, his expression mirroring her own unease. "I'm Elizabeth Bartlett, an attorney," she said briskly, walking over to sit in the only chair in the cell and motioning him to sit on his bunk. He didn't. He continued standing instead, towering over her and adding to her discomfort. "I was asked to come and talk with you by, uh, relatives of Ms. Maudie Brewster, Jacinda Phillip's employer."

"You talked to Jacinda?" he asked in a deep baritone voice.

"Uh...no. I only talked with Thea Richards, Miss Maudie's niece."

"Then I have nothing to say to you."

"*What?*"

"You heard me."

Elizabeth got up again. "Look, I'm no more excited about this arrangement than you are. But I promised the family that I'd at least talk to you...because Jacinda's so upset," she added as a sudden thought struck her.

"She is?"

"That's what I was told. They said she goes around crying all the time."

Lance looked as if he was about to cry, too. Elizabeth hoped he wouldn't. "So don't you think that the two of us could bury our differences long enough to talk to each other for a bit...just long enough for me to see if I can help you?"

Lance shook his head sadly. "I don't think anybody can help me."

"But we won't know that for sure unless we talk about it, will we?" Elizabeth asked. "Besides, anything you say to me will be completely confidential. They *did* tell you that, didn't they?"

Lance nodded affirmative.

"Okay," Elizabeth said, sitting back down again and taking out her notebook. This time Lance sat down, too. "I'll need a little background information. How old are you, Lance?"

"Twenty."

Elizabeth looked at him, raising an eyebrow. "Almost," he added.

"How almost?"

"Next February."

"Who are your parents?" she asked, writing in her notebook.

"I don't have any."

She looked at him again. "You mean you suddenly sprang forth on this earth . . . just as you are now? Did they write you up in the *Guinness Book of World Records*?" She was delighted when Lance snickered. A sense of humor was always a good sign as far as she was concerned.

"You know what I mean," he said. "I don't know who they were. I was brought up in foster homes."

Homes, plural, she thought. "Where are you living now?"

"The county jail."

"I mean before this."

Lance shrugged, looking uncomfortable. "Here and there."

"Could you be more specific? The most recent place," Elizabeth said, hating to have to badger him, but feeling that they might be getting close to something.

"I lived out of the backseat of my car, okay?"

Elizabeth leaned her head down, pretending to write in her notebook, but the only thing she could think about was an overwhelming sadness and the only thing she wrote was a question mark. She swallowed and lifted her gaze to face Lance again. "Do you have a job?" she asked quietly.

"Yeah. I work at a service station."

Oh, dear Lord, she thought. *Cal.*

She really wasn't up to this. Not only was she rusty in criminal law, after years spent catering to the needs of corporate clients, but she was also beginning to realize that her personal defense mechanisms were sadly in need of repair and shoring up. Lance needed—and deserved—much more than she had to offer.

"I'll be honest with you, Lance..." she began, preparing herself to tell him she couldn't handle his case.

"I know," he said. "You can't handle my case."

Elizabeth blinked. "Why do you say that?"

"Because people always say, 'I'll be honest with you,' when they're getting ready to dump on you."

She took a deep breath. "I *was* going to say something about not being able to represent you. But it wasn't because of you. It was because of me... because I don't feel qualified."

"Why not? Are you saying this is your first case?"

Elizabeth looked at him closely, and honestly couldn't tell if he was deliberately trying to flatter her or not. "Are *you* saying that I look young enough to be fresh out of law school?" she asked.

"No. All I meant was... Hey. Things are tough all over. Maybe you couldn't get a job or something."

Elizabeth suppressed her smile, wondering if she'd ever had a put-down as nice as his had been. "I had a job, Lance, a good one. But then... something happened. And I found myself not only without a job but... a lot of my self-confidence was gone, too."

He nodded. "Yeah. I've been down that road myself before, a couple of times."

Elizabeth found herself watching Lance with new interest, admiring his astuteness, respecting his tough veneer and the keen intelligence that lay beneath it. "What kind of a case do they have against you?" she asked abruptly.

He shrugged. "They pulled me over for driving a '76 Chevy with only one headlight. Then they checked and said it was stolen."

Elizabeth hesitated a moment. "And what did you tell them?" she asked, phrasing her question with care. There was no way she was going to ask him if he was guilty.

"I told them the truth."

"Which was...?"

"That a guy brought the car into the station for a tune-up, then called later to ask if we'd deliver it, which I was doing when they pulled me over."

"And they arrested you on the strength of *that?*"

"Well...there was a little more to it. It turned out that there was no such place as the address the guy gave me."

"Who was they guy?"

"I, uh...I forgot his name."

"What did he look like?"

"I'm not sure about that, either. We were really busy that day, with a lot of people coming and going...."

"How about your boss, the owner of the station? Did the police ask him if he remembered that particular customer?"

"Yeah. But he was busy down in the pit almost all day, changing oil. I was the only one who talked to the guy."

Elizabeth took a deep breath, and understood for the first time that Cal might have been trying to do her a favor by suggesting that she shouldn't get involved in this case.

WHEN ELIZABETH CALLED for Cal to come let her out of the cell later on, she still hadn't made up her mind whether she would defend Lance, and had told him as much. If nothing else, she could at least give him honesty.

"I understand," Lance said. "You have to..." He broke off abruptly, staring at something behind her. She turned and saw Deputy Siddons coming down the hallway toward them, probably to let her out.

She turned to Lance. "You were saying...?"

"Nothing." He quickly walked away from her, to the opposite side of the room, where he stared out through the bars of the cell's single window.

Elizabeth frowned. Before Lance had turned away, she had seen a brief flicker of something—fear? anxiety?—in his eyes. She had only caught a momentary glimpse, though...so perhaps she was imagining it. She must be. She followed Deputy Siddons back to the front office of the station, where Cal was waiting to drive her to the automobile graveyard.

"Would you like to go in my new car?" Elizabeth asked as she and Cal stepped outside into the bright sunshine.

"You have a new car?"

"Since yesterday...when I finally gave up on recovering the old one."

"Oh, ye of little faith," Cal said, shaking his head. Then, spotting the gleaming Jeep Cherokee, he asked, "Is this it?"

Elizabeth nodded. "Isn't it a beauty?"

"Not bad."

"*Not bad?* It's gorgeous!"

"If you feel that way about it, we'd better go in my car. It looks like we might have some rain later on, and you wouldn't want to get your new plaything all muddy out in the junkyard."

Elizabeth looked up at the blue sky overhead and started to protest; then she saw dark clouds building on the horizon and changed her mind. She climbed into the passenger seat of the sheriff's car. Cal folded his long frame into the driver's seat and started the car, guiding it smoothly out of the parking lot and heading for the highway going south.

They drove in silence for some minutes. "What did you think of Lance Strickland?" Cal finally asked.

She opened her mouth to speak, then closed it again. "I'm not sure," she said, glancing at him in time to see the sudden tightening of his jaw. "That's the truth," she added. "I'm not trying to be evasive. And for what it's worth...I decided that you were trying to do me a favor by warning me against the case."

He didn't speak, merely nodded his head, but Elizabeth saw his jaw relax. She smiled to herself. "What do you think about him?" she asked after another moment.

"I'm not completely sure, either. The evidence against him—did he tell you about that?"

"Yes."

"It's fairly solid."

"But not conclusive."

"Perhaps. But my gut feeling is...he's hiding something. I'm not sure what."

Elizabeth nodded in agreement. Then, realizing that Cal couldn't see her nod, she said, "I had the same feeling. And there was something else..." She frowned.

"What?"

"It was so trivial. I'm not sure that I didn't imagine it."

"Tell me anyway."

"Well, when Deputy Siddons came into the cell area to let me out, I thought...but it could have been my imagination..." She took a deep breath and quickly expelled it. "Anyway, I either thought or imagined that I saw a glimpse of fear in Lance's eyes. Is there any reason you can think of for that?"

Watching Cal's profile, she saw him frown, too. "No. None that I know."

"I probably imagined it."

"Maybe. But if you see anything similar to that again, would you let me know, Elizabeth?"

Suddenly, from out of nowhere, she remembered the feeling she'd had when she first went to the sheriff's office to report the theft of her car...the feeling that Cal had some personal cat-and-mouse game going with Winston Siddons. "Yes," she said after a moment. "I'll let you know."

Cal slowed down the car and pulled onto a graveled area in front of a small cinder-block building. "This is it," he said, releasing his seat belt. "I'm going inside to check the exact location of the car, but I should only be a minute. We might as well leave the engine running so you can be cool while you wait. It's still hot as blazes.''

He was out of the car almost immediately, heading for the junkyard office. Elizabeth watched him. She saw the outline of his long legs encased in the smooth chinos he seemed to favor instead of the blue uniforms his deputies wore. She saw the muscles of his rear end as he walked...saw the trim waist and broad shoulders that complemented the high, tight rear end.

She sighed, thinking how ironic it was that even now— after all these years and all that had happened—she would still think that Cal had the best-looking body she'd ever seen. She heard a rumble of thunder, and almost at the same time, the sun disappeared behind a cloud. Tilting her head to look up at the sky, she saw that the clouds that had been on the horizon were now much closer, and coming closer still. Rain seemed to be definitely on the way, and heavens knew the farmers needed it.

Cal returned with directions to the place where the car was located. They drove down a road that gradually narrowed to an aisle with cars parked close together on both sides of it. Then they turned left onto another aisle, right onto another and stopped, because there was no place else they could drive. They were completely surrounded by automobiles—old ones, almost new ones, wrecked ones and abandoned ones that had been towed in. Getting out of Cal's car and looking around, Elizabeth could see why people called it an automobile graveyard. The place was so spooky-looking that no other word would have described it half as well.

"I think your car is over in this direction," Cal said, pointing to his left.

"If it *is* my car," she corrected him.

"Right."

They started walking, but Elizabeth found herself lagging behind, fascinated by the array of automobiles, not to mention the sheer number of them. "Wait!" she said suddenly, coming to a halt. "Doesn't that look like Chip Webster's old convertible?"

Cal stopped, too, and studied the car. "I thought his was a darker blue than this."

"Well...it might have faded through the years." *Was it the same car?* Elizabeth wondered, remembering a glorious spring day, the last day of school, when they'd all piled into the convertible that Sally Webster had borrowed from her older brother, Chip. They were headed out to Paradise Lake, where there was going to be a grand party. She'd been with Cal, of course, as she always was in those days, but that particular day was something special. It was the first time Cal told her he loved her, and the first time she told him she loved him.

"You might be right," Cal said, still looking at the car, a thoughtful expression on his face.

Was he remembering the same thing she was? A loud rumble of thunder brought her back to the present. Then she felt a drop of rain on her arm. "We need to move along," Cal said. "It looks like we're finally going to get some rain."

It seemed to take forever, and they had to backtrack a couple of times, but they finally reached the car that Cal had thought might be hers. It was. Sort of. The frame was there, but almost everything else was missing. Tires, engine, radio, chrome, even the interior seats. "There's not much left," she said.

"I know. Is there enough that you can make a positive identification, though?"

"Yes. This is...was...my car."

Cal cleared his throat. "I don't want to question you, Elizabeth, but...how can you be sure? When there's so little left of it?"

"Because of this," she said, pointing to a deep dent on the door beside the driver's seat. "It, uh, occurred when my ex-husband and I were arguing one time."

Cal's eyes widened. "Your ex-husband did *this* damage...with his fists?"

"No. I did it. With a baseball bat."

He blinked. She laughed. "Want me to tell you about it?" she asked.

"I think not."

Rain started coming down in big drops then, and they both looked up at the sky, then at each other. "We'd better get back to the car," he said, taking her hand to pull her along.

Elizabeth felt a shock of surprise when he touched her, and automatically started to protest, but stifled her protest before she could utter it. What, after all, was wrong about his holding her hand while they ran back to the car? Nothing. Absolutely nothing. And not only that... but it *felt* good, too; his touch was warm and comforting. Familiar.

Familiar? she asked herself. How could that be? After all these years? She couldn't answer the question. She only knew that it was.

They were running faster now, and the rain was coming down harder, drenching Cal's short-sleeved cotton shirt and chinos, drenching the businesslike linen dress she'd worn to meet her prospective client. To make matters worse, she'd worn heels today, too. She tried to run on her toes, but could feel her heels digging into the wet soil every time she allowed them to touch the ground.

Cal veered to the left, pulling her along with him, and her right heel snagged on something, causing her to stumble. She almost fell, and would have if it hadn't been for Cal holding on to her hand, pulling her against his chest and halting their progress. He was breathing hard. So was she. Then she stopped breathing, holding her breath. The world stopped.

There were only the two of them, standing in a drenching rain in the middle of an automobile graveyard. Cal was still holding her hand, and his other hand was around her arm, where he'd grabbed her to keep her from falling. Her other hand was pressed against his chest, where she could feel the rapid hammering of his heart, echoing her own.

Chapter Nine

Cal knew he should move—say something or do something to get them out of the rain that was soaking them both to the skin—but he did nothing. He merely stood there, feeling suspended in time and space, watching Elizabeth as the rain beat against her face and plastered her hair to her head.

Suddenly he was gripped by an incredible sense of déjà vu as he remembered another time the two of them had been caught in such a rain. It had happened on the day they'd gone out to Paradise Lake, the first time he'd told her he loved her, and the first time she told him. Searching her upturned face and seeing the unreadable expression in the depths of her green eyes, he wondered if she was remembering, too....

A loud rumble of thunder, punctuated by a sharp crackle of lightning, broke the spell. Cal blinked. "Are you okay?" he asked.

She nodded. "Yes."

"I'm sorry. I should have realized you couldn't run in those high heels...."

"I'm okay. Real— Aaagh!"

"What is it?"

"I don't know. Something ran across my foot...."

They both looked down at the ground.

Elizabeth screamed.

Cal felt a voice deep inside himself screaming, too, when he saw what had caused her reaction—*rats*. There were rats on the ground all around them . . . rats everywhere, scurrying in all directions. They'd probably been driven out by the rain and were looking for a safe place to hide, but knowing that didn't even begin to ease his revulsion. Seeing the rats brought back all the old horrors, making him feel that he was reliving his own worst nightmares.

All he wanted to do was get the hell out of there. Fast.

"Don't be afraid," he told Elizabeth. "I'll carry you back to the car."

"You can't—"

"Of course I can," he insisted, suppressing a shudder as a large rat ran past. "I'll carry you piggyback."

"My skirt's too tight to—"

"Then pull up your skirt!" he shouted, barely able to keep his own panic under control. "And stop arguing with me." He turned and waited, then breathed a silent prayer of relief when he felt her climb onto his back. "Okay?" he asked, looping his arms around her legs.

"Yes," she whispered.

Cal started walking quickly, trying not to think about the disgusting furry rodents all around them. He didn't look down.

Elizabeth's arms were wound around his shoulders, her body pressed against his back, and he suddenly felt a violent shudder go through her. He thought about trying to say something to comfort her, but what could he say? He felt the same way she did about the rats . . . probably more so. He walked the rest of the way to the car in silence, barely noticing the rain pounding down against his face. He concentrated all his energy—all his willpower—on trying to avoid thinking about the rats.

Finally reaching his car, he opened the door on the passenger side and backed up to it so Elizabeth could lower herself to the seat without having to touch the ground. Then he walked around to the driver's side and got into the car himself, closing the door behind him. Only then did he allow himself to think, and react.

He took a deep breath and held it. He clenched his eyes tightly shut and clenched his fists so tight that he could feel his stubby nails biting into his palms. Then he started to shake. After a moment he clenched his hands around the steering wheel, clutching it as if it were life itself. And maybe it was, he thought, lowering his forehead to touch the steering wheel, too, as the memories—the nightmares—crowded in on him, and the shudders grew even stronger, racking his body. He was back in the jungle again... in the rain that never stopped, only coming down less or more... in the steaming heat... the smell of unwashed bodies ... and most of all, the stench of fear. Everywhere.

He didn't know how long he remained like that, motionless, lost in his own private hell. Finally a muffled sound caught his attention. Elizabeth. He'd forgotten she was here, and would gladly have given anything he owned if she weren't. Of all people on earth, he hated that she was the one to see him lose control the way he had. There was no help for it now, though.

He heard the muffled sound again, seeming to come from far away, although he knew she was sitting right beside him. He finally lifted his head to look at her. And when he saw her, she broke his heart.

She was huddled against the door with her knees drawn up to her chest and her arms wrapped tightly around them. She wasn't crying, but was trembling all over, so hard he could see it. And again, for the second time that day, he was reminded of that other time at Paradise Lake so long ago. She *had* cried then, until he had gathered her into his arms to comfort her.

He wanted to comfort her now, but didn't know how. He certainly couldn't put his arms around her. Could he? She might read something into it that wasn't there. She might even think he was trying to take advantage of her when her defenses were down. He waited, hoping her trembling would go away soon. It didn't.

He had to do *something*. "Elizabeth," he said, touching her shoulder.

For a time he thought she wasn't going to respond. Then she did. "I'm all right," she said in a muffled voice.

He saw a tremor go through her. "You're *not* all right," he said, awkwardly putting his arm around her. "So stop trying to pretend you are. Stop trying to fight it by yourself."

With a little sob, she turned to him then, burying her face against his chest instead of against her knees. After a moment's hesitation, he put his other arm around her, too, pulling her closer. And after another moment, he felt her arms go around his waist, and tighten.

They held onto each other. There was nothing sexual or sensual or even romantic about it. It was simply one human being offering comfort and another human being accepting it. Cal understood Elizabeth's need because he knew something about isolation and loneliness himself, knew it from years back. At times, especially after a period of exposure to danger and fear, he had actually ached with the need for human contact.

That's what he tried to offer Elizabeth now—healing closeness, with no strings attached.

Gradually, though, as her trembling subsided, he became aware of another need building inside him. He didn't want it to happen. It was the last thing on earth he would have wished. But he smelled the sweet, fresh scent of her hair, and felt the warmth of her body through the wet clothes she wore.... He closed his eyes, but immediately opened them again when the image he saw was one of Elizabeth—soft and warm and completely bare—lying in bed beside him.

"You're trembling, too," she said suddenly, lifting her head.

"Yes," he admitted. "Seeing the rats got to me, too." That wasn't a total lie. Seeing the rats *had* caused him to shake, except it had happened much earlier. "They made me remember the jungle...when I was in the army." He relaxed his arms and moved slightly away from her. "Are you okay now?"

"Yes," she said, moving back to her side of the car, looking endearingly self-conscious and unsure of herself. "Thank you."

For a wild, insane moment, he considered pulling her back into his arms again. "You're welcome."

"You saw rats in the jungle...?"

"Everywhere. Hordes of them. You wouldn't believe the horror stories we heard." He stopped himself, unsure whether it was for her sake or his own.

"And then today... How horrible for you." She brushed her wet hair back from her forehead with an impatient gesture. "I'm sorry, Cal."

He shrugged.

"Would you like to talk about it?" she asked.

Would he? She'd given him the perfect opportunity to open up the subject of the past, their past. And he hesitated, knowing there'd be no turning back once that door had been opened. Everything would have to come out. All the old hurts, the old wounds. *Was it worth it?*

"Did you know that your father forced me to join the army in the first place?" he asked, making his decision.

She flinched, as if he'd struck her. "He...told me something like that."

Cal was surprised for a moment. Then, remembering her father, he became suspicious. "What *exactly* did he tell you?"

"He said that...that he offered you the option of either marrying me or joining the army," she said in a rush.

"What?" Cal asked incredulously, feeling the old, familiar outrage. "He told you *that?* And you believed him?"

"No! I didn't believe him. I didn't believe him then, and I never changed my mind. But..."

"But what?"

"But I never heard from you!" she said. "Not one single word."

"You know that your father wouldn't let me come within a mile of your house."

"You could have called."

"I *tried* to call. Time and again. You must have known that."

"I *didn't* know that! I mean, I wasn't sure."

"How can you say that? Your parents wouldn't let me talk to you, but you must have heard the telephone ring. I kept hoping *you'd* be the one to answer. Why didn't you ever answer?"

"I . . . I couldn't."

"Couldn't? Or wouldn't? Maybe you simply decided that was a nice convenient time to be rid of me, once and for all."

"That's not true!"

"Then why *couldn't* you answer the phone?"

"Because they locked me in my room and took away my phone!" Elizabeth shouted, her words reverberating through the car.

Cal stared at her. She looked away. He blinked. He knew she was telling the truth, not only because she had no reason to lie about it at this late date, but also because she wouldn't have been so embarrassed if it hadn't been the truth. And that particular truth was something he'd never considered. He took a deep breath.

"But I wasn't talking only about the telephone calls, when I said I never heard from you," Elizabeth said after a moment.

Cal looked at her again and saw that she was still staring out the car window. "What *were* you talking about?"

"I was talking about later, and all the letters I wrote you from Switzerland. All the letters you never answered . . ."

Cal's head was swimming, and he felt as if he were suffocating. "I never received a letter from you, Elizabeth. Not a single one."

She turned to him then, looking as taken aback as he felt—stunned, shocked speechless. She shook her head. "I don't understand. I mean . . . Surely you don't think I'd lie about something like that." At that particular moment, Cal wasn't sure what he thought—about her, about himself, about anything.

"I think we need to talk some more," he said finally.

She nodded her agreement. Then she wrapped her arms around herself and shivered.

"But maybe we should do it another time . . ." he began.

"No," she insisted. "We need to do it now. Right now, while we're both a little . . . vulnerable."

"Vulnerable to pneumonia, you mean. You need to change out of those wet clothes."

"So do you," she said, looking at him. "But we still need to talk and we can't go to my place." She hesitated and Cal was afraid he knew what was coming next.

"Where do *you* live?" she asked.

Cal was almost sure that wasn't a good idea. "My cabin's not too far from here. It's on the way back to town actually, but . . ."

"Do you have any dry towels?"

"Yes."

"So?"

He sighed. "We'll go to my place."

ELIZABETH TRIED TO HIDE her discomfort from Cal, but she was so cold in her wet clothes that her teeth were chattering by the time they pulled up to a stop in front of his cabin, a rustic A-frame nestled in a clearing bordered by tall, stately pine trees. She managed to smile in spite of her discomfort, because Cal's home suited him so well. If she'd had to guess, this was exactly the kind of home she'd imagine he would choose for himself.

"It's still raining," he observed, opening the door on his side. "Do you want to wait while I get an umbrella?"

"What for?" she said, getting out of the car. "I'm already as wet as a person could be . . . except maybe you." She raced for the shelter of his screened porch and arrived there at the same time Cal did. Both of them were slightly breathless.

After fumbling for his keys, Cal unlocked the front door and moved aside for Elizabeth to enter first. She stepped into the cabin, which seemed to have only one huge room downstairs and a sleeping loft overhead. Much of it was hidden in late-afternoon shadows until Cal flicked a switch and the room was bathed in the warm glow of several lamps.

Elizabeth blinked in the sudden brightness, then blinked again as the room came into focus. She saw soaring ceilings, white walls and natural hardwood floors. Solid, unpretentious comfort. She liked it. To one side, she could see stairs leading to a sleeping loft. The stairs angled above a kitchen alcove and, beyond that, a door that probably led to a bathroom. Somebody—Cal?—had built bookcases to fit into one of the angled walls.

There was a large stone fireplace in the center of the back wall, flanked by a leather sofa on one side and two comfortable chairs on the other. The furnishings were decidedly masculine with a lot of leather and glass, but there several surprises, too—an elegant étagère, an antique rolltop desk and a colorful oriental rug that appeared authentic from where she was standing.

"I like it, Cal," she said, voicing her opinion aloud.

"There's still a lot more to be done."

"What?"

"The dining room table, for one thing," he said, pointing to the glass-topped table and four wrought-iron chairs. "I plan to move these out to the porch when I find what I'm looking for."

"What are you looking for?"

"That's the trouble. I don't know."

She started to say something automatically—something innocuous about knowing it when he saw it—but stopped when she saw the expression on his face. She had the distinct impression that he wasn't talking about the dining table any longer...or at least not entirely. Her mouth suddenly felt dry. She swallowed.

"But I'm sure you're not interested in my decorating plans," he said abruptly. "I'll get you a dry towel."

"I'll need more than that. My clothes are wet, too," she added when she saw his surprised look. "Do you have anything I could borrow?"

"I don't own a robe."

"How about a long-sleeved shirt then?"

He nodded. "They're in the closet in the sleeping loft. I'll go up and—"

"There's no need for you to do that. I'm sure I can find it and change clothes while I'm up there." Seeing his sudden frown, she added, "I mean...unless you'd rather I didn't go up there."

"It's not that. It's just...the sleeping loft is a disaster area."

She was surprised to see him suddenly unsure of himself. "I promise not to look," she said, trying to make a joke of it. He didn't even smile.

"I'll get you a towel to carry up with you," he said, heading for the bathroom.

Elizabeth frowned, wondering why he seemed so nervous. If even half the rumors she'd heard about him were true, he must have entertained women here before, and under much more romantic circumstances than this. Maybe that was it. Always before, Cal had had women here for romance, pure and simple. Whereas this was ...what? An unpleasant chore? Something that needed to be done in order to put the past to rest, and gotten over with as quickly as possible? She was still thinking about it when Cal returned with a fresh towel.

"Here," he said, thrusting the towel into her hands. "If you need anything else..."

"Thank you," she said, starting for the stairs and wondering what had come over him.

The sleeping loft wasn't a disaster area as Cal had claimed. It was mostly taken up by one gigantic bed, as

wide as it was long. The bed was unmade, so maybe that
was what he'd had in mind. She looked at the rumpled
covers, then her gaze went to the pillows. As far as she was
able to determine, only one of them had been slept on, but
that didn't mean anything because it only covered *last*
night.

She continued staring at the huge bed, wondering what
activities it had seen in the past. She could imagine Cal in
the bed—Cal with his gorgeous body, in the nude, his long
legs entangled with...whomever. She sniffed with self-
righteousness, then immediately chastised herself. Who did
she think she was to criticize him in such a way? Cal was
free, unattached and over twenty-one, so why shouldn't he
have a bed this size? Or even the size of the Atlantic Ocean?
And why shouldn't he enjoy it properly, as such a bed was
meant to be enjoyed?

Still... Looking at the bed, she suddenly found herself
frowning. She erased the frown immediately, but not before she recognized it for what it was. Jealousy.

She sighed and quickly walked over to double louvered
doors, the only doors in the room, figuring the closet must
be behind them. Everything inside was immaculate, with
shirts on one side, trousers in the middle, coats on the other
side. She selected one of Cal's white, long-sleeve oxford
shirts and flung it onto the bed, hanger and all. Then she sat
on the bed, shucking her wet shoes and panty hose.

She got up and removed her dress, slip and bra. She felt
her panties and discovered that even they were damp, so she
removed them, too. Surely Cal had a pair of shorts she
could borrow around here somewhere. She dried herself
with the towel he'd given her, then took his shirt from the
hanger and pulled it on. She buttoned it all the way to the
top at first, but then changed her mind and unbuttoned the
top two buttons. After hesitating a moment, she unbuttoned the third one as well.

She walked over to a small chest, the only piece of furniture in the room except for the bed, and opened the top
drawer. She saw socks, keys, handkerchiefs and a bunch of

coins, both foreign and domestic. She closed the drawer and pulled open the second one, finding what she was looking for. His undershirts were stacked neatly on one side of the drawer, his shorts on the other side. Seeing that he had both boxers and briefs, she thought for a moment and decided on briefs. She pulled out a pair of white cotton ones and felt a shiver of excitement run through her. *Don't be silly,* she told herself. *It's just underpants.* She stepped into them, pulling them over her hips as far as they'd go, and smiling when she found that they were bikini-cut. She let her hands linger on the smooth cotton fabric for a moment, imagining how Cal would look in the briefs... then guiltily dropped her hands.

She looked around but there was no mirror in the room and she hadn't brought her purse, so she had no way of knowing what her hair was doing. She ran her fingers through it a couple of times, fluffing it out and hoping she looked carefree and exotic rather than wild and abandoned. With her hair, it was a toss-up; it could go either way.

She rolled up the cuffs of Cal's shirt a couple of times, folded her own clothes into a neat bundle and carried it with her when she started down to meet him. Halfway down the stairs she stopped, suddenly remembering why they'd come to his house in the first place. She felt a tightening in the pit of her stomach and wished she was someplace else. Anyplace else.

She forced herself to continue down the stairs and after a couple more steps she saw Cal. He was standing by the front windows overlooking the porch, staring out into nothingness, as far as she could tell. She'd almost be willing to bet that he was thinking about why they'd come here, too. She walked slowly down the last few steps and over to him.

"I see you found some dry clothes, too," she said, commenting on his jeans and polo shirt.

He turned to face her. "I remembered that I had some clean ones in the clothes dryer. Here," he said, reaching for her clothes, "I'll take yours and put them in to dry now."

"I can do it."

"It's no problem. Besides, you don't know the settings for my machine. Gentle?"

"Yes. Please," she said, relinquishing her clothes and wondering why he insisted on taking them rather than allowing her to do it. Perhaps there was incriminating evidence in the bathroom—women's underwear and such—instead of in the sleeping loft, where she'd found none at all.

And perhaps he's merely being a proper host, she told herself sternly. Why couldn't she put a stop to all this fantasizing about Cal and other women? His affairs were none of her business. *He* was none of her business, or would be after their discussion today, after they'd finally buried the past once and for all.

And why did that fact fill her with sadness so deep that it bordered on desolation?

CAL FINISHED LOADING Elizabeth's clothes into the dryer and set the dials to start the machine. Then he took a deep breath before going back to face her again, hoping he wouldn't make an even worse fool of himself than he'd already managed to do... acting like an awkward schoolboy, and at his age! It was because he'd been thrown off guard, first by what she'd said about writing him letters—*all* the letters, she'd said. How many was that? And then, to make matters worse, they'd wound up coming here, wound up with her waiting for him now, dressed only in one of his shirts and nothing at all underneath it, judging by the clothes she'd handed him to put in the dryer. He swallowed.

Now he not only had to confront her with the truth after all these years, but he had to do it in the sanctity of his own home, his own private domain where he'd never brought a woman before. Ever. He saw other women, of course, but always at their homes or on neutral territory. Never here in the one place he treasured the most, the place he carefully guarded for himself alone. And a few good friends such as Lum and Quint.

He hadn't wanted to bring Elizabeth here, either, but at the time it had seemed the logical thing to do. Refusing would have seemed silly.

There was no help for it now, though, and no turning back, so he squared his shoulders and marched out to face her. He was surprised to find her in the kitchen alcove and his first reaction was: *She has no right to be here.* Who did she think she was, waltzing in here and acting as if the place belonged to her? "Looking for something?" he asked.

She whirled around, a guilty expression on her face. "I, uh, was thirsty."

"What would you like to drink?"

"A glass of water? Please?" she said in a small voice.

Looking at her—seeing her standing there in her bare feet, her hair in wild disarray, seeming more like a lost child than a desirable woman, with only his shirt for protection—Cal suddenly knew that she was as uncomfortable as he was, probably more so. And instead of trying to ease the situation, he was acting like a selfish, inconsiderate creep.

He cleared his throat. "I could make us a cup of instant coffee, if you'd like that better."

She closed her eyes for a brief moment. "It sounds heavenly."

Cal put a pot of water on to boil, measured instant coffee into two cups, then turned to face Elizabeth, who had moved to the edge of the counter and was silently watching him, a distinct expression of unease in her eyes. He knew how she felt. Exactly. And he knew they could go on the way there were doing indefinitely. "Cream for your coffee?" "Yes, please." "Sugar?" "Thank you." "Maybe some cookies to go with it?"

The possibilities were unlimited; they might even be able to go on that way forever, delaying, denying, hedging. And it would be the cruelest thing they could do... for both of them.

"After your parents discovered us in bed together," he said, plunging into the deep, dark uncharted waters, "your father took me down to the police station."

He paused long enough to allow what he had said—and his intention to continue—to register. Elizabeth's eyes widened. After a moment, she nodded her head. *Good,* he thought. *She understands what I'm trying to do... and approves.*

"Sheriff Buck Maxwell was on duty himself that Sunday morning."

"Mayor Maxwell?" Elizabeth asked.

He nodded. "One and the same. Your father told the sheriff what had happened—that he'd found us in bed together, without any clothes on...." He was watching her and saw her blink once, twice, but she continued meeting his gaze, and he felt a wave of admiration. Then he remembered: In spite of the years that had separated them, she was, after all, still Elizabeth. Of course she would continue to meet his gaze, the same as she would have done back then, daring him to be the first one to look away.

"The sheriff asked your father how old you were. Your father said that you were only seventeen, and asked the sheriff if I could be charged with statutory rape."

"Oh, dear Lord!" Elizabeth said.

"The sheriff said that wasn't possible, but that they could certainly nail me for contributing to the delinquency of a minor and other things. He also mentioned how a trial would attract a lot of publicity, and that judges had become too lenient.

"Your father said the thing he wanted was for me to be put away somewhere... safely away from you, I think he said. And the sheriff finally came up with the idea of having me join the Army Rangers for four years."

"What were you doing while that... that *farce* was going on?"

"I was simply standing there, listening. What could I do?"

"But they couldn't actually *force* you to join the army."

Cal rubbed his chin, remembering. "Sheriff Maxwell could be pretty persuasive."

"You mean he *beat* you?"

"Yes. Did a pretty good job of it, too, as I remember."

"But..." she began indignantly. "*Now?* In this day and age?"

"You seem to have forgotten how powerful Sheriff Maxwell was during his terms in his office. From what I've heard since, I got off light with only a black eye and a few busted ribs."

"That... That's horrible," Elizabeth whispered.

Cal heard the sound of the water boiling and turned away to make their instant coffee. Elizabeth was silent. "Would you like sugar or cream?" he asked after a moment.

"No. Plain black, please."

He handed her a steaming mug. "We can take these into the living room..." he began.

She shook her head, obviously still disturbed, and placed her mug on the counter. "My father," she said. "What did he do while... while the sheriff..."

"He wasn't there," Cal said emphatically, trying to be fair. "He left as soon as he and the sheriff finished talking, and I never saw him again."

"Still... He must have known..."

There was nothing he could say to that, so Cal shrugged.

"I'm sorry, Cal," Elizabeth said. "I know it's totally inadequate but... I'm sorry."

He shrugged again, and picked up both their mugs. "We should drink our coffee while it's still hot," he said, heading for the living room and feeling rather than hearing her follow him. He placed the mugs on the coffee table in front of the sofa. "Is this okay?" he asked.

She nodded and sat down on the sofa. He chose a spot a few feet away from her, not quite within touching range, figuring that would be more comfortable for both of them.

He watched as she lifted her mug and took a sip of the coffee, saw his shirt pull against her shoulders as she moved, saw the outline of her narrow back....

"You said you wrote me from Switzerland," he said. "Letters, plural?"

"Yes," she replied, cradling the mug between both her hands, as if seeking warmth from it. "Dozens of letters."

Dozens? "Where did you send them?"

"I didn't know where you were, had no way of knowing, so I sent them to you at your mother's address."

He shook his head. "That couldn't be."

"*I'm not lying!* Could your mother have—"

"*No!* Absolutely not."

"But—"

"My mother loved me. The same way I loved her. She would never have kept something like that from me. Besides..."

"Besides what?"

Cal hesitated. "I asked her a direct question about letters. By that time I was almost frantic...unable to get in touch with you because your parents wouldn't let me...wondering where you were...what had happened to you... And then I realized that even though I couldn't get in touch with you, you were still able to write me. So I called my mother."

Elizabeth was leaning forward on the sofa, her eyes blazing with intensity. "And what did she say?"

"She said that no letters had come for me." He hesitated again. "I believed her."

He could hear the sound of Elizabeth catching her breath, even if he hadn't been able to see it. And the pain in her eyes... He swallowed.

She didn't speak for a long moment. Then, when she did, the anguish in her voice tore straight through him. "Are you saying you don't believe me?"

He didn't answer. He wasn't even sure he was able to talk.

"But I tell you I wrote you...dozens of times...until I finally gave up."

"Maybe...maybe something happened to them on the way to the post office...where you were..." he said, trying to offer an explanation, solace—he wasn't sure what—just *something* to erase that look in Elizabeth's eyes.

"No," she said. "I wasn't able to mail the letters myself, because my parents had left specific instructions with the school authorities, but I gave them to someone I trusted completely. I'm certain they were mailed properly."

Cal frowned, trying to readjust his conception of the school that Elizabeth's parents had sent her to in Switzerland. He'd always assumed that it was an expensive playground, a place where children of the rich and famous went to emulate their parents' life-styles. But if she wasn't even able to mail letters—having to smuggle them out through *someone she trusted completely*—then his entire thinking had to be off base. Way off.

"Maybe..." he began tentatively. "Maybe you misplaced your trust."

"No! I couldn't be wrong about that. I couldn't."

"Why are you so sure?"

"Because Sis— Because the person I trusted so completely was a *nun!*"

If Cal had been a smoker—a habit he'd picked up in the army and finally been able to shake—he'd have chosen this as the perfect time to light a cigarette. Since he wasn't a smoker any longer, he didn't know what to do with himself. There wasn't anything else to say—he *knew* he'd never received any letters from her, and was sure his mother would have told him if she'd seen any—and Elizabeth seemed equally positive that her letters had been mailed. *If...* He hated to think what he was thinking, but couldn't escape the idea. *If she had written any letters addressed to him in the first place.*

Suppose she was mistaken? Suppose she was so upset, suddenly being sent to such a terrible place as that so-called school seemed to be, that she'd lost touch with reality? *And suppose the moon is made of blue cheese, Potts,* he told himself. *You're grabbing at straws, making excuses for her. Why?*

He had no answer for that. And no answer for the disappearance of the dozens of letters she'd supposedly written to him from Switzerland, letters he'd never received.

Chapter Ten

"I think we've reached an impasse," Elizabeth said. "I know I wrote the letters, and I'm certain they were mailed. Yet you claim you never received them."

Cal blinked. "Are you suggesting that *I'm* lying?" he asked, astonished.

"Can you think of another explanation?"

"That's ridiculous! Why would I lie about it?"

"Because you're still angry about something that happened to two kids seventeen years ago...so angry that you cross the street in order to avoid meeting me!"

So she'd noticed that. But of course she would. He hadn't tried to hide the fact that he wanted to avoid her; on the contrary, he'd flaunted his aversion. "You might think of it as merely *something* that happened between two kids," he said. "But it meant much more than that to me."

"It meant more than that to me, too! But I don't revel in bitterness, the way you do. I don't still carry a grudge around because of it."

"Maybe that's because you didn't find yourself shipped off to a stinking jungle the way I did."

"There are all sorts of jungles out there, Cal. Mental as well as physical."

"Sure. Tell me about it," he said sarcastically.

"I intend to," she said, ignoring his sarcasm. "I was so unhappy—so miserable—that I thought I'd die when my parents separated us the way they did. And the place they sent me in Switzerland was more a prison than a school...at least, it seemed that way to me. It was dark, damp, lonely...and always cold...so very cold..."

"Funny thing," he said, interrupting. "The jungle was dark and damp, too, but it was hot as hell, and never lonely. We always had enemy soldiers around to keep us company...plus the rats, of course."

She took a deep breath. "I'm sorry. I really am. But the point I was trying to make was...I suffered, too. Not in the same way you did, but..."

"Are we going to turn this into a game of who suffered the most?"

He was sorry he'd said that as soon as the words were out of his mouth. He knew he more than deserved the look of scorn she gave him.

"No," she said, getting up. "I think we've both said enough. And you've made your point. And I think my clothes are probably dry by now...or dry enough. So I'm going to your bathroom to get dressed, and then I'd appreciate your driving me back to my car."

Her chin was high and her voice was firm, but Cal saw the slight tremor in her right hand before she clenched her fist. Seeing it, he felt even worse than he'd already felt, if that was possible. He thought about apologizing to her, but then realized he couldn't do that in good conscience. It would have been hypocritical. Even though he'd been too blunt, he hadn't said anything he didn't mean and feel.

He nodded. "I'll be ready to go whenever you are." He watched her go, shoulders back, head held high...his shirt flapping against her thighs as she moved. He was disgusted with himself for noticing her legs at a time like this, but he should have expected it. In spite of everything, he still thought she was the most perfect creature God ever created. He closed his eyes. *Heaven help me.* Then, remembering the hurt he'd caused her, he amended that. *Heaven help us both.*

Cal picked up their mugs from the coffee table. Before he could take them to the kitchen, the front door flew open and Lum stepped inside, grinning, carrying a huge pot. "I made us some chili," he said. "Thought it'd go down good on a raw day like—"

Lum stopped talking, staring instead at something—someone—behind Cal.

Cal knew what his old friend must be staring at, but turned around anyway. Sure enough, Elizabeth was standing in the doorway to the bathroom, barefoot, still wearing his shirt, her hair even wilder now that it had started to dry. She looked more like a waif than a woman. "Listen," she said. "Before I leave there's something—" She stopped abruptly and stared at Lum, the same way he was staring at her. "Lum!" she said.

"Hello, Elizabeth. Didn't expect to find you here today."

"I didn't expect to be here, either," she said. "Cal and I got caught in the rain . . . but you'll be happy to know that he found my stolen car."

"That right? What kind of shape was it in?"

"A complete wreck. But that wasn't his fault."

"Win some, lose some, I guess," Lum said, and she nodded her agreement.

Cal watched the exchange, impressed by how quickly Elizabeth had recovered her composure.

"What's in the pot?" she asked.

"Mess of homemade chili," Lum replied. "Want some?"

Cal knew exactly how *homemade* Lum's concoctions were—straight out of the can, with extra hot seasonings added. He thought about saying something to warn Elizabeth but didn't want to call attention to himself—especially since she was handling the potentially awkward situation just fine—so he kept quiet.

"It sounds good but, uh, you sort of caught Cal and me at an awkward moment," Elizabeth said.

Cal caught his breath so fast that he started coughing.

"That right?" Lum asked.

"Yes," she replied. "We'd been having a heart-to-heart talk."

"About that business that happened all those years ago?" Lum asked.

"Yes."

"It's about time," Lum said, nodding his approval at Elizabeth, then at Cal. "Mind if I put this pot on the stove? It's getting heavy."

Cal was still coughing and couldn't speak, so he nodded and gestured toward the kitchen. Lum took the pot around and placed it on a burner before turning to Elizabeth again. "So did you two finally get everything out in the open?"

"Yes," Cal said, finally able to speak again.

"Not exactly," Elizabeth said.

"What happened?" Lum asked Elizabeth, ignoring Cal.

"We started off okay," she replied. "Then we ran into a stone wall...in the form of each other."

Lum stomped his foot. "I knew it! I knew Cal would blow the whole thing, letting his silly pride get in the way again."

"No, Lum!" Elizabeth said, surprising Cal by grabbing the old man's arm. "It was as much my fault as his. More. That's what I was coming out to tell him when you came in."

"You're just trying to protect him 'cause you know I'll give him hell later."

"No, I really mean it. Honestly. Do you want to hear what I was going to tell him?"

Lum nodded, keeping quiet for once in his life, Cal noted with relief.

"I wasn't going to say I was sorry," Elizabeth said, giving Cal a brief glance before turning her attention back to Lum. "I'd meant everything I'd said up to that point...just as I'm sure he meant everything he said." She glanced at him again, but focused on Lum before Cal had a chance to reply, even by a nod.

"The thing is...after I'd stormed off into the bathroom to get dressed and go home...I remembered something. Something very, very important...something I should have remembered in the first place.

"Cal had lost me because of my parents, just as I'd lost him...but somehow, along the way, I'd forgotten that Cal had lost much more than that. He'd also lost *his entire future*. He had dreams of going to college.... You remember that, don't you, Lum?"

Lum nodded.

"Cal was going to be the first person in his entire family to go to college. The very first! And my father...my entire family, including me...robbed him of that dream." She turned around to look at Cal then, her eyes brimming with tears. "There's...no comparison between what each of us lost, Cal. None at all. And I don't blame you for being bitter...." She sniffed. "And that's what I was going to say."

Cal didn't know what to say. And for once in his life, Lum seemed to be at a loss for words, too.

ELIZABETH HELD HER BREATH for what seemed an eternity, waiting for someone to speak. Cal opened his mouth, then closed it again. Lum traced a pattern on the kitchen floor with the toe of his boot. Finally Cal cleared his throat and she lifted her head to look at him.

"Thank you," he said.

Short. Simple. Honest. The most touching words anyone had ever said to her in her entire life. She bit her bottom lip, fighting back tears that threatened to overflow, and attempted a smile that didn't quite come off. "I meant it," she said.

"I know." Cal gave her one of his rare smiles then, a smile that was bright enough to light up the entire world...or at least her small part of it.

She felt her throat tighten, so hard that it ached. And the ache filled her with happiness, because she was *feeling* again, after living for a long time in an emotionless void.

"Does this mean that you two are friends again?" Lum asked, breaking the emotion-charged silence.

Cal and Elizabeth continued looking at each other for a long moment. "I think it does," he finally said.

"So do I," she agreed.

"Good," Lum said. "Maybe we can have supper now. I'm starving."

"Lum and I are in the habit of eating early," Cal explained to Elizabeth. "We'd be happy to have you join us but..."

"But what?" she asked.

"You might not be hungry. It's only a little after six..."

"I'm starving," she said, suddenly realizing she really was hungry. Then she remembered that she hadn't eaten lunch today because she was nervous about her upcoming meeting with Lance. And perhaps over the possibility of seeing Cal again, too? "And chili sounds marvelous, Lum," she added.

She didn't offer to help serve the meal, seeing right away that Cal and Lum took up all the space there was in the kitchen alcove. She stood to one side, trying to keep out of their way as they reheated the chili and set the table. She saw a frown on Cal's face once when he glanced her way, and wondered what had caused it. Then, remembering the way she was dressed, she decided he must be worried about her underclothing—or lack thereof. The first chance she got, she pulled him aside as he was carrying glasses from the kitchen to the dining table.

"Don't worry," she whispered. "I'm decent underneath your shirt. I borrowed a pair of your briefs, too."

She saw him open his mouth to speak, but nothing came out. Then... she wasn't sure, but could almost swear that he blushed. Cal? With his reputation, blushing? She decided that she must have been mistaken.

The two men finished serving the meal and the three of them sat down to eat. Elizabeth picked up her soup spoon and dipped it into her steaming bowl of chili. "This looks delicious, Lum," she said.

"Might be a tad hot," Lum cautioned.

"Hot food will taste good on a rainy night like this," she said, bringing the spoon to her mouth. "I know the hot coffee did, earlier."

"That's not what he meant," Cal said. "He—"

Elizabeth swallowed the spoonful of chili. She started to smile, to tell Lum how delicious his chili was...but something happened to her voice before she could speak. In addition to that, she felt that her entire mouth, along with her throat, could ignite at any moment. She reached for the tall glass of iced tea Cal had placed beside her plate and gulped down half of it. When she finally lowered the glass, she looked at Cal with tears in her eyes.

"I think that Lum was trying to tell you the chili was hot like pepper, not hot like fire," he said, his lips twitching.

She nodded, wiping away the bead of sweat over her upper lip. "It is that. But good," she added, turning to Lum.

He rewarded her with a half-toothless smile. "Glad you like it," he said. "Eat up."

She did, managing to finish her entire serving with the help of saltine crackers and iced tea to keep the fires under control. She got up and reached for her soup bowl. "I'll do the dishes," she said.

"No, I'll do them," Cal said, standing up, too.

"I'll let you two fight it out," Lum said, heading for the living area, where he turned on the television, plopped himself into a comfortable chair and started watching the evening news.

"Lum made the food and you served it," Elizabeth told Cal. "I really wish you'd at least let me—"

"Okay, you can help clear the table," he said, interrupting her. "But I insist on washing the dishes. I'm the only one who knows where everything goes."

Elizabeth picked up bowls and took them to the kitchen alcove, feeling hurt by Cal's attitude. Was he such a perfectionist about where his dishes were stored, or was it simply that he didn't want *her* handling his things? Then she wondered when she'd become so thin-skinned that she'd worry about such a minor thing. At one time, she'd simply have asked him—or anyone—about it.

"Are you so possessive about your house and your things with everyone?" she asked. "Or is it just with me?"

He wheeled around from the kitchen sink and stared at her, obviously surprised. "I . . ." he began, then stopped. "It's not just with you," he finally said.

"I'm glad to hear it."

"And I don't owe you an explanation."

"I know that."

"And you're still asking the same kind of nosy, none-of-your-business questions you used to ask."

"I know that, too."

He sighed. "I *do* feel protective about this place. I guess you could call it possessive. I think it's because...this is the first home I've ever owned, just me and nobody else."

She thought about that, and what she knew about the past seventeen years of his life. She knew about the jungle in Central America, of course, where he'd served in the army and been decorated as a hero. After that, according to bits and pieces she'd been able to pick up from various sources, he'd joined the Army Special Forces and had served in various hot spots around the world, until he'd come back to Planters' Junction several years ago. He'd claimed this land, land that had belonged to his father, and had built a house on it. Then Quint had persuaded him to run for sheriff because Buck Maxwell was finally retiring to run for mayor. Both Cal and Buck had won their respective races.

Those were the bare facts, as far as she knew them. But what about all the missing pieces? For instance, what had he *done* in the Special Forces for all those years? And he'd been back in Planters' Junction for almost five years now— so why was he still defensive and uncertain at times? Was it because of what he'd seen, and done, during those years away?

And why couldn't she stop analyzing the past and get on with the future, as she hoped to do today?

"I don't think you owe me—or anyone else—an explanation for the way you treat your personal possessions," she said. "But thank you for telling me about your home, Cal. And did I tell you that I like it a lot?"

"Yes."

"Good. I'm still of the same opinion." She took a deep breath. "And now I think I really *will* get dressed in my own clothes while you're finishing the dishes." She turned to go, and immediately turned back to him again. "But there's one more thing..."

Cal turned back again to face her, too, waiting silently.

"A little while ago, when I told you I was wearing your briefs in addition to your shirt, I thought you *blushed.* Could that be, or was I mistaken?"

"You were mistaken."

"You're sure?"

"Positive, although it's possible that my face did change color. But it wasn't a blush, Elizabeth. What some people call it—and what it really is, I guess—is a *flush*... of sexual awareness."

"Oh." At that, she could feel her own face growing warm. She hurried away before he could see it, not knowing whether it was a flush or a blush, or possibly both.

By the time she finished dressing, this time with a mirror to guide her and the contents of her purse to help, too, she felt much more confident. Stepping out of the bathroom, she saw that Cal had already finished the dishes and put them away. He was sitting on the sofa, watching the last of the evening news with Lum, and the cozy domestic scene made her smile. She hated to interrupt it.

Cal must have heard her because he suddenly looked in her direction and got up. "Ready?" he asked.

"Yes, I—"

"Get him to show you our workshop before he takes you home, Elizabeth," Lum said, his gaze still fixed on the television.

She lifted her eyebrows in a silent question to Cal. He shrugged. "I'd like to see it," she said. "Aren't you coming, too, Lum?'' she asked the old man, who'd made no move to get up.

"Not me," he replied. "I've already seen it and besides, there's a rerun of *Beverly Hillbillies* coming up next and I sure don't want to miss *that.*"

"Absolutely," she agreed, suppressing her laughter when she saw Cal roll his eyes. "I'll say goodbye to you now, in that case."

"Come again soon," Lum said, waving his hand in dismissal as he continued watching TV.

Elizabeth and Cal waited until they were outside with the door closed behind them; then they both laughed at the same time. "He's wonderful," she said.

"Incorrigible, you mean."

"That, too. Does he come over often?"

"Several times a week," Cal said. "Whenever he gets the notion. And he usually knows when I'm on duty, or when I have something else planned."

Something else planned, Elizabeth thought, picking up on the phrase. *Planned*—as in big date, big rendezvous, big seduction scene? *And big mistake to continue thinking in that direction,* she told herself, wondering why she continued to punish herself by fantasizing about Cal's romances. "I'm glad Lum happened to come by tonight," she said.

"Oh?"

"We were making a pretty big botch of things until he showed up to get us talking again."

"I guess so. Although you *had* come out of the bathroom to apologize before you knew he was here..."

"I *hadn't* come out to apologize. I told you that."

"But still..."

"If Lum hadn't been here, we'd probably have argued again, just like we're doing now, and I'd never have said what I came out to say."

He nodded. "You might have a point."

"You know I do."

"For what it's worth... I'm glad he was here, too, Elizabeth, if that was the prod that caused you to say what you did about my...my plans for the future being lost at the same time...you know."

She took a deep breath. "You mean the same time that we lost each other?"

"Yes. I think all of it together...sort of built up over the years, feeding on itself...making me more and more bitter, just like you said. And then tonight—what you said— I know it took a lot of courage on your part..."

"But did it help?"

"Yes," he said. Then he nodded again. "I really think it did."

"Then it was worth it."

They stood completely still, looking at each other, and Elizabeth could hear the night sounds starting up—the chirping of crickets, the soft dripping of raindrops off the pine trees onto the earth beneath, the gentle rustle of a breeze.... "The rain's stopped," she realized, voicing her thought aloud.

"So it has," Cal said after a moment. "But look," he added, "we don't have to do a big tour of the workshop if you're not interested. It's mostly a lot of junk...."

"I'd like to see it. Really. And if you try to renege," she added, lifting an eyebrow, "I'll tell Lum."

Cal put up both his hands in a gesture of surrender. "Heaven forbid."

HE WAS STILL uncomfortable showing Elizabeth into the inner sanctum of his world, not because he had anything to hide but because he dreaded the thought of her disapproval. He didn't know why her opinion mattered so much to him. He only knew that it did.

Holding his breath, he opened the double doors to the garage he'd built for Lum and himself, and switched on overhead fluorescent lights. The workplace was relatively neat, almost pristine if you compared it with Lum's old garage in the back of his service station, but when you disassembled an old car, you had to put the parts someplace...and the most convenient place to put them was on the floor surrounding the car. Cal tried to view the antique Lincoln Continental—their current project—through Elizabeth's eyes, and could only come to the conclusion that it looked like a piece of junk, as he'd described it earlier. Lum and he could see beyond the mess, of course, but he couldn't expect her to.

"What kind of car is that you're working on?" Elizabeth asked.

"An old Lincoln Continental."

"I knew it!" she said, rushing over to the car. "We used to have one almost like it. I mean, my father did. I thought it was the grandest automobile ever made." She rubbed her hand along the one rear fender that was still intact. "It must be a little frightening to work on a car like this."

"Why do you say that?"

"I mean the challenge—actually bringing it back to life. It's almost as if you were recreating a work of art."

Cal was surprised that she'd picked up on that angle. It was exactly the way he felt. "Lum does most of the work. And of course we take it to a professional body shop after we've restored the engine."

"You mean you trust it to *strangers?*"

"Then we bring it back here for the finishing touches," he admitted.

"That's more like it," she said, caressing the car one more time before she walked back across the concrete floor to where he was standing. "I can understand why you're so protective of this place. I would be, too."

Cal was surprised again, but only briefly this time because he suddenly remembered how she always used to be able to pick up on his thoughts and what he was feeling...sometimes even before he knew it himself. She'd known him so well back then, just as he'd known her, and that special closeness was the single thing he'd missed the most after they were torn apart.

"I, uh, think that another reason I have a special feeling for this place is because the land belonged to my father," he said, feeling a little awkward about telling her something so personal. And after he'd said it, he wondered why he had.

She nodded. And smiled. And Cal was glad he'd told her, after all, because she understood.

"I don't know how Mom managed to hold on to it all those years she was married to Luther," he said. "But she did. And when I came back home after she died, I found out that it belonged to me. Of course it's only a few acres...."

"The size isn't important, Cal, and you know it. The important thing is that it belonged to your daddy, and now it belongs to you. *You.*"

"Yeah," he said, suddenly feeling lighthearted. "And I'll admit I like the idea of having my own place—my own space—after all the years I spent living like a nomad."

"So you've decided to settle down back here in Planters' Junction, then?" she asked, her face completely somber, so somber that it made him wonder what she was thinking, remembering....

"At least for the time being," he replied, hedging. "What about you? Are you planning to stay here, too?"

"Are you hoping to get rid of me?"

"I would have been, up until a couple of hours ago," he replied truthfully. "But not now."

"Thank you for that." She took a deep breath. "I imagine I will leave here soon...as soon as I get myself back into some kind of shape to cope with the outside world again. I originally thought I'd be gone ages ago, but it's taken longer than I thought it would to regain my self-esteem."

"You?" Cal asked, honestly surprised. "Was your divorce *that* devastating?"

"You want to know the truth?"

Cal wasn't sure whether he did or not, but nodded anyway.

"The divorce itself was a relief. It meant everything was finally over at last. All the lies, the deceit..." She caught herself then, and took a deep breath. "But I know you don't want to hear all the gory details. And to answer your question—no, the divorce wasn't devastating."

She closed her eyes. "It was the loss of my law practice that did me in, Cal. That was the toughie. The real toughie."

She was hurting. Bad. Cal knew it. He could almost feel it himself, the same way he used to be able to do when they were teenagers—the way they *both* used to be able to do. He wished she would cry because that might help ease the hurting, but he knew she wouldn't. She always cried for other people, but almost never for herself...except that one time at Paradise Lake.

He stood silently watching her, feeling completely helpless, until she finally opened her eyes. They were unusually bright, but there were no tears in them, just as he'd known. "One good thing has come out of all my trouble," she said.

"What's that?"

"My mother and I have finally made peace. Remember how the two of us were always fighting when I was a teenager...on the few occasions when we were even on speaking terms?"

"I remember."

"Well, she's come around now. Or I have. Or both of us have. Anyway, we actually *talk*. We tell each other things. I even like her. I never thought it would happen, but it has."

"What caused the change in her after all these years?" he asked, not convinced.

"I'm not sure about all the reasons, but getting out from under the shadow of my father was one of them. It allowed her to open up more. She told me that he was one of the reasons she was always so *guarded* with me before."

"And you believe her?"

"Of course! I *trust* her, don't you see? None of the other changes would have been possible without that."

Cal didn't comment, but crossed his fingers in hope that Elizabeth wasn't misplacing her trust. From what she'd confided to him years ago about both her parents, he was skeptical. And he wished with all his heart that she wasn't opening herself up to further pain by trusting her mother now.

"I'm happy your relationship with your mother seems to be working out better," he said, choosing his words with care. "And if it continues...why should you leave, or even consider leaving? You could practice law right here."

She shook her head. "I still have to prove something...to myself, if nobody else."

Cal could understand that. He knew the feeling well. Too well. He was only sorry that Elizabeth seemed to be going through the same kind of pain he had to endure. But there was a difference. He'd have to go on proving his worth, to himself, until the day he died, whereas there might be a chance for Elizabeth to escape the terrible burden. "Some people already believe in you," he said.

She narrowed her eyes. "Who?" she asked, challenging him.

"Quint, for one."

"Him," she said, shaking her head. "He doesn't count."

"Why not?"

"He was always the nice guy, remember? Much better than you and me, the two-of-a-kind rebels. And since he married Thea..." She rolled her eyes. "They're so smitten with each other that they're both convinced the whole world is as sweet and good as they are. They make me sick...with envy, of course."

Cal had to laugh, but sobered again immediately. "I believe in you, too."

He saw Elizabeth catch her breath...saw her blink a quick couple of times while she stared at him...then saw her lower her head and shrug. "What do you know?" she asked in a husky voice.

He didn't know which of her gestures got through to him, causing something long buried deep inside him to snap. Maybe it was her catching her breath, the way she had a habit of doing when something took her by surprise. Or maybe it was blinking, which was something she did when she was unsure of her emotions. Or maybe it was the shrug she often gave when she was fighting those same emotions.

Maybe it was none of the gestures that caused him to suddenly reach out for her. Maybe it was all of them. He didn't stop to examine the causes and consequences; he only knew he *had* to put his arms around her. He pulled her close against him, and they were standing chest to chest, heartbeat to heartbeat. She lifted her head, and he saw her eyes widen with surprise.

Then he kissed her.

He didn't kiss her wildly. Or passionately. He touched his lips to hers gently, tentatively, at first, and only increased the pressure when he felt her respond, her mouth softening under his, adjusting itself to his and finally, clinging to his. He closed his eyes tightly shut, and felt her hands touch his face, the back of his head, and then felt her arms encircle his neck.

He made no effort to deepen their kiss. It wasn't necessary. He was already experiencing more emotion than he could handle. He was lost in her, lost in the feel of her body pressed against his, lost in the warmth of her arms around him, lost in the sweet softness of her mouth. Every muscle in his body was tensed to the breaking point.

He didn't know how long they kissed. It could have been forever... or only a matter of minutes. He felt Elizabeth tremble in his arms, and knew she must be feeling some of the same fierce emotions he felt. He also knew he had to end the kiss soon ... for his own self-preservation and sanity if nothing else.

Finally, regretfully, he lifted his mouth from hers, and pressed his forehead against hers instead, keeping his eyes closed. He might have moved completely away from her if he'd had the strength to do so, but he didn't. By then they were both trembling, and Cal felt shaken to the very core of his being.

Neither of them spoke.

Elizabeth was the one who finally moved away first, removing her arms from around his neck and stepping back out of his loose embrace. Their glances met briefly before she quickly looked away, one of the few times in their acquaintance that he'd ever seen her do that. Under the circumstances, he found it totally understandable.

"I, uh, really need to get home," she said. "I didn't tell my mother I'd be late, and she might be worried."

Cal drove her back to his office, where she'd left her car. On the way, they even managed to start up a casual conversation, although later Cal couldn't remember what they'd talked about.

He did remember one thing. Clearly. Neither of them said a single word about their kiss.

Chapter Eleven

Elizabeth stepped into the library, where her mother was sitting at the desk working on her household accounts. Frances looked up and removed her reading glasses.

"I just wanted to let you know I'm leaving now," Elizabeth said.

"So soon? I thought your luncheon with Thea wasn't until one."

"I'm going by the jail first. To see Lance Strickland."

"Oh? Does that mean you've decided to defend him?"

"I might," Elizabeth said. "He certainly needs *someone*. And I need the work."

"That's impossible! You have—"

"I didn't say I needed the money, Mother. I said I needed the *work*... as in, getting back into the swing of it again."

"I can understand that," Frances said. "And I agree. Still..."

"I haven't decided definitely yet, and I'm merely going by to talk to him again today. So don't worry."

"It's not that," Frances protested. "It's just that I want the best for you, Elizabeth, because... I care about you."

Her mother's words were so unexpected—and so close to affectionate—that they caught Elizabeth completely by surprise. "Thank you," she muttered, unsure what to say in response.

"You seem surprised," Frances said. When Elizabeth didn't respond, she continued. "I know we haven't been demonstrative in the past, but I thought I explained to you that my reserve was because of the situation between your father and me."

"I know. I mean, we did. You did." Elizabeth knew she was babbling, and tried to collect her thoughts. "It's just that I still find myself having a little trouble getting adjusted to our new relationship after all these years. But I like the way we get along now," she added self-consciously.

"Me, too," Frances said, smiling. "So," she continued brightly after a moment, "will you be seeing Sheriff Potts again today, too?"

All of Elizabeth's senses sprang to immediate, all-out alert. "It's possible," she said. "I'm not sure whether he'll be on duty at the station or not."

"I always liked him, you know," Frances said.

Elizabeth shook her head, unable to accept that statement. "No, Mother. You didn't even—"

"But I *did!* Although I'll admit that I disapproved of his taking advantage of your age and inexperience."

"Nobody took advantage of anybody, Mother," Elizabeth said. "And if anybody *had* taken advantage, it would have been me, not Cal."

"You're still in love with him."

"No!"

"Are you sure?"

Elizabeth hesitated, wanting to be honest as her mother was trying to be with her, but finding it difficult after all the years and the deep chasm that had been between them. "I admire him as a person, and for what he's made of his life on his own." She took a deep breath. "And I'll admit that I'm still physically attracted to him," she added, thinking about their kiss, which had absolutely shattered her two nights ago.

"I might even have found myself falling in love with him again if..."

"If what?" Frances asked.

"I'm almost convinced he's lying to me. About something very important. You see, I wrote Cal letters from

Switzerland, Mother,'' she admitted. "I know I was forbidden to write, but I was so much in love with him and so desperate . . .'' She closed her eyes for a brief moment. "So I wrote him. Letters, plural, pouring my heart out to him. And I managed to get the letters mailed. But he never answered. He says he never received them."

"And you don't believe him?"

Elizabeth swallowed. "I don't know. I sent them to his mother's address, and the two of them were so close that I think she would have gotten them to him. But who can be sure about something like that? And she died in a house fire about a year later, so we'll probably never know."

She turned to her mother again, and found Frances watching her, eyes alert. "What do you think, Mother?"

"I, uh, it's hard to say," Frances said, obviously hedging. "I'd hate to make a judgment, and it would only be my opinion . . ."

"I know," Elizabeth said, going over quickly to give her mother a hug. "I'm sorry I put you on the spot that way."

"I don't mind. I only wish I could have helped."

"You already have . . . by being on my side." She kissed her mother's forehead. "And now I really have to be off."

"Give Thea my regards," Frances said. "And Cal, too, if you see him."

Elizabeth nodded, and blew another kiss to her mother as she left the room, smiling. Her smile faded as soon as she thought about her upcoming meeting with Lance Strickland. She planned to make a definite decision on whether or not she'd accept his case today, and then tell Thea her decision over lunch. She had grave concerns about the young man's future, no matter who handled his pending case of car theft. The magistrate was almost certain to bind him over for probable cause at his upcoming hearing.

After that, there'd probably be at least a couple of months before his arraignment hearing before a grand jury . . . and where would Lance live in the meantime? In the backseat of a car, as he'd been doing before he was arrested? And that was the *best* scenario, assuming that he was able to come up with the money for bail.

On the other hand…assuming that the magistrate bound Lance over to the grand jury…wouldn't he be more safe and secure, and as free from temptation as he could be, if he remained in the county jail until his grand-jury hearing? He'd have a dry place to sleep and three meals a day guaranteed. There was a lot to be said for the arrangement, especially if it kept Lance out of even worse trouble than he was already in.

But she was getting ahead of herself. After all, she hadn't even decided if she would accept Lance's case.

She drove to the county jail, enjoying the slightly cooler temperature and lower humidity they'd had since the hard rains of two days ago—the rains that had helped clear the air in many more ways than one. Elizabeth thought again about her talk with Cal, although she'd already gone over everything they'd said a dozen times or more.

Being on good terms with him again was the best thing that had happened to her in a long, long time. She had missed him. Lord, how she had missed him! After the initial sharp pain of their separation and even after the deeper hurt of his not responding to her letters had diminished, she had continued to miss him. Cal had a special place deep in her heart, close to her soul, that no one else had ever been able to fill. And all these years that special place had remained empty, sometimes achingly so. Until now.

Knowing they could never be lovers again didn't change that; if anything, it enhanced it, she thought, pulling the Cherokee into a parking space beside the jail and killing the engine.

Locking all her car doors, she started walking toward the jail, but stopped when a man on a huge black motorcycle pulled up beside her. The driver, hidden from view behind one of those big dark helmets that looked like something out of *Star Wars*, revved the engine, eased off for a moment, then revved it again.

Elizabeth frowned with annoyance and took a step to one side, planning to go around the obnoxious biker. As soon as she moved, he revved the engine another time, much louder than before... so loud that she almost jumped out of her skin.

"Wanna go for a ride?" he asked in a deep, dangerous voice.

"I most certainly do not!" she said indignantly. "And if you..."

The biker laughed then, and something familiar about his laugh caught her attention. She leaned closer to him, narrowing her eyes while she tried to make out the face behind the dark mask. "Cal?" she asked.

He flipped back the visor on the helmet, still laughing.

"It *is* you!" she said. "You almost scared me out of my wits."

"You? I don't believe it. You were always completely fearless."

Elizabeth couldn't help feeling pleased by his assessment of her, even though it wasn't entirely accurate. "Is this yours?" she asked, gesturing toward the throbbing black machine and thinking that Cal looked long and lean and dangerous sitting astride it, almost the same as he'd seemed to her years ago on the Harley he used to have.

"Not yet," he said. "But I'm seriously considering buying it. Want to go for a ride with me and help me make up my mind?"

"You have to be kidding," she said, halfway wishing that he wasn't. "Can't you just hear the town gossips? 'The *sheriff*, for goodness' sake... and that scandalous Elizabeth Bartlett, up to her old tricks again! What's the world coming to?' They'd have a field day, Cal, and you know it."

"Wouldn't bother me," he said. "Would it bother you?"

She noticed the glint in his gray eyes. "Is that a challenge?"

"Could be," he said. "But it's also an invitation. What do you say?"

"I have to go in and talk with Lance Strickland. He's expecting me."

Cal shrugged. "What about after that? This is my day off, so I have plenty of time."

He was serious, she suddenly realized with a rush of excitement... and of pleasure. Maybe... "I'm supposed to have lunch with Thea at her house," she said with regret when she remembered the appointment.

"That's perfect."

Elizabeth was totally confused. "Why do you say that?"

"Because Thea's house—Miss Maudie's house—is miles away from town. You'll be able to leave from there without any gossips around to watch. And nobody could recognize you behind one of these dark helmets. Remember how much trouble you had recognizing me? And I was only a couple of feet away."

"I don't know..." Elizabeth said. The idea was tempting. Roaring off on a motorcycle again...enjoying the speed, the excitement, the sense of flying free in the face of the wind... And she'd even worn slacks today, so her clothes were appropriate for a bike ride. "You really want me to go?"

"I wouldn't ask if I didn't, Elizabeth."

"Okay," she said, making her decision. "We should be finished with lunch by about two-thirty."

"I'll be outside Miss Maudie's house a little after that, then. Revving my engine," he added, giving it a rev now by way of illustration.

Elizabeth laughed. "Crazy man."

"Not as crazy as you."

"Oh? Why do you say that?"

"Because I'll be doing the driving!" With that, he flipped his visor back down and roared off, giving a last farewell wave of his hand to Elizabeth, who stood in the parking lot watching him leave. She smiled and shook her head. Then she sighed and headed for the jail again.

She hid her displeasure when she saw that Winston Siddons was on duty at the front desk. He was her least favorite of all of Cal's deputies. "Hello, Deputy Siddons," she said, walking up to him.

"What are you doing here?" he asked rudely. "I thought Sheriff Potts already showed you your—"

"I'm here as an attorney this time," she interrupted him, hoping that Cal *was* building up a dossier on Siddons in order to fire him . . . and the sooner, the better. "I'd like to see Lance Strickland."

Siddons narrowed his eyes. "You visited him a couple of days ago. Are you his lawyer?"

Elizabeth was tempted to tell him she was, in order to aggravate him if nothing else, but resisted the impulse. "It hasn't been decided definitely. That's why I need to talk to him."

"You can't come in here soliciting business. . . ."

Damn him! Maybe she'd just beat him up right now and save Cal the trouble of firing him. "I was *asked* to come here," she said, managing to control her temper.

"I don't remember seeing your name on the list of approved visitors," Siddons said, jutting out his jaw and giving her a glare that he probably thought was fierce.

She glared back at him and shook her head, letting him know that she was fully aware no such list existed and never had. "Nice try. But it won't work."

He blushed, but tried to stand his ground. "You can't visit an accused felon unless—"

"I just talked to Sheriff Potts outside, no more than two minutes ago," Elizabeth said, slowly and distinctly. "I told him that I was coming in to see my prospective client, Lance Strickland, and he had no objection. None whatsoever. Do *you* intend to keep me waiting while you track him down . . . on his day off . . . and verify that?"

"I told you—"

"Do you?"

She saw Siddons start to sweat, but had to grudgingly give him credit when he *still* tried to ward her off. "Strickland already has a visitor," he said. "It's against the rules to allow more than one in at a time."

She wanted to call him a liar to his face, but again resisted the impulse. "Who's with him now?"

"Lum Starr," Siddons said, surprising her. "That silly old man who—"

"I know who Lum Starr is," she said, interrupting, detesting Winston Siddons as much as it was possible for one human being to detest another. "He's a very dear personal friend of mine." She paused a moment to allow that statement to penetrate Siddons's thick skull, then continued. "I'm sure Lum won't mind if I interrupt his conversation with Lance... *whom I'll very probably represent.* In fact, I'm almost sure of it." She hadn't been sure at all up to that moment, but now she was. And she was going to give Lance Strickland the best representation that any lawyer alive or dead could have done! She made it a promise—to Lance and to herself.

"And now, unless you've come up with still more objections, I'd like to see Lance Strickland."

Siddons shot her a brief look of pure venom, then turned and started walking toward the door leading to the cells. She followed closely behind him, still quivering with suppressed fury. She tried to will herself to relax, but wasn't able to manage it until she saw Lum's familiar face. He was sitting on the bunk beside Lance, and the two of them seemed to be having a spirited conversation... probably about cars, if she was any judge of things.

Deputy Siddons stopped at the entrance to Lance's cell and Elizabeth took the opportunity to move a step ahead of him, so she'd have a clear view of the cell and its occupants, as they would have of her. "Hello, Lum," she said. "I didn't know you and Lance were friends."

Lum looked up at her and immediately broke into a grin. "Sure. We go way back. At least a coupla days, wouldn't you say, Lance?"

"At least that," Lance agreed, also grinning.

"I met him when I came by to visit Cal and the three of us got to talking about cars," Lum explained to Elizabeth.

"I can imagine how that conversation went," she said with a laugh.

"I'll just bet you can," Lum agreed.

"What do you plan to do?" Deputy Siddons said briskly. "Stand around here and jibber-jabber all day?"

Elizabeth shot him a brief look, then turned her attention back to the occupants of the cell again. "I think what Deputy Siddons is *trying* to say, is that he won't allow the three of us in the cell together at the same time. *I* personally can't imagine what he thinks the three of us would do, but maybe my imagination isn't what it used to be...."

Lum whooped at that. Elizabeth noticed the angry flush on Siddons's face, but she didn't care. He more than deserved all the ridicule she could heap on him.

"Anyway," she continued after Lum's laughter had died down, "would you mind leaving the cell for a short time, Lum, while I talk with Lance?"

"Nah," the old man said, getting up. "I need to be going anyway."

A little while later when Elizabeth and Lance were alone in his cell she turned to him. "Well, Lance," she said, "now that you've had time to think about it some more...are you still sticking with the story you gave me the other day?"

She saw the sudden fear in his eyes, and saw him quickly look away, obviously trying to hide that fear from her. "What do you mean?"

"I think you know. It was a simple question."

"I told you the truth the other day."

She waited a moment, staring at him, trying to impress him with the seriousness of his situation...but she had the distinct feeling that he already knew what deep trouble he was in. The question was—why wouldn't he do something about it? Why wouldn't he at least *try* to help in his own defense?

Lance turned to her and their glances met for a brief second before he quickly turned away again. The brief glimpse she had of the fear and uncertainty in his eyes was enough to convince her that she'd been correct in her assumption. Lance knew full well what a mess he was in, but didn't know how to get out of it...and was scared to death because of both those factors.

Elizabeth took a deep breath. "You'll have a preliminary hearing before a magistrate in a couple of days, Lance, but that's merely a formality. You know as well as I do that he'll most likely bind you over for probable cause." She hesitated. "What you and I need to talk about is what you're going to do after that."

Lance listened to every word she said, and nodded a couple of times. "Does this mean you're going to handle my case?"

"It sure looks that way," she said with a rueful grin. "Unless you have a serious objection."

"Well, no. I mean I'd be happy. I *am* happy..."

"Then let's get to work."

They talked for almost two hours, and when Elizabeth finally left she was as frustrated as she'd been in her entire life. She hadn't been able to shake Lance from his farfetched story about a man leaving the stolen Chevy to be serviced and then calling later to ask Lance to deliver the car to an address that turned out to be phony.

To make matters worse, Lance had been the only person to see the man at the station that day. And to compound the damage, Lance continued to insist he couldn't recall what the man looked like, and had either lost or accidentally destroyed the work order with the man's name on it.

Not likely, a jury would say to that story. And Elizabeth would agree with them.

On the other hand, she felt in her heart that Lance was innocent of car theft. And if that was the case, why was he lying? In order to protect someone? Probably. But whom? And why?

Unless she could find some way to convince Lance to tell her the truth—or at least give her *something* to work with— he'd likely be convicted and sentenced to a prison term.

Based on the evidence against him, what jury in its right mind could do anything *but* find him guilty?

She sighed, determined to have another go tomorrow at trying to shake Lance from his story.

In the meantime, she needed to hurry so she wouldn't be late for her luncheon with Thea, where she'd tell her friend that she had decided to accept Lance's case, for better or worse.

And after lunch, Cal would be picking her up for a ride on the motorcycle he might buy, she remembered. Not that she'd ever completely forgotten his invitation; it had been in the back of her mind all the time she was talking to Lance. She knew she shouldn't go, just as she'd known it all along, from the moment she'd impulsively accepted his invitation.

Riding behind Cal on a motorcycle again wasn't safe... not in the physical sense because he was an excellent driver, but in the more complex emotional sense. She had only recently begun to realize how fragile she was in that area. Now that she *had* realized it, she knew that flying off with Cal on a motorcycle was neither a sane nor a rational thing for her to do.

But when had she ever played it safe—or been sane or rational—when it came to Cal Potts? She quickened her step, heading for her car.

CAL COASTED THE BIKE to a stop beside Elizabeth's new car parked under a shade tree in the big side yard at Miss Maudie's house. He grinned, feeling sure that she'd chosen that particular spot because it offered protection from the sun. She'd lived in the city too long, and must have forgotten that the birds nesting in the tree could do more damage to the finish on her new car than the sun ever would.

He flipped up the visor of his helmet and looked at his watch. Two-thirty. Exactly. And getting hotter by the minute. The rains had cooled things off a couple of days ago, but now South Georgia was feeling like South Georgia again. Hot. He wondered how much longer Elizabeth would be. In the old days she was almost always on time and early more often than not.

But that was then and this is now.

And what am I doing here? he wondered, not for the first time since he'd impulsively asked Elizabeth to go for a bike ride with him. He knew it wasn't a good idea. It was a very bad idea. Spending any appreciable amount of time with her doing *anything* was a bad idea—bad for his health, bad for his peace of mind—but riding on a motorcycle with her was the very worst idea he could have come up with.

He took off the bike helmet and ran his fingers through his hair, thinking about Elizabeth, and himself, and their situation.

Finally talking with her again after all the years they'd been apart, he'd come to realize she wasn't all that different from the girl he'd once known and loved with all his being. And knowing that, he also knew he had to be on his guard so the same thing didn't happen to him again. And what if it happened to her again, too? His falling in love with Elizabeth would be bad enough, but her falling in love with him would be disastrous. He had nothing to offer her, not now and not ever. He inhabited the shell of the person he'd once been, and that was all. It was all he was, too, a shell. The rest of him had been ripped out in a jungle in Central America.

In his own defense, he hadn't *intended* to ask her to go for a ride. He'd only been teasing her at first, but one thing had led to another and she'd suddenly seemed to be considering his outrageous suggestion seriously and he certainly wasn't going to be the first one to back off...and here he was. Waiting for Elizabeth. Again. When was the last time—"*No,*" he said out loud. Going for this bike ride was stupid enough, but he drew the line at allowing himself to be drawn into that particular trap of remember-when.

The two of them would go for a bike ride today, and that would be the end of that. It was sort of a fitting finale, actually. Some of their best times—and worst—had been spent astride the old Harley he used to have. And today, they could have one last ride together—one last fling—thumbing their noses at the whole world as they roared past it.

"Hello, Cal!"

He'd been so caught up in his own thoughts that he hadn't seen Elizabeth come out of the house. But it wasn't she who'd called out to him. Elizabeth was already halfway along the path, and it was Thea standing in the open doorway who'd shouted a greeting. He waved back to her.

"Have a nice ride!" Thea shouted. He nodded.

"Have you been here long?" Elizabeth asked, walking up.

He looked at his watch again. "Three and a half minutes."

"Good timing."

He nodded. "Ready to ride?"

"As soon as I put on the helmet from outer space that I see you've brought for me. I feel a little underdressed, though."

"Oh?"

"This bike—and particularly the helmet—cry out for black leather, don't you think?"

He grinned and handed her the helmet without comment. What he really thought was that she'd look sensational in anything she wore . . . and better still in nothing at all. He pushed the thought from his mind and put on his own helmet, then waited for Elizabeth to climb onto the passenger seat behind him. He saw her hesitate. *She feels a little awkward about this, just like I do,* he realized.

"I'll bet you a quarter it starts on the very first try," he said. He'd lost a lot of quarters to her back in the days when he drove the Harley. He still considered it the finest motorcycle ever made, but the one he'd owned had been used and abused so much it was on its last gasp when he bought it. It was only due to Lum's genius—and the Harley's durability—that the machine was able to run at all.

''You're on,'' she said with a laugh, swinging one of her long legs over the bike and settling behind him.

Checking first to make sure Elizabeth's feet were in place on the unfamiliar vehicle, Cal started the engine. It roared to life immediately, but he gave it a little extra rev for emphasis. ''You owe me,'' he said over his shoulder.

''I'll deduct it from what you owe *me!*'' she said, pinching his middle.

Cal caught his breath, almost gasping aloud. He looked down and saw that her arms and hands were in place around him—just as they were supposed to be. But until she pinched him, he hadn't known they were there. When had she snaked them around him the way she had? He swallowed and took a deep breath. ''Ready?'' he said over his shoulder.

''You bet.''

He took it easy going down Miss Maudie's long graveled driveway, and only sped up slightly when they reached the macadam access road to the main highway. He finally turned onto the main highway and was getting ready to speed up when Elizabeth pinched him again. He half turned his head in her direction to hear what she wanted to say.

''Will it go any faster?'' she shouted, repeating the same words she'd said to him the first time he took her for a ride on the Harley, so many years ago.

Cal felt a sudden, unexplained lump in his throat and swallowed it away. He nodded. ''Hold on!'' he shouted over his shoulder, and felt Elizabeth's arms tighten around him.

He gave the engine more gas, and felt the bike respond immediately. He sped up a little more...then still more, until they were zooming along the sparsely traveled highway, fairly flying past the tall pines that bordered the road on both sides...escaping the past...outrunning the present...rapidly gaining on the future....

He felt exuberant, exhilarated beyond reason or caring, with the sun beaming down on his face and the warm wind caressing his body as they roared along the highway. This was what life was all about.

Elizabeth squeezed her arms tighter around him for a moment, and he knew she was feeling the same thing he was feeling. He smiled, happy that he'd suggested this ride, after all, because it was giving her such pleasure. She deserved a little pleasure, after what she'd been through. And so did he.

He drove for miles, pushing the motorcycle all out for most of them, not wanting the ride to end, not wanting to have to come back down to earth and face reality, but knowing he'd have to do it sooner or later. Finally he did.

He turned the bike onto a side road and slowed down, following the rutted dirt tracks until they dead-ended beside a small lake. He stopped and idled the engine, then flipped up his visor and swiveled around to look at Elizabeth. "What did you think?" he asked.

She flipped up her own visor and Cal saw that her face was flushed. "About the ride or the bike?" she asked.

"Both."

"I think the ride was the most fun I've had in years."

"And the bike?"

She shrugged. "You know I don't know anything about motors. But I think you could probably win a lot of quarters with this machine."

He laughed and shook his head. "Would you like to stop and take a breather before we go back?"

"Sure. Where are we, anyway?"

"At my place. On the back side," he added when he saw her look of surprise. "There's a natural spring running through the property and I brought in some bulldozers and had a lake dug out a couple of years ago."

"Really?" she said, dismounting the bike and removing her helmet, draping it over the handlebars.

Cal killed the engine and removed his own helmet, hanging it beside hers, then pushing the kickstand into place with his foot. Out of the corner of his eye, he saw that

Elizabeth was still looking at the lake and the property surrounding it. He walked over to her.

"It's nice, Cal. Really nice." She turned around abruptly, almost bumping into him. "But I thought you told me your father only left you a few acres."

"About twenty-five...which isn't considered much around here."

"Still—"

"You don't need to tell me that I should appreciate what I have, Elizabeth. I already do. I promise."

She looked at him for a long moment, then arched an eyebrow. "And don't you ever forget it," she said sternly.

"Yes, ma'am," he said, giving her a mock salute.

She walked down to the lake and Cal followed her. He saw her reach down and pick up a small rock, then try to skip it on the water. It sank without a single bounce. "I never could do that," she said.

"What? This?" He picked up a small, flat rock and skipped it expertly across the lake.

"Yes, that! How come mine never bounces that way?"

"Probably because you're using the wrong kind of rock."

She narrowed her eyes. "C'mon, Cal, give me a break."

"I'm serious. It's almost impossible to do without the proper rock." He bent over and searched the ground until he found another flat stone and scooped it up. "It needs to be reasonably flat...like this one. And I always hold it a certain way in my hand." He demonstrated. "See?"

She nodded.

"And finally, you shouldn't throw it the way you ordinarily would. What you want to do is try to *sail* it out...like this." He demonstrated again, but didn't let go of the rock. He handed it to her. "Now you try it."

She placed the rock in her right hand. "Is this the way to hold it?"

"Almost." He took her hand in his, readjusting her fingers slightly. "More like that."

"Okay. Here goes."

Cal watched her, smiling as he saw her compress her lips, the way she had a habit of doing when she was really concentrating on something. This time, the rock bounced once before it sank. "Not bad," he said.

"Not very good, either," she disagreed. "Yours skipped a lot more times than that."

"I think your problem might have been in the wrist action. Here, let me show you." He scooped up another rock and moved behind her, placing the rock in her hand and then guiding her arm with his to show the proper movement. "Like that. See?"

She nodded, continuing the motion, moving his right arm along with hers, and his hand along with hers. He glanced down and saw the sunlight reflecting off the top of her head, picking up the reddish highlights in her hair. She moved again and her hair brushed against his cheek. He caught a brief scent that reminded him of fresh apples. He felt the warmth of her back where it touched against his chest, and the smoothness of her arm, the softness of her hand beneath his.

Oh, dear Lord. What am I doing? he thought. The same thought—or something similar—must have hit Elizabeth, too. At almost the same time. She stopped moving her arm, and he could feel her catch her breath.

She turned her head to look back at him, her lips slightly parted, her eyes wide. With surprise? With wonder?

He covered her mouth with his, and turned her around in his arms. One of them made a small sound that was almost a moan. He didn't know whether she had made the sound or he had.

Chapter Twelve

A miraculous thing happened. The world didn't suddenly stop—or turn on its axis—but Elizabeth imagined that this was the way she would feel if it had. She had been lost, cast adrift for years on a perilous sea, but now was home. She was safely back in Cal's arms, where she belonged. Where she'd always belonged.

She wanted to laugh, to cry, to shout out loud with sheer joy.

She lifted her arms to encircle his neck, and realized that she was still holding a rock in her hand—the same rock that Cal had been trying to teach her to skip across the water. She clutched the rock tighter, tightening her arms around him at the same time.

She closed her eyes, remembering all the times she'd thought about him. And in spite of everything, she *had* thought about him. Especially in her dreams. She'd thought about the very thing that was happening between them now, and the two of them being together again like this. Exactly like this, with his arms holding her tightly—as if he'd never again let her go—and with his mouth laying claim to hers, branding her as his.

The reality was even better than the dream.

His arms were warm and strong. His mouth pressed against hers was warm, too. And insistent. Demanding. She didn't resist. She welcomed his embrace, reveled in it, gloried in it. She opened her mouth beneath his, then murmured her pleasure when she felt his tongue inside her—exploring, seeking and finally finding.

She felt his hand touch her breast and cup around it, and heard his own murmur of pleasure. She buried her hand in the thick hair at the back of his neck, pulling him closer, increasing the pressure of their coupled mouths, wanting more of him. Wanting all of him.

And then—suddenly, abruptly, almost violently—he pushed her away from him.

She was left with only the rock clutched in her hand, trembling. Her legs were so weak that she wondered if she might not crumble to the ground. She looked at him, waiting for him to speak. He said nothing. He wouldn't even raise his gaze to meet hers. Why?

Damn him! He could at least look at her.

When she couldn't bear the silence any longer, she finally spoke. "Are we going to talk about it?" she asked quietly. "Or pretend it never happened, like we did the last time?"

"It shouldn't have happened," he said at last, his voice raspy.

"But it did," she said, trying to channel her hurt into anger.

"Yes." He finally looked at her and his look broke her heart. "I wasn't trying to start up anything. I mean . . . it's too late for that."

"Then why?"

"I merely wanted to kiss you. So I did. It's as simple as that."

He was lying—perhaps to himself, too—because there had been nothing simple about their kiss. Gathering all her courage and what little was left of her pride, she managed a small smile. "I see."

"I'm sorry."

"Don't be. No permanent damage was done," she said, secretly wondering if that wasn't a lie, too.

He cleared his throat. "Do you want to go back now?"

"Not yet." She didn't think she could cope with being in close contact with him on the motorcycle at the moment. She needed to shore up her defenses first. "I'd like to stretch my legs before we start back. If you don't mind."

"Okay. Shall we walk?"

What she really wanted was to go off by herself someplace, but she couldn't tell him that. She started walking along the shoreline of the lake and he fell into step beside her. Neither of them spoke.

"How did your talk with Lance Strickland go today?" Cal asked at last, breaking the silence.

She glanced at him, wondering whether he really wanted to know or was merely making small talk to ease the awkwardness between them. "Not too well," she said. "But I've decided to represent him. I told Thea at lunch."

"Are you sure you made the right decision?"

"No. But I'm doing it anyway."

"He's a loser, Elizabeth. Why do you want to defend him?"

She shrugged. "He needs my help. And nobody else is beating a path to my door asking for my legal services."

She felt his fingers close around her arm, pulling her to a halt. "Don't put yourself down that way," he said.

She looked at his hand and he quickly let go of her arm. "Why do you say he's a loser?" she asked.

"You've talked to him," Cal said. "You've seen how surly and uncooperative he is."

"I'd probably be surly and uncooperative, too, if I were in jail for car theft, and if I were innocent, like Lance is."

"Maybe he's not innocent."

"How can you say that?" Elizabeth asked. "You and I already agreed that he's hiding something...probably in order to protect someone."

"It could be that he's trying to hide the fact that he's guilty...in order to protect himself."

She shook her head. "I'm convinced he's innocent. He got caught up in something over his head, and he's trying to bluff his way out of it by acting tough. In some ways he reminds me of you at that age." She was sorry she'd added that last remark, even before she saw the look of surprise on Cal's face, then the slow flush of anger.

"He's a punk. A loser. Is that what you think of me?"

"No! I meant that he works in a gas station, the way you did. And he's in love with Jacinda, the way... the way we used to be. He worries about losing her, now that Miss Maudie is paying Jacinda's way to college.

"He's mixed up, Cal. And afraid. And because of that, he has a chip on his shoulder. But that doesn't make him a thief!"

She looked at him, waiting for him to say something. He turned away and looked out at the lake. "I'm sorry, Cal," she said after a moment. "I didn't mean to offend you. In any way. I certainly don't think you're a punk or a loser. I never did. When we were..."

She caught herself, stopped then started again. "Back in school, you were a hero to me." He wheeled around and glared at her, shaking his head. "I mean it," she said. "You were all the things I admired. I would have followed you anywhere, done anything you asked.

"And now, today, I admire you even more. But for different reasons. For what you've made of yourself. For what you've done with your life."

"*Don't!* You of all people should know that this isn't the life I intended for myself."

"I do know. But don't you see? That's what makes what you've done all the more impressive. You did it *in spite of* what my father and Sheriff Maxwell did to you. You succeeded in spite of everything."

"You call *this* succeeding—being a podunk sheriff in a town so small nobody ever heard of it?"

"*Yes!* I most certainly do! And so should you!"

"Evidently your sights are set a lot lower than mine are. Maybe that was what caused your trouble in—"

"Don't, Cal. Please don't try to hurt me. Because you can, you know. Easily. And it still wouldn't change my opinion about what you've accomplished."

She saw him take a deep breath, and saw the muscles working in his jaw as he struggled to regain control of himself. "I'm sorry," he said in a choked voice. He took her hand in both of his. "And thank you." He squeezed her hand and she winced. He looked at her hand again, then gently opened her fingers one by one.

"The rock," he said, giving her a heart-shattering smile. "I forgot to drop it."

"Maybe you could make it skip this time."

She lifted her eyebrows in a silent question.

"Just remember what I told you," he said.

She nodded, concentrated for a moment, then flung the rock out across the lake. It took four quick skips, another much longer skip, and arched into the clear sunshine one final time before it finally settled on the water and sank beneath the dark blue surface, making a small ripple that spread out in ever-widening circles.

CAL TRIED TO CONCENTRATE on his driving on the way back to Miss Maudie's house, but he kept thinking about Elizabeth. She was sitting behind him on the motorcycle, her arms around his waist. He could feel her warmth against his back. It was a distraction, but it wasn't what was bothering him the most.

He'd hurt her today. Twice.

One of those times was unintentional. When he'd pulled away from her during their kiss—when he was in eminent danger of losing control of himself and doing something they'd both regret later—it hadn't been because he wanted to hurt her. It was because he wanted to protect her. And himself. Both of them.

The other time was a different story. She'd hurt him when she'd made the comparison between him and Lance Strickland, and he'd deliberately lashed out at her in retaliation . . . not because she was wrong, but because she was right on target. He'd already noticed the similarities between Lance and himself. *The young man reminded him of himself.*

That's why he had such a low opinion of Lance. He didn't like himself very much, so how could he possibly like Lance, who had many of the same personality traits? The young man tried to act tough, but underneath the macho exterior he was scared to death. Lance was a coward. *And so am I.*

Elizabeth had tried to excuse Lance's failings—explain them away—but there was no excuse for cowardice. Cal had tried to run from the truth, too—tried to prove himself over and over for years now—but maybe everything was catching up with him. At last. It might almost be a relief.

Wouldn't it be appropriately ironic if that young punk Lance Strickland—so much like Cal had been at the same age—should finally be the cause of his exposure? It was enough to make you laugh. Or cry.

Cal spotted the turnoff to Miss Maudie's house and slowed down, following the graveled road and coasting to a stop beside Elizabeth's car again. He turned off the engine and waited until Elizabeth dismounted to secure the bike. By the time he'd finished, she had already removed her helmet. She handed it to him.

"What can I say?" she said. "The bike ride was wonderful, Cal. Better than that."

"For me, too, Elizabeth," he said, meaning it, suddenly wishing that this was the beginning instead of the end of something that had obsessed him for almost half his life.

"Will you buy it?" she asked, gesturing toward the motorcycle.

He thought for a few seconds, then nodded his head. "Probably."

"Good."

They grinned at each other.

"About today," he said, clearing his throat. "I didn't want to stop our kiss. It might have been the hardest thing to do that I've ever done in my life."

"Thank you for that," she said, blinking rapidly.

"I mean it."

"It still sounds a lot like goodbye."

"No," he protested automatically. Then, reconsidering, he said, "I mean, we'll probably see each other from time to time when you come to the station to talk to Lance."

"I understand."

"And even after that."

"You mean you won't cross the street to avoid me anymore?" she asked.

"No," he promised, swallowing the huge lump in his throat. "Never again. I'll cross the street to say hello instead...for as long as you're here, and whenever you come back."

She nodded and Cal saw that her eyes were unusually bright, but she didn't cry. He was afraid that he would, though, if she didn't leave soon. She did. "I'll hold you to that," she said, turning and walking quickly toward her car. She lifted her hand in the air and waved to him without looking back.

Cal closed his eyes with relief. And when he opened them again, his vision was blurred. He reached for his helmet and put it on, hiding his pain behind the tinted visor.

ELIZABETH MANAGED TO WAIT until she was out of Miss Maudie's driveway, out of view of any eyes that might still be watching. Then she allowed herself to do what she'd been wanting to do for hours. She cried.

She brushed her tears away with the back of her hand, and as soon as she did, more tears replaced them. Finally, when she could no longer keep the road in focus, she pulled off onto a side road and leaned her head against the steering wheel. Then she cried in earnest.

CAL SAW ELIZABETH a couple of days later at Lance's preliminary hearing before a magistrate. He thought she looked a little strained and tense, but maybe he was reading things that weren't there, because of the way he was feeling himself. Still, he sought her out afterward. "Are you okay?" he asked.

"A little disappointed," she said.

"It's not as if you didn't expect him to be bound over," Cal pointed out.

"No. But I kept hoping for a miracle—like the guilty person coming forward and confessing."

"That doesn't happen in real life."

"I know. More's the pity, don't you think?" she asked with a smile that was so wistful it made him want to take her in his arms and tell her everything would be all right.

He nodded. "I thought about you last night."

She lifted an eyebrow. "Oh?"

"Yes. Lum brought over some jambalaya for supper."

"Uh-oh," she said, her eyes crinkling at the corners. "Was it hot?"

"You might say that. The two of us drank two gallons of iced tea and finally had to resort to tap water to keep the fires under control."

They both laughed. "Well..." she said, looking at her watch "... I guess I'd better..."

"Yeah, me too."

She started to leave but immediately turned back to him. "I just remembered something. Did you buy the motorcycle?"

"Yes."

"That's good. Congratulations."

"Thanks," he said. She did leave then, because there was nothing more for them to say. Watching her straight, narrow back as she walked down the corridor, Cal felt an incredible sadness.

IT WASN'T AS IF they'd fallen in love again, or started up a romance, Elizabeth kept telling herself. All they'd done was share a kiss, and she'd read more into the kiss than Cal wanted or intended. So why did she continue to feel this terrible sense of loss, all over again?

It was stupid to feel this way. Senseless. *So stop it,* she told herself. She needed to think about something else, such as trying to prepare a defense for Lance. The trouble was,

she needed a law library for that and all her books were still
crated in boxes, where they'd been for more than two years.

Then she thought about Quint. Although he was the
district attorney and ordinarily would have been her op-
ponent, he'd already taken himself off Lance's case, so
maybe she could use his law library. She talked to Thea, and
Thea talked to Quint, and soon it was all arranged.

She felt good getting back to work again after so long a
time. Or reasonably good. Better, anyway. And she knew
from past experience that time would help, too. Maybe in
another seventeen years she'd be completely over Cal.

"AREN'T YOU GLAD now that I insisted you come with me
to the Rockwells' house tonight?" Frances Bartlett said as
Elizabeth guided the Cadillac to a stop in their driveway
and killed the engine.

"I had a nice time, Mother," Elizabeth said, getting out
on the driver's side and locking the door, something she
never used to do before her car was stolen. Actually, going
out for dinner and bridge at the home of her mother's
friends *hadn't* been bad. At least it had kept her from
moping in her room, something she'd done too much of
lately.

"I hope my bridge playing didn't embarrass you too
much," Elizabeth added.

"Don't worry," her mother said, looping her arm with
Elizabeth's as they walked up the steps to their front door.
"I know it's been a while since you played, but it'll come
back to you in no time."

She sounds as if she expects us to be doing this a lot, Elizabeth thought with a sinking feeling. She could see it now—
mother and daughter, two lonely women, out on the town
for another wild night of dinner and bridge. She felt a chill
run up her spine.

"That's strange," Frances said as Elizabeth fumbled in
her purse for the front-door key. "I could have sworn I left
on the outside light, and one in the hall as well."

"Maybe you forgot," Elizabeth said, looking at the dark house. "It *was* still light when we left."

"No, I'm almost positive. I always leave lights burning when I go out on the housekeeper's night off."

"Or maybe the bulb's burned out."

"Both of them?"

Elizabeth shrugged. She finally found her keys and unlocked the front door, then stepped inside and flipped a switch beside the door, flooding the foyer with bright light. Her mother followed her inside and Elizabeth closed and locked the front door.

"Elizabeth?"

"Yes, Mother?" she said, turning around in time to see her mother pick up something from the marble floor.

"This is strange," Frances said, holding up a woman's bra. "Did you . . . ?"

"No," Elizabeth said in a strangled voice, feeling her blood run cold. "I didn't."

"Then—"

"You'd better wait here, Mother. I'll—"

"*No!* Somebody might still be in the house!"

Elizabeth swallowed, trying to calm down, trying to think. "We have to do something."

"Call the police," Frances said.

"We can't do that, not until we know for sure," she said, thinking of what Cal's reaction might be if she called him in the middle of the night. "It could be nothing."

"You call this nothing?" Frances said, holding up the bra with her thumb and forefinger.

Elizabeth looked around for a weapon and finally picked up an umbrella from the stand beside the front door. "I'll take a quick look in the hall," she said, glancing toward one of three closed doors leading off from the foyer.

"But suppose—" Frances began.

"That's where the closest telephone is, Mother. Besides, I can turn on the hall light from out here."

Frances nodded and Elizabeth moved slowly to the light switch for the hall. Suddenly realizing she was tiptoeing, she almost laughed but didn't. Laughing would make noise. Taking a deep breath, she slowly reached out her hand to switch on the light.

"*Wait!*"

Elizabeth caught her breath and almost screamed out loud. Finally recognizing that it was her mother who'd spoken to her, she closed her eyes for a moment while she waited for her racing heart to slow down. Then she turned to her mother.

"What now?" she asked, not bothering to disguise her annoyance.

"The doors leading off the foyer," Frances whispered. "They're all closed."

Elizabeth glanced around and saw that what Frances said was true. All three doors were closed, something that everyone in the household knew not to do, especially in the summer. Frances insisted that all the doors be left open for air circulation.

"Someone *has* been in this house," Frances said in a fierce whisper. "They're probably still here!"

Be calm, Elizabeth told herself, trying to swallow her fear. "You go outside and wait for me," she told her mother. "If you hear anything, or if I don't come back out in a couple of seconds, start running."

"No!"

"I'll be all right," she said, patting Frances's hand.

"I'm *not* leaving you."

Elizabeth hesitated, torn between gratitude to her mother for not leaving and fear for their safety. She wasn't as brave as she'd tried to sound. She patted Frances's hand again, then squeezed it. "Here we go, then."

She reached out her hand for the light switch again, and after pausing a brief moment flicked it on. Then she held her breath, waiting. After she'd silently counted to thirty, she pressed her ear to the door and listened for sounds coming from the hall. She heard nothing. After a full minute, she turned to her mother.

"If anybody was in there, they've had plenty of time to get away," she said. "I'm going to open the door now."

Frances nodded. Elizabeth opened the door. Frances screamed. Elizabeth gasped and covered her mouth with her hand to keep from screaming herself.

The hall looked as if a whirlwind—a tornado—had been through it, destroying everything.

"MY MEN ARE STILL going through the upstairs bedrooms," Cal said. "But from the looks of things so far, I'd say that no burglary has taken place here."

"What?" Elizabeth exclaimed indignantly.

"What makes you think that?" her mother asked in a much more reasonable tone, Cal noticed.

"I've been going through the list you gave me," he said, glancing down at the typewritten sheet of paper in his hands, "and so far, we've found no valuables missing. It's lucky you had this list made, Mrs. Bartlett."

"It was for insurance purposes," she said. "I happened to remember it was in the wall safe."

"The wall safe that hadn't even been touched," he said to Elizabeth.

"They could have overlooked it," she replied.

"Not likely. But the point is, we've accounted for almost every item on the list. So judging by that, I'd guess this was the work of vandals."

"Vandals!" Elizabeth exclaimed. "Just look around you, Cal. There's wholesale destruction here."

"I agree. And that makes me even more sure it's the work of vandals. Burglars as a rule are much neater."

"How do you know?"

"I've seen both." *And done both,* he thought, recalling his years of undercover work with distaste. He saw Elizabeth's mother lift up her hand to smother a yawn. Elizabeth was looking tired, too, although she didn't appear to be sleepy. Adrenaline was probably keeping her going.

"I'm sorry to keep you up so late," Cal said. "I wish we could hurry things up so we could leave and you could go to bed, but it's important that we go through everything with a fine-toothed comb before it's disturbed. I mean...anymore than it already is."

"We understand, Cal," Elizabeth said. "And thank you."

"Besides," Mrs. Bartlett said, "we aren't staying here tonight anyway."

"We're not?" Elizabeth said.

"You're not?" Cal said at the same time.

Frances Bartlett shuddered. "Certainly not! I've already talked to the Rockwells and they're expecting both of us at their house as soon as we finish up here. I called while you two were talking in the foyer," she added, looking at Elizabeth, who was frowning. "Surely you didn't expect us to spend the night in this ...this *bedlam,* this crime scene."

"I guess I wasn't thinking clearly, Mother. Of course you can't stay here...*we* can't stay here."

Cal watched the exchange with interest, then took a deep breath. "In that case, may I make a suggestion?" he asked. "Why don't you two pack some things in an overnight bag and I'll drive you over to your friends now. There's really no need for you to hang around here, all worn out like you are."

"Thank you, Cal," Mrs. Bartlett said. "That's a wonderful idea. Don't you think so, Elizabeth?"

Elizabeth appeared skeptical. "Don't worry," Cal said to her. "I'll come back here as soon as I've dropped you off. I'll make sure everything's secure before I leave."

"It's not that," she said.

"What, then?"

"I don't know." She shrugged. "Nothing, I guess."

"Then go upstairs with your mother," he said, wanting to hold her in his arms, but knowing he couldn't. Barring that, he wanted to touch her—on the shoulder, on the arm, the hand, anywhere—but knowing he couldn't do that, either.

"Pack," he said gruffly. "I'll come up with you."

"That's not necessary," Elizabeth said.

"Just in case," he said. "There's a pretty bad mess up there."

Cal followed Elizabeth and her mother upstairs, but stepped in front of them before they could enter Mrs. Bartlett's bedroom, which seemed to have received the worst destruction. "George, come out here with me while Elizabeth helps her mother pack a few nightclothes," he said to his deputy.

"Sorry this happened to you," George said to Elizabeth as he came out of the room.

"Me, too, George," she replied, touching his hand. "And thank you." She looked into the bedroom then, and Cal watched her catch her breath when she saw the senseless destruction for the first time.

"Mother—" she began, but Mrs. Bartlett was already beside her, pushing her way past her.

"Don't try to spare me, Elizabeth," she said.

Cal watched closely, and was surprised when Mrs. Bartlett's only reaction on seeing her room was to shake her head. "What a mess," she finally said. Then she sighed. "Well, come along, Elizabeth. Help me pack."

Elizabeth looked back at Cal and shrugged before she followed her mother into the room.

Cal breathed a sigh of relief that Mrs. Bartlett was taking it so well. He turned to his deputy. "Did you turn up anything missing yet, George?"

"Not me. And the last time I checked, Travis hadn't found anything either. Looks like it was vandals, just as you thought in the first place."

"But keep looking, all the same," Cal cautioned.

"Sure."

"I'm going to drive Elizabeth and her mother over to some friends' house after they've finished packing. But I'll come back as soon as—"

"Where did you get these?"

Cal stopped talking, then moved quickly toward the bedroom when he realized that the shrill voice belonged to Elizabeth.

"Give them to me!" he heard her mother demand.

"What's going on?" Cal asked from the doorway, seeing Elizabeth and her mother facing each other. As far as he could tell, both of them were breathing fury.

"I asked you a question!" Elizabeth shouted, ignoring Cal and waving something she held in her hand. She jerked her hand back as soon as Mrs. Bartlett reached for it. "Where did you get these?"

"Elizabeth!" he said in a louder voice. "What are you doing?"

That finally caught her attention and she turned to him, her face contorted with anger. "It's not what *I'm* doing," she said. "It's what *she's* doing. What she's done!"

"You're talking nonsense," he said soothingly, trying to calm her down. The shock of having her house burglarized must have gotten to her, causing her to lose control, he decided.

"Yes, you are," Mrs. Bartlett said, agreeing with Cal.

"*Shut up!*" Elizabeth shouted at her mother.

"*Elizabeth!*" Cal shouted at her, shocked.

She turned to him then, waving whatever it was she was holding in her hand. "Do you know what these are?"

"No, but—"

"They're *letters,* Cal. The letters I wrote you from Switzerland. The ones I told you about but you didn't believe me. You thought I was lying when I told you I wrote them and I thought you were lying when you said you never received them. And *she* had them all along...."

Elizabeth seemed to run out of steam then. Cal hesitated a moment, then walked over to her and gently took the letters from her hand. She didn't resist.

They were neatly stacked and held together by a rubber band. He glanced at the one on top. It was written in a girlish scrawl that he immediately recognized as Elizabeth's—Elizabeth at seventeen.

He caught his breath and felt the hairs prickle at the back of his neck.

The letter on top was addressed to him—Cal Potts—at his mother's old address, the place where she'd lived until she died in a terrible house fire sixteen years ago.

Chapter Thirteen

Cal looked down at the letters in his hand, then at Elizabeth, who was watching him. "You found these here in your mother's bedroom?"

She nodded. "They were on the floor beside her dresser. The burglars must have dumped them out, along with everything else."

He finally turned to Mrs. Bartlett. "I don't understand," he said to her. "How do you happen to have these?"

She lifted her chin defiantly. "Give them to me. They're mine."

"I think not. They're addressed to me."

"But they *belong* to me," she said, narrowing her eyes. "I bought and paid for them."

Cal heard Elizabeth's gasp but he continued staring at her mother. "What are you saying?"

"I bought the letters. Now give them to me."

"Are you claiming that *my mother* sold these to you?" he said, feeling himself losing control. "I don't believe you."

"How dare you call me a liar!" Mrs. Bartlett said.

"My mother wouldn't do that to me," Cal said. "Never in a million years."

"It wasn't your mother. It was your stepfather."

Cal blinked. He knew his mother wouldn't do such a thing... but Luther might. "I think you'd better tell us the whole story, from the beginning."

He saw Mrs. Bartlett take a deep breath. "Your mother brought the first letter to me the day after it arrived."

"No!" Cal exclaimed. "You're not—"

"She told me she was afraid of what my husband might do to you if he found out that you and Elizabeth were keeping in touch with each other behind his back."

Cal started to protest again but stopped himself when he realized Mrs. Bartlett might be telling the truth. He'd told his mother the whole story about being beaten and forced to join the army... including why it had happened. He could see how she'd be worried for his safety if Mr. Bartlett found out that Elizabeth was writing to him.

"I told her she'd done the right thing in bringing the letter to me," Mrs. Bartlett said. "I told her it would be our secret, and she agreed to bring me any future letters that might come to her address. I offered to pay her, but she refused. After that... your stepfather brought me the letters, one by one as they received them."

"And he *did* accept your money," Cal said.

"Yes."

The room was quiet, so quiet that Cal could hear the rapid hammering of his own heart. Then, out of the corner of his eye, he saw Elizabeth take a single step toward her mother.

"How could you do that to me?" Elizabeth asked, her voice choked with anguish.

"I was trying to protect you... and Cal as well," Mrs. Bartlett said.

"No! Tell the truth for once in your life, Mother. You hated Cal, the same as my father did, but at least he was honest about it. He didn't try to hide it, or tell lies the way you've done all these years."

"Don't you *dare* talk to me that way!"

"There are worse things I could say, Mother. Such as . . . what would you call a person who reads another person's mail? Those letters *have been opened.*"

"I wasn't the one who opened them," Mrs. Bartlett insisted.

"My mother would never have done it," Cal said with certainty.

"Your stepfather—" Mrs. Bartlett began.

"Why would Luther open them?" Cal said. "He couldn't even read."

"*You* did it, Mother," Elizabeth said. "You read those letters—letters I'd intended for Cal alone."

"Yes, I read them!" Mrs. Bartlett finally admitted. "And they made me sick. To think that my own daughter would write such—"

"*I meant every word I said!*" Elizabeth shouted. "And . . . and you make *me* sick. If you read those letters, you know how much I loved Cal. Yet you deliberately tried to keep us apart."

"It was for your own good. You were too young."

"Was I *still* too young a week ago, Mother?"

"What are you talking about?"

"I told you about the missing letters then. Remember? I even asked your opinion on what could have happened to them. You could have told me you had the letters then. But you didn't."

"I . . . I was afraid to."

"Afraid?" Elizabeth repeated. "Afraid of what?"

"Afraid that you'd hate me and say terrible things to me, just like you're doing now."

Elizabeth shook her head. "I might have been upset if you'd told me then. But nothing like this. I might have forgiven you then. But not now."

"*Do* forgive me, Elizabeth!" Mrs. Bartlett said. "Please. I'm sorry."

Cal almost forgave Elizabeth's mother then. She suddenly looked old. And afraid.

"I'm sorry, too, Mother," Elizabeth said. "But it's too late now to ask forgiveness."

"It's only been a week—" Mrs. Bartlett began.

"Yes. But a week ago, I trusted you. And I gave you a chance to be honest with me, like I was trying to be with you. Maybe...maybe living a lie with my father all those years has made you incapable of honesty. I'm sorry," Elizabeth said again, looking as if she might cry. She quickly turned and headed for the bedroom door.

"Elizabeth!" her mother shouted, but Elizabeth was already gone. "Cal, do something!" Mrs. Bartlett screamed.

"I intend to," he said, starting for the door. "I'm going after her. I'll tell one of my men to drive you wherever you want to go."

Cal paused briefly to speak to George, who was waiting in the hallway outside the bedroom. "You heard?"

George nodded.

"Good," Cal said before he heard the front door slam. "You drive Mrs. Bartlett to her friends' house and then come back here and help Travis finish up. I doubt that I'll be back tonight," he added, remembering the last look he'd seen on Elizabeth's face.

George nodded again. "Not much left of the night anyway."

Cal didn't reply. Instead he raced down the stairs after Elizabeth. He caught up with her beside her new Jeep Cherokee, trying to open the door on the driver's side. When she couldn't get the door to open, she started pounding her fists against the roof of the car.

"Elizabeth," he said, taking hold of her wrists and gently but firmly pulling her away from the car.

She looked at him, tears streaming down her cheeks. "It's *locked!*" she said. "The damned car's locked."

"It's okay. I'll drive you."

"But don't you see?" she shouted. "I don't even know where my keys are. *I have no idea!*"

She collapsed against his chest then, crying heartbrokenly. Cal released her wrists and wrapped his arms around her, pulling her close and then closer still, holding her tight. "Elizabeth," he murmured against her hair. "Oh, Elizabeth. What has she done to you? What have we all done to you?"

OPENING HER EYES, Elizabeth felt disoriented. She saw dashboard lights and knew she must be in a car, but whose? And how had she gotten there? She tried to focus on the dashboard lights but her vision was blurred. She blinked and then realized she had tears in her eyes. Why had she been crying? She brushed away the tears with the back of her hand.

"Elizabeth?"

That was Cal's voice. Cal was sitting next to her. And it was Cal's arm she felt around her shoulders. But why were the two of them in a car? And where were they going?

"Where are we going?" she asked, voicing her question out loud in a croaky voice.

"To my place," Cal said.

"Oh." She closed her eyes again, and leaned her head against his shoulder, feeling as tired as she'd ever felt in her life. But everything was okay. They were going to Cal's place. Maybe Lum would be there, too. She smiled, and felt the smile pinch her parched lips.

Then she thought of her mother and the thought caused a sharp pain inside her and made her want to start crying all over again, although she couldn't remember why it did. "My mother!" she said.

"She's all right, Elizabeth. Much better than you are, I imagine. I told one of my deputies to drive her to her friends' house for the night."

She nodded, and relaxed her head against his shoulder.

The car wasn't moving anymore. Elizabeth blinked her eyes and realized she must have dozed off to sleep. "Where are we?" she asked Cal, who was sitting beside her.

"My place," he said. "I told you we were coming here. Remember?"

"I'm not sure." She blinked again, trying to remember but drawing a blank. "*Why* did we come here?"

"Because you're tired and you need to sleep," he said. She noticed his voice was very gentle. Why was Cal being so nice to her? Wasn't he supposed to hate her and want nothing more to do with her? She tried to think....

"My head hurts," she said.

"That's because you're so tired, and you had quite a shock tonight."

"Something about my mother."

"Yes. But don't try to think about it now. Wait until you've rested," he said, helping her across the seat to get out of the car on his side. "You'll have plenty of time to think about it later."

She tried to stand and her legs were wobbly. "I'll carry you," Cal said.

"You can't—" she started to protest, but he'd already scooped her up in his arms before she could finish. "Really, Cal."

"I'm playing macho tonight," he said. "You can tease me about it later."

He put her down while he opened the door, but kept an arm around her and she was thankful he did. She felt weak as dishwater. Maybe she was coming down with something. She felt herself being lifted in his arms again. "What...?"

"I'm taking you up to bed," he said.

"But—"

"I'll sleep down here on the sofa."

She had no more strength left to protest, so she closed her eyes again.

CAL LOOKED DOWN at Elizabeth asleep in his bed, something he used to dream about. *And still did,* his conscience reminded him.

But not like this. His heart went out to her, crying along with her for what she'd been through tonight. *Last night,* he corrected himself, glancing at his watch. Dawn would break soon, and the sun would be up in only a couple more hours.

He looked at her one last long time—curled in a fetal position at one edge of his big bed—and then made his way out of the loft and down the stairs quickly and silently, as he'd been taught to do in the special forces many years ago.

He stood in the middle of his living room, unsure what to do with himself. He could try to get a little sleep on the sofa, but there were two problems with that. One was that Elizabeth might need him and call out to him. The other was that he wasn't the slightest bit sleepy. He was wound tight as a tick, totally awake and alert.

He suddenly remembered the letters, the ones Elizabeth had written him seventeen years ago. He'd stuffed them into his back pocket when he raced out to get her at her mother's house. He pulled them out of his pocket and looked at them, still bound together with a rubber band.

He walked over to the sofa and sat down, placing the letters on the coffee table in front of him. After a moment he picked them up. He turned them over in his hands, then turned them over again. She had written them years and years ago, when she was much younger. For him to read them now would be... What? Dishonest? A violation of trust or confidence?

Not really. She had written them to him, and wanted him to receive them, to read them. She'd gone to great pains to make sure he received them, placing them in the care of someone she trusted.

Should he read them, now that he had the opportunity? *Her mother had.*

But he wasn't like her mother. He'd done some bad things in his life—some really terrible things if you wanted to get down to cases—but he'd never been as cold-bloodedly malicious as Elizabeth's mother.

So what other excuses are you going to invent for yourself, Potts?

He removed the rubber band and opened the envelope on top. Then, with shaky hands, he unfolded the letter inside. He started to read.

Much later he folded the last letter and inserted it into its proper envelope. He stacked the letters together, replaced the rubber band, and put them on the coffee table.

He sat silently, not moving, for several minutes. The he placed his elbows on his knees and lowered his head to his upturned hands. He started to cry, something he hadn't allowed himself to do in a long, long time.

"CAL!"

He sat up abruptly on the sofa, trying to rub the sleep from his eyes, unsure whether he'd dreamed that Elizabeth had cried out for him.

"Cal!" he heard again. That was no dream. He jumped to his feet and bounded up the stairs to the sleeping loft. Elizabeth was thrashing about on the bed, making small sounds like a hurt or wounded animal would make.

She must be having a nightmare, he thought, noticing that her eyes were closed. He sat on the bed beside her, trying to pull her into his arms. She resisted with almost superhuman strength, pushing and flailing wildly. He caught one of her hands in his and held on to it until he finally managed to capture the other one. Then he pushed her back in the bed, holding her in place by covering her body with his.

"Elizabeth," he said. "It's me, Cal. You're having a nightmare. *Elizabeth.* Listen to me. Do you hear me?"

She gradually stopped struggling, and finally opened her eyes. She was breathing hard, almost panting. "Cal?"

"Yes. It's me. You were having a nightmare."

She nodded. "Yes." She took a deep breath. "I was dreaming about my mother..." She stopped suddenly, closed her eyes, then opened them again. Wide. "But it really happened, didn't it?"

Cal swallowed. "Yes."

Elizabeth closed her eyes again, tightly, and Cal could see tears starting to roll down her cheeks. "She destroyed my life, Cal. She did it deliberately."

"I know," he said, moving off her, lying in bed beside her and gathering her into his arms. "And I know it hurts. So cry. Cry, Elizabeth, as much as you want to. It won't change the past but maybe it'll help wash away the hurt. And if it helps, I'll cry along with you."

He held her while she cried, and continued holding her until she finally stopped trembling and appeared to be sleeping soundly at last. Then he closed his own eyes, allowing himself to relax but not releasing his hold on her, knowing she might need him more than ever when she woke up and was thinking clearly.

He must have drifted off to sleep again, he realized when he opened his eyes and saw the first faint traces of dawn through the skylight above the bed. He shifted his head slightly and saw Elizabeth sleeping beside him, her head cradled in the crook of his arm. The arm was asleep, too, and he longed to move it but didn't because that might disturb her. He knew that healing sleep was the most precious thing he could give her at the moment.

Later on, she'd need more from him. And he'd give it. Gladly. He could do that for her, even though he couldn't give her a lifetime. Whatever chance of happiness the two of them might have had together had been wiped out long ago in a steamy jungle. He had to live with the memory of what had happened there for the rest of his life, but that was his guilt. His alone. And he'd never ask her to share it, not the woman he loved.

Yes, he finally admitted to himself. He loved her.

He'd probably never stopped loving her, he thought, looking at her face only inches away from his. Even when he'd tried to convince himself he hated her, he'd still loved her.

And now he had one last chance to demonstrate it. He couldn't offer her a future, but he could take care of her today—maybe for a few days—however long it took until she got over the worst of her hurt.

He continued watching her, feeling an incredible tenderness as he examined the contours of her face while she slept. He saw her long, dark lashes, spiked from the tears she'd shed last night and this morning. He saw her pink lips, soft and full, and remembered how they'd felt under his.

He felt a stirring inside him—a deep longing for something that could never be—and looked away in pain and denial. He took a deep breath. Another one. Then something caused him to look back at Elizabeth again.

He saw a familiar pair of green eyes. They were awake and alert, watching him.

"I hope I didn't wake you," he said.

"No." Her voice was deep and throaty.

"How are you?"

She didn't reply immediately. "I'm not sure." After a moment she added, "Thank you for taking care of me last night. I don't know what I would have done if. . ." She left the sentence unfinished.

"I'm glad I was there."

"I must have been in pretty bad shape. I don't even remember a lot of what happened."

"You were in shock. But I imagine most of it'll come back to you in time."

"Unfortunately."

He nodded, agreeing with her.

"One thing I wonder about," she said hesitantly. "The last I remember, I had on the same clothes I'd worn out to dinner. But now. . ."

She was covered by a sheet, but even if he hadn't still had his arms around her, Cal would have known what she was wearing now—her panties and one of his undershirts. Nothing else. "I, uh, tried to make you comfortable when I brought you up to bed."

"Oh."

"I thought it might help you sleep better," he added.

"Thank you."

He was suddenly more acutely conscious of his arms around her than he'd been before, and of her supple body stretched out next to his. Although he was completely dressed except for his shoes, he could feel their bodies touching in several places, and could feel the heat of her burning through his clothes every place they touched, adding fuel to the fire within him. He thought about moving away from her, but that would be too obvious.

"Cal?"

"What?"

"Would you like to make love with me?"

He caught his breath. "I don't think that would be a good idea."

"Because I'd like to make love with you," she added, as if he hadn't spoken. "I'd like it very much."

"You're still upset about last night, Elizabeth. If...if we made love, you'd regret it later."

"Are you saying you don't want me?"

He knew she could feel his arousal. "No. You know better than that."

"Then why won't you?"

"Because you're still on shaky emotional ground and I'd be taking advantage of that. It would be a cheap, shabby thing for me to do."

He jumped with surprise when she suddenly touched his chin. "If that's what's stopping you, then let me take advantage of you," she said.

He swallowed. "Elizabeth, there's no future for the two of us together. We—"

"I'm not asking for the future," she said, moving her hand along his cheek. "Only the present. Here. Now."

He covered her hand with his, trying to halt its motion which was making him crazy with wanting her. *God, how he wanted her.*

"I need you, Cal," she whispered. "And you need me, too, whether you know it or not."

He did need her. And he knew it. Knew it in his heart . . . in his aching body that was screaming with need of her . . . knew it in his soul.

With a deep moan—almost of pain—he gave in to that need and crushed his mouth to hers.

He kissed her hungrily, and she kissed him back with equal intensity, their tongues thrusting wildly, their bodies straining for more intimacy. She pulled him closer to her, first with her arms, then with her legs wrapped around him. He was drowning in her—in the touch and taste of her— and went willingly, only wanting more of her.

Elizabeth. *His* Elizabeth. He'd thought they could never be together again, and certainly not like this. But how many times had he dreamed of it in spite of the sure knowledge it couldn't happen? How many times had he longed for her? Physically ached for her?

He touched her and she touched him and they seemed to realize at the same time that their clothes were a hindrance. They helped each other remove them, working with urgent intensity. And when they were both completely naked, the urgency suddenly vanished. He lay down on the bed beside her, not touching, loving her with his eyes, and feeling her loving gaze warming him in return.

They smiled at each other.

After several moments, he leaned over to kiss her. As soon as their lips touched, the urgency returned. And the desire. Stronger than ever. When Cal felt that he couldn't stand not being inside her a second longer, he raised himself up on his arms, hovering above her, asking a silent question with his eyes.

"Yes," she said. "Oh, please. Yes."

And finally, after so many years apart—years when longing often bordered on desolation and pain often bordered on heartbreak —Cal and Elizabeth made love to each other.

Chapter Fourteen

Elizabeth shivered one last time, not with pain but with delight, and kissed Cal's forehead, tasting the salt of his sweat on her lips. She kissed him again, trying to show him how much pleasure he'd given her. And was still giving her. He hadn't moved away after the lovemaking was over, and she loved the prolonged closeness, the intimacy.

She loved him.

Thinking about it, she knew that she always had loved him, in spite of everything. And always would. Until the day she died.

She frowned, thinking it strange that she hadn't recognized she was in love with him before now, because she usually knew herself so well. *Too* well.

Perhaps she'd subconsciously been trying to protect herself, after the trauma of believing Cal had abandoned her all those years ago. *And also knowing he wouldn't welcome her love now.*

He'd made it clear—painfully clear—that he wouldn't get involved with her again. "There's no future for the two of us," he'd said. And she'd told him she wasn't asking for a future, only the present. She hadn't known at the time that she was lying. She *did* want a future. With Cal.

But she couldn't tell him that, not now, after what they'd both said. Could she? She closed her eyes, wishing with all her heart that things were different. They weren't, however, and there was no point in worrying about it anymore now. In fact, she didn't want to worry about anything at the moment. She didn't even want to *think*. She wanted to feel, savor, enjoy.

That's what she wanted, but suddenly she was hit with a new set of worries. She and Cal would probably talk soon—after they'd both had a chance to catch their breath and return to earth from the intense experience they'd just shared—and she didn't know what she could say to him. She wanted to let him know how deeply, truly moved she was, but since she couldn't tell him she loved him, how could she express her feelings in a way that wouldn't embarrass him?

What *do* you tell a man after the most incredible lovemaking experience of your life? "It was wonderful for me. How was it for you?" She cringed and shivered at the thought, not with pleasure this time.

"Elizabeth?"

She didn't answer.

"I know you're not asleep," Cal said. "So don't pretend you are."

She opened her eyes. "I wasn't pretending to be asleep."

"What were you doing, then?"

"If you must know the truth, I was trying to think of something to say to you."

"Oh?"

"Without sounding too corny," she added, relieved when she saw his eyes crinkle at the corners with amusement.

"What sort of lines were you thinking along?"

"Well..." she said, pretending to think about it. "How about *wonderful?*"

"That's *all?*" he asked, going along with the joke and pretending to be shocked.

"Terrific?"

He shook his head. "Not nearly descriptive enough."

"Beautiful?"

"Better," he said giving her a quick kiss.

"Fantastic?"

"Better still," he said, kissing her again. "But how about *incredible?*" he murmured against her lips.

"Yes," she said, kissing him back. "Oh, yes. My sentiments exactly."

They kissed for some minutes, their tongues exploring each other, their legs intertwined. Elizabeth felt herself heating up, especially when she felt him growing harder inside her, where he'd been since the last time they made love.

Growing? She pulled back slightly and looked at him, her eyes wide.

"Yes," he said in answer to her silent question. "And if you say, 'So soon?' I'll strangle you."

She struggled to keep a straight face. "You know I wouldn't say something as corny as that."

"You better not," he said, kissing her and beginning the whole incredible lovemaking process all over again.

BEING CAREFUL NOT to awaken Elizabeth, Cal got out of bed, scooping a pair of khakis from the floor, and quickly descended the stairs, pulling on the trousers as he went. Cursing himself for oversleeping, he picked up the telephone and punched out a series of numbers, breathing a sigh of relief when he heard the voice on the other end.

"George, it's me. Cal. Did you get Mrs. Bartlett delivered to her friends last night?"

"Yeah."

Cal heard the edge to George's voice. "But...?"

"From the way that woman acted, you'd have thought I was a mass murderer instead of a sheriff's deputy."

"Sorry about that. But you know the way some people are—taking their feelings out on anybody that's around. I'm the one she'd *really* like to see hanged...and tarred and feathered beforehand, if she had her way about it."

He heard George's deep chuckle. "Did you and Travis get finished at the Bartletts' house last night?"

"This morning, you mean. And we didn't find a single thing missing from the list that woman gave us. Musta been the work of vandals, like you thought. You suppose she did it herself?"

"You wish," Cal said, laughing. "But seriously," he added, sobering quickly. "I'd like to ask a favor of you, George. If you're agreeable to the idea, I'd like to put you in charge of the station while I take a few days off. I've already made out the duty schedule, so there shouldn't be too much extra work for you."

"Well...sure, Cal. And you sure deserve a vacation. You haven't had a real one in three years, and I know that for a fact. Have a good 'un."

"Thanks. And, uh, there's one more thing. You can always call me here in case of an emergency, but—"

"I know that. Let's hope I don't have to."

"Right. But the thing is..." Cal hesitated and took a deep breath. "Elizabeth is here, too. She was in pretty bad shape last night and—"

"You don't have to tell me," George interrupted. "I saw and heard what happened. It made me want to wring that scrawny woman's neck with my own hands...treating Elizabeth like that..."

"Yes," Cal said. "Well...as I started to say, I'm going to try to persuade Elizabeth to stay here a few days. Just until she's feeling better. And I thought you ought to know in case her mother comes around raising Cain about it."

"I'll tell her that Elizabeth's okay and that she's staying with a friend," George said.

"That sounds good."

"But I'll tell you something, too, Cal," George continued. "If you're as smart as I always thought you were, you won't let Elizabeth get away from you this time."

"George, I don't think—"

"I remember how the two of you were back in high school. Her as pretty as a picture and sweet as honey. All the guys were after her, and she wouldn't even *look* at anybody but you. She thought you were rained down from heaven."

Cal tried to talk around the huge lump in his throat. "Listen..."

"I know it's none of my business, but I just wanted to remind you."

"I appreciate it, George. But..."

"I won't call you unless it's necessary. And good luck."

Cal tried to say something—anything that would correct George's misconception—but his deputy had already hung up before he could get the words out. Cal stood there, staring at the receiver he still held in his hand. Finally he replaced it in the hook.

George was just what he needed—somebody else to remind him of how much he cared, or should care, about Elizabeth. As if he needed reminding. Cal shook his head, then padded into the kitchen alcove. He pulled out the electric percolator and added water up to the eight-cup rim. Thinking about it some more, he added water up to the twelve-cup rim, measured coffee into the basket, and plugged it in to perk.

He walked to the bathroom and turned on the shower in the tub, holding his hand under the water while he adjusted the temperature. Shucking his khakis, he stepped into the tub, ducking his head under the shower spray and waiting for the water to wash away all his cares, all his woes, as it had done so many times before.

But something was wrong this time.

The water wasn't washing away all his cares and woes. In fact, he didn't even seem to *have* any woes at the moment. He was happy, happier than he'd been in many years, and his cares were buried so far back in his mind that they were almost out of sight. What was wrong with him?

Then it came to him. Nothing was wrong. Something was right for a change. Because Elizabeth was here. Right here in his house. Sleeping upstairs in his bed. At this very moment. And maybe she'd be staying here for a few days—nothing permanent—just until she was fully recovered.

He ducked his head under the water again and started humming to himself.

WHEN CAL EMERGED from the bathroom a short while later, he saw Elizabeth sitting at the kitchen table drinking coffee. She was wearing another of his shirts with the sleeves rolled up to her elbows. She also had on something that looked suspiciously like a pair of his boxer shorts.

She smiled at him. "The smell of coffee woke me up."

He smiled back at her. "How about something to go with the coffee? Bacon and eggs, for instance. I make a mean breakfast."

"Maybe later. I'd like to shower first," she said, her eyes trained on his bare chest.

"All my shirts were upstairs and I didn't want to run the risk of waking you," he explained.

"I'm not complaining," she said. "I'm all in favor of casual attire around the house."

He saw the mischief in her eyes then. And something else, too. He moved quickly to the table and put his hands under her elbows to guide her to her feet. He put one arm around her waist and tilted back her chin with his other hand. "How do you feel about casual kisses before breakfast?" he asked.

"I have no objection to them, either," she said huskily.

He lowered his mouth to hers, gently at first, intending to keep the kiss casual. But as soon as their lips met, and as soon as he felt her lightning-like response to his touch, his good intentions vanished. Soon he was kissing her hungrily, thrusting his tongue inside her to taste the coffee she'd drunk earlier, greedily drawing her tongue into his mouth, acting as if he hadn't touched her in years instead of only a few hours.

The bed upstairs suddenly seemed too far away—miles away—so Cal scooped Elizabeth up into his arms and carried her to the sofa instead, keeping their kiss going while he walked, and even after he'd placed her on the sofa and knelt on the floor beside her. He finally moved his mouth from her lips to her breast after he'd unbuttoned her shirt and pushed it aside. Then he trailed his lips along her flat stomach . . . down to his boxer shorts which she wore.

"I knew these were mine," he said, slipping his hand inside the shorts and lifting his head to look at her.

"Why don't you take them back, then?" she whispered. "Now."

He removed the shorts, and his own trousers as well, and then kissed her all over before he finally joined her on the sofa.

IT WAS ALMOST NOON before they finally got around to eating breakfast.

"I've been thinking," Cal said after they'd done the dishes together and moved outside to the screened porch. "And I have an idea I'd like to discuss with you."

"Again?" she teased. "So soon?"

"That wasn't the idea I was talking about," he said. "But I might change my mind if you don't watch it."

Elizabeth laughed, still slightly amazed that she *could* laugh today after the way she'd felt last night. *That's what love will do for you.* She sighed. "Tell me your idea, Cal. The original one."

"Well..." he began, then stopped, seeming to be unsure of himself or what he wanted to say.

"It's okay," she prompted. "I promise I won't tease anymore."

"I was thinking that after last night you probably won't want to go back to your mother's house for awhile."

"I'll never go back there, except to get my personal belongings and then leave again immediately," she said with certainty.

"Yes," he said. "I can see how you'd feel that way. And that made me think...made me wonder...if you'd given any thought to where you'll live now."

Elizabeth caught her breath, feeling a pain so sharp it almost made her cry aloud. "What you mean is...I can't stay here," she said in a small voice.

"*No!* That's not what I meant at all. I *want* you to stay here. Not permanently, of course, but—"

"Of course."

"But you could stay here for several days—or even several weeks—until you've had time to decide what you want to do. That's what I was trying to say."

"Thanks, Cal, but no thanks."

"Don't make a rash decision. Think about it some more."

"I don't need to think about it. I'm not staying."

"But I told you... I *want* you to stay."

"What? So you can have a compliant, willing, live-in sex partner for a few days?" Elizabeth heard the sound of her own voice growing more shrill with each word, but didn't know how she could control it, even if she wanted to. "Or a few weeks? Isn't that what you said?"

"It wasn't what I meant! *At all!* We don't have to have sex. I won't even come near you if that's the way you want it. I'm simply inviting you to stay here until you've had time to make a rational, long-term decision on what you want to do. I'm trying to do you a favor, Elizabeth."

"Why?"

"What?"

"Why are you doing this, Cal? Why are you inviting me into your home, into your life? Why are you inviting me to invade your precious privacy?"

"Because I *care* about you!" he shouted. He took a deep breath, then another one. "It's as simple as that. I care about you."

"Then that's all the more reason why I can't do it, Cal."

"I don't understand."

"I mean, with you, *caring* would be all there was. But there's something you need to know about me." She hesitated, gathering her courage. "I'm in love with you."

"No," he said, shaking his head in denial. "You don't really mean that. You're simply feeling—"

"I *do* mean it. And don't tell me what I'm feeling. I'm in love with you. Even if you don't want me to be. Even if *I* don't want to be."

He blinked. "I don't know what to say."

"I think you just said it."

"I wish I could offer you more, Elizabeth, but I can't. Please believe me."

"I do believe you, Cal. And I appreciate your honesty...as well as your offer."

"The offer's still open. And you have to stay somewhere."

"You mean that? In spite of everything?"

"I mean it," he said. "Especially in spite of everything."

"And you mean what you said about no sex between us if I stayed here?"

"Yes," he said, taking a deep breath. "I promise. We won't make love."

She stayed.

But before she agreed to stay for a few days, she made Cal retract his promise not to make love with her.

"THIS IS THE BIGGEST bed I've ever seen," Elizabeth said to Cal that afternoon when they were relaxing side by side in it after having made love.

"I like to stretch out," he drawled lazily.

"Even stretched *all* the way out, you couldn't touch both sides at the same time."

"Also, with a bed this size, I can always root around and find a cool spot in the summertime."

Elizabeth giggled. "I'll bet you couldn't find a cool spot on it right now...not after what we just put it through."

He leaned over and kissed the tip of her nose.

"Still...it *is* nice having a bed this size," she said. "I, uh, imagine you've enjoyed it a lot."

He propped himself up on one elbow and looked down at her. She saw that his gray eyes seemed both tender and amused. "Elizabeth, if you're trying to quiz me about previous times I might have used the bed for the particular purpose *we've* just used it..."

"I'm *not!*"

"Okay, you're not. But if you were, I'd tell you that I've never brought anybody into this bed before. Only you."

That was a nice thing for him to say. He might be lying, but even if he was, it was still nice, she thought, feeling pleased.

"I'd tell you that," he said, as if reading her mind, "and it would be the truth."

That was even better, and pleased her even more. *Face it,* she told herself. *Everything about Cal Potts pleases you.*

During the days that followed they spent a lot of time in the big bed. They spent *most* of their time in the big bed, getting up only for necessities—to eat, to go to the bathroom and shower, and occasionally to walk outside and make sure the rest of the world still existed.

They made love in the big bed, time and again—under the stars shining through the skylight at night and under the sun beaming through it in the daytime. But making love wasn't all they did. They slept occasionally, usually in small snatches, and they talked. And talked.

"I've been wanting to ask you about the baseball bat," Cal said one morning.

"You mean the one I used to bash in the side door of my car?"

"Yes. That one."

"I'd been out playing ball with some neighborhood kids that afternoon," she said. "In a park close to our house. When I got home, my ex-husband was sitting in the driveway in my new car, waiting for me. There was a woman in the car with him and—"

"Hold on," Cal said. "Back up. You lost me a long time ago. What was your *ex*-husband doing in *your* new car?"

"He wasn't my ex at that time. We were only separated. And I'd loaned him my car because his was in the shop being repaired. Plus, he needed a car and I didn't. I was staying at home, hiding out you might say…while I waited for the decision on what action the bar association was going to take against me. And him.

"So I saw him parked in the driveway when I came home. He and a woman."

"The same woman who—"

"No. A different one. That other woman had already taken a reading on him by then. She was the one who sued the firm for malpractice."

"Okay. I think I understand now. You came home and your husband was parked in the driveway with another woman—a *different* woman—sitting in the car beside him and you went crazy."

"Cal," she said, shaking her head. "That wasn't the way it was at all. Not a bit of it. I never saw that woman before and I've never seen her since. She's a nothing."

Cal frowned. "Then I don't understand what happened."

"I told you I was waiting to hear what the bar association was going to do. I'd been waiting all day... for days... weeks. And I knew that Tate was going to tell me. So I rushed up to the car when I saw him there. But he didn't tell me right away. He started talking chitchat, making me wait.

"I was so tense I didn't know what to do with myself, so I started swinging the bat back and forth—the way they do on TV when they're waiting for the pitcher to throw the ball. I was trying to relax, and also hide the fact that the suspense was killing me.

"And finally Tate told me. He told me that he'd been disbarred... which was something we'd both been expecting, but I told him I was sorry anyway. And after that he told me I'd been censured, too. I couldn't believe it. He said it was true:.. and then he laughed. *He laughed.*

"That's when I swung the bat and hit the car as hard as I could. It was either that, or hit him... and I figured he wasn't worth what it'd cost me if I hit him."

Cal leaned over and kissed her. "I think you made the right decision."

"CAL?"

"Hmm."

"I don't want to sound like I'm complaining," Elizabeth said, leaning over him and making lazy circles on his bare chest with her finger. "Because I'm not. But you—haven't left the house in days."

"There's no need to. We still have plenty of food left in the freezer and refrigerator."

"But aren't you supposed to go to work or something?"

"I'm on vacation."

She let out a sigh. "That's a relief. I thought maybe you'd quit your job."

"Why would you think that?"

"Well…I remembered what you told me not long ago—the day we went for a bike ride—about not feeling you were a success because you were only a sheriff in a small town…and about this not being the life you'd planned for yourself."

He nodded. "I remember saying those things. But do *you* remember how angry I was when I said them?"

"Yes. You were furious with me."

"I'm sorry about that," he said, touching her cheek. "If it helps any…I was even more furious with myself. You'd just said that Lance Strickland was a lot like I was at his age and I got mad, not because you were wrong, but because you were right. And I overreacted."

"And you don't really feel that way about this town…and about your job?"

"No. I started seriously thinking about it the other day when some people called and offered me the job of assistant chief in Macon."

"They did?" she asked, surprised to find herself distressed at the idea of Cal moving someplace else. It wasn't as if she harbored any idea of the two of *them* making a life together here. *Or maybe she did.* Maybe—buried so deep inside her that she didn't even know it was there—she'd secretly hoped for just such a thing to happen. "What did you tell them?"

"I told them I'd consider it. There's no rush. The job won't open up for several more months."

"It sounds like quite an opportunity," she said, trying to put some enthusiasm in her voice.

"I suppose. But then I got to thinking about this job, and this town. Actually, there's a lot to be said for both of them."

"All bad?" she said, repeating the joke they used to make about Planters' Junction years ago.

He laughed. "Not *all* bad. I enjoy the work here most of the time. And I have this cabin..."

"And this wonderful bed."

"Yes. And the garage out back and the lake for fishing. And my friends Lum and Quint..."

You could have me, too, Cal. If you'd ask. But she knew he wouldn't.

Cal pulled her close and kissed her. "Do you think you'll ever forgive your mother?" he asked, changing the subject.

"I don't see how I can. But I imagine we'll start speaking to each other again in time," she added after a moment. "And we'll probably eventually work our way back to the way we used to be when I was growing up."

"Do you mean you intend to move back to her house?"

"No," she said emphatically. "Never. And is that a hint that I've overstayed my welcome here?"

"Don't start that again," he warned, tightening his arms around her. "You're staying with me until *I* say you can leave."

"Oh? When will *that* be?" *Please say never,* she thought.

"I'm not sure. But I think you and I will both know when it's time."

"And what if we don't? What if I'm never ready to go out on my own?"

"You will be. I know you've had some tough blows, especially lately...."

No. The toughest blow was losing you, and that happened a long time ago.

"But you've survived," he said. "And you have so much going for you. You're smart as hell—"

"Smart mouth, you mean?"

"*Intelligent,* dammit! And stop making jokes. I'm serious."

"What makes you think I'm intelligent? I've made some really stupid mistakes in my life."

"You were second in your class at the top law school in the whole country. What would *you* call it? Good luck?"

"How did you know about that?"

"I've forgotten. But that's not the point...."

Yes, it was. Very few people had known about her success in law school, and if Cal knew about it, that meant he must have kept track of her, even back then.

"The point is—you're intelligent, you're beautiful...not to mention sexy as hell—and you can't let it all go to waste. I won't let you!"

He loves me, even if he won't admit it, she thought. And in that instant she realized something else. She hadn't loved *herself,* not in a long, long time. But now—with Cal feeling the way she was almost sure he did about her—maybe she could.

CAL BROUGHT HER BREAKFAST in bed one morning, and had even put a tiny wildflower in a jelly glass to decorate the tray. Elizabeth burst into tears when she saw it.

"Listen, I didn't mean to upset you," he said, his voice tinged with uncertainty.

"I'm not upset. I'm touched. Nobody's ever done anything like this for me before."

"It's no wonder, if you carry on this way. Should I go downstairs and bring up a bucket for your tears?"

"No," she said, lifting up her arms and silently inviting him to come inside them. He did. "Now be quiet and let me thank you properly," she said. He did that, too.

The breakfast was ice-cold by the time Elizabeth finally got around to eating it much later, but she swore it was the most delicious food she'd ever had.

After breakfast they went for a walk in the woods, then came back to the cabin, where they settled on the sofa, Elizabeth leafing through a magazine at one end while Cal read the newspaper at the other end, their legs stretched out comfortably between them. "I've been thinking," she said after a moment.

"Again?"

She threw the magazine at him. It missed. "Seriously," she said. "I've already agreed to handle Lance's case, and I'm determined to follow through on that."

Cal nodded. "I agree you should ... even if he doesn't deserve you."

"And after that, I have to make a decision. I'm not going back to Atlanta...." She waited for his reaction, and saw him raise one eyebrow. "I know you might think I'm merely being a coward, but it's more than that. Believe it or not ... I've decided I really *like* living in a smaller town. So I've narrowed it down to two options. I can either set up a practice here on my own in Planters' Junction, or look to join an already established firm in someplace nearby. Maybe Albany."

"Albany's a nice place," Cal said. "And it's a good size, not too large and not too small."

"Yes," she agreed. *It's almost the size of Macon, where you might possibly go,* she thought.

"And your cases might be more varied there than they would be here," he said. "More interesting."

"Not necessarily more interesting. There'd just be more of them," she said. *But I wouldn't mind staying here, if it's where you decide you want to stay,* she thought. "What do you think?"

Cal rubbed the back of his neck, the way he always did when he was seriously considering possibilities and weighing consequences. Elizabeth held her breath while she waited for him to say something. She'd deliberately given him an opening. This was the perfect opportunity for him to tell her that he wanted her to be with him—either here or in Macon. Or anywhere. She wouldn't care as long as they were together.

"I think you couldn't go wrong either way," he finally said.

She wanted to cry.

CAL WANTED TO CRY when he thought about Elizabeth leaving him and knowing that this time it truly would be forever. She'd be lost to him as soon as she left his house, even if she decided to settle in Planters' Junction.

He'd known from the beginning that she couldn't stay with him permanently, but he hadn't known how quickly he would get used to having her around. She showered with him. She used his toothbrush. She wore his clothes.

How could he bear to let her go? How was he going to be able to survive without her? *Not very well,* he admitted to himself later that afternoon.

"Why doesn't Lum ever come over anymore?" Elizabeth asked that night at dinner.

"I'm sure he'll turn up again soon," Cal replied.

"After I'm gone?"

"He likes you. You know that," he said, hedging.

"Then why doesn't he come over while I'm here?"

Cal sighed. "He's got this crazy idea in his head—that if he gives us enough time alone, something…something will work out between us."

"Yes. That *is* a crazy idea."

Her voice sounded so wistful, and she looked so forlorn, that Cal wanted to hold her in his arms and never let her go. But he couldn't do that. He loved her too much to do that.

The telephone rang and Cal jumped up to answer it, almost with relief. "That's probably one of my deputies checking in."

"Cal, it's Travis," he heard a voice say as soon as he answered the phone. "Who's on duty at the station tonight?"

"Why? Is something wrong?" Cal asked.

"I'm not sure. I'm supposed to relieve whoever's on duty and I called a minute ago to say I'm running a little late. I let the phone ring and ring. But nobody answered it."

Chapter Fifteen

"What's wrong?" Elizabeth asked after Cal hung up.

"Nobody's answering the phone at the station," he said, already on the way upstairs for his service revolver.

"Is that bad?" she called after him.

"Somebody is supposed to be on duty all the time, twenty-four hours a day," he said, putting on the holster as he descended the stairs. "I'm going down to check."

"I'm coming with you."

"It might be nothing," he said, although he had a feeling that something was wrong, terribly wrong.

"If so, I can talk to Lance while we're there. And I'm even dressed in my own clothes for a change."

He saw that she was. They'd washed her clothes the day after she came to the cabin, but this was the first time she'd worn them since then. She'd seemed to prefer wearing his instead. "Let's go, then," he said.

He hurried out to his official car. When they were both belted in their seats, he started the engine and turned on the flashing light mounted on top of the car. He thought about turning on the siren as well, but decided against it. There was no need to alarm the whole town...not yet, anyway.

Traffic was light, and Cal kept the gas pedal pressed all the way to the floorboard for most of the ride to town. He was thankful that Elizabeth didn't try to talk, leaving him free to concentrate on driving. He didn't allow himself to think about what might be waiting for him at the station.

It seemed like hours but was only a matter of minutes until he screeched to a halt in front of the station. "Wait here," he told Elizabeth tersely, unbuckling his seat belt and running for the front door, removing his revolver as he ran. He hesitated briefly outside the front door, then flung it open. The big room was deserted, not a soul in sight.

Then he saw something that made his blood run cold. The door leading to the cell area was open . . . the door that was always supposed to be kept locked, with the key to unlock it in the possession of the officer on duty. Cal took a deep breath and silently made his way across the room, his revolver poised to fire.

Reaching the open door, he stood beside it, hidden from the view of anyone who might be inside. "Siddons," he called out to the deputy who was supposed to be on duty. "Siddons," he called again. There was no answer. He waited another moment, then darted his head around the door frame, jumping back again immediately. From his brief glance, he'd seen no one. But he had caught a glimpse of the door leading to Lance Strickland's cell. It was wide open.

Cal wiped the sweat from his upper lip, then took another, slightly longer look inside the cell area . . . and saw a body. A body lying beside the bunk in Lance Strickland's cell. Still holding his revolver in front of him, he finally moved into the open doorway. The entire cell area was deserted except for the body lying on the floor. He walked toward it.

When he was still several yards away, he caught his breath because the body looked familiar. He moved faster for a few steps, then stopped. "Oh, no," he said. "Oh, hell, no!" He lowered his gun and ran toward the still, silent body of Lum Starr, his best friend on earth, the man who'd been like a father to him.

Cal knelt down beside Lum, placing his gun on the floor and tenderly touching the old man. His skin was warm, and Cal could see blood still pumping out from a nasty gash on the side of his head. Maybe... Cal touched Lum's neck, feeling for a pulse, praying that he'd find one.

"Cal!"

He recognized Elizabeth's voice. "I'm back here!" he yelled as loud as he could. "Come quick!"

He heard the sound of her running footsteps, then heard them stop beside the cell. "Cal, what happened? Who... *Oh, God!*"

"It's Lum. He's still alive, but just barely. Call an ambulance." Elizabeth didn't move; she seemed paralyzed. *"Now!"* he shouted and that galvanized her into action. Cal pulled out his handkerchief, pressing it against Lum's wound to stanch the flow of blood.

Elizabeth returned in only a matter of seconds. "They're on their way," she said. "I told them it was a matter of life and death."

"Good thinking."

"Is there something else I can do?"

"I need to call my deputies," Cal said. "I hate to ask you, but—"

"You want me to hold the compress against Lum's head while you call?" She knelt on the floor beside him. "I'll be glad to do it. Lum's my friend, too, you know."

"Thanks." Cal showed her where to apply the pressure, and was just getting up to leave when Travis Lovejoy, one of his deputies, raced in.

"What happened?" Travis asked breathlessly.

"There's been a jailbreak," Cal explained. "Lum Starr was hurt, but we've already called an ambulance. I'd like you to call the other deputies and tell them to get over here as fast as they can. We need every man."

"Right," Travis said. He started to leave, then stopped for a moment. "Did you find out what happened to Siddons?"

"No. But I'd guess that he's gone after Lance Strickland."

Travis nodded and left.

"Lance didn't do this, Cal," Elizabeth said.

Angrily, he wheeled around to face her. "How can you say that? You claimed Lum was your friend. Just look at him!"

"I know what bad shape he's in. And it breaks my heart to see him that way, just like it does yours. But I also know Lance didn't do this to him. He wouldn't, he *couldn't*... because he was Lum's friend, too!"

Cal clenched his fists. "What is it with you, Elizabeth? Why do you keep defending that young punk, even now?"

"Because I don't believe he did this to Lum!"

"Okay. Then answer me one question. If Lance Strickland didn't do it, *who did?*"

She blinked.

"Well?" he demanded.

"I...I don't know."

"Exactly. He's the only one who could have done it, the only one who would have done it."

"Look who just walked in the door to give himself up," Travis Lovejoy said.

Cal saw Elizabeth's eyes widen and heard her gasp as she looked at something—somebody—behind him. He knew who it was, of course, long before he turned around. And when he did turn, he had to take several deep breaths before he was able to speak.

"Hello, Strickland," he finally said, surprised that his voice sounded so calm when he felt like a raging volcano inside. "I ought to kill you with my bare hands for what you've done to Lum."

"I wouldn't blame you," Lance said. "I wish you would."

Cal was surprised by that. Taking a closer look at Lance, he saw that the young man was filthy dirty, his long hair hanging in wet strings around his face and his clothes caked with mud. He looked as if he'd been crawling through a swamp.

"So you admit that you're responsible for this," Cal said, coming out of the cell to confront Strickland.

Lance looked at the floor, his shoulders drooping like an old man's. "Yes. It was my fault."

Cal had calmed down for a moment, but now felt his rage return in full force. "If Lum dies, I'm going to throw the book at you. I'm going to charge you with first degree murder."

Lance's head suddenly jerked back up. "Murder? No!"

"You just admitted it."

Lance shook his head. "I said that what happened was my fault. I didn't say I was the one who hit him. Siddons did it."

"Siddons?" Cal repeated blankly.

"Yes. Winston Siddons. Your deputy."

Cal simply stared at Lance, speechless, and continued staring at him as the ambulance emergency crew rushed in, pushing him out of their way and heading for the cell where Lum was lying. Elizabeth appeared at Cal's side a few seconds later.

"They told me to get out of their way," she said to him before turning to Strickland. "It was a very brave thing you did tonight, Lance, coming back here. I'm proud of you."

"There's nothing to be proud of. I was a coward out to save my own skin. I only sneaked back to see if Lum was okay."

"Don't be too hard on yourself," she said. "Choosing to survive doesn't make you a coward. It proves you're a sensible human being. I'm proud of you for that, too."

"What do you want me to do with him, Cal?" Travis asked.

"Uh...lock him in another cell for the time being. I'll talk with him as soon as I can."

Cal watched his deputy lead Lance away and then turned to Elizabeth. He was torn with conflicting emotions. "I don't know what to do," he admitted to her. "I know I should stay here and try to find out exactly what happened tonight, but..." He stopped and glanced toward the cell where the technicians were working on the man who meant the most to him in the world.

"Cal," she interrupted. "I'll go to the hospital with Lum. And I'll stay with him all the way, for as long as they'll let me. I promise. And I'm sure that he'd understand, too."

Cal closed his eyes for a brief second. "Thank you."

"You needn't thank me. I'd already decided that I was going along to the hospital, whether you wanted me to or not."

He placed his hand on her cheek, loving her, wishing the two of them could be together always. But they couldn't.

ELIZABETH MIGHT HAVE spent more anxious moments in her life, but if she had, she couldn't remember them. She was worried for Cal, who'd had such a fierce hatred in his eyes that she'd wondered for a moment if he might not kill Lance when he was brought in. She was worried for Lance, obviously scared to death, who'd had the courage to come back and face his accusers anyway, because he was concerned for his friend.

And most of all, she was worried for Lum, the dear old man who'd been almost a father to Cal, and whom she'd come to love, too. She was thankful that the emergency crew had allowed her to ride with Lum on the way to the hospital in Planters' Junction and later on to accompany him on the helicopter to the better-equipped hospital in Albany. But the last time she'd seen him, he had looked so gray—almost like a person who was already dead. And his lips had been blue.

She shivered. Then she stood up, casting aside the dog-eared magazine she'd been holding in her hands for hours without turning a page. She stretched her arms above her head, then walked over to the picture windows in the waiting room and stared out into the darkness.

Later—she had no idea how much later—something caused her to turn around and she saw him. Cal. Cal, looking as tense and wiped out as she felt. Then he crossed the room in several long strides and she was in his arms, holding on to him for dear life, the same way he was holding her, squeezing the breath out of her.

Finally he relaxed his arms slightly and looked at her. "Lum?"

"He's in the operating room. His skull was fractured and they're doing emergency surgery to relieve the pressure. They promised to let me know as soon as . . . as soon as he was out of surgery." She lifted her arm and looked at her watch. "It shouldn't be too much longer now."

"You look dead tired," Cal said.

"Thanks," she said, managing a weary smile. "You don't look so hot yourself, either." Holding his hand, she pulled him to one of the sofas and they sat down. "You talked to Lance?" she asked.

"Yes. And I'm convinced now that you were right all along. He's innocent of car theft, and he wasn't the one who beat Lum. It was Siddons. We're looking for him right now. We've called in the state authorities to help, too, so it shouldn't be long before we catch him."

"What about Lance? Where is he?"

"He's locked up in a cell."

"But—"

"We still have minor charges against him—concealing information, abetting a criminal—but a smart lawyer like you should be able to get him off easily, especially since he's cooperating with us. The main reason I locked him up is that I thought jail was the safest place for him right now. Okay?"

She nodded. "What actually happened, Cal?"

"Well, to begin with, there's a car theft ring operating in this area. Lance wasn't a member of it, but he knew someone who was—his girlfriend Jacinda's cousin. The cousin stole a car, got scared, and asked Lance to hide it for him and deliver it after dark. But we caught Lance on a safety violation before he could make the delivery.

"Siddons is involved in the theft ring, and he threatened Lance's life unless he kept quiet. Lance also told us that Siddons made veiled threats against Jacinda."

"That . . . that *scum!*"

"Yes," Cal agreed. "And that's not even the worst of it. When Siddons was on duty alone last night, he went to Lance's cell and opened it. He told Lance he was setting him free, and that he'd help him get away. He gave Lance the keys to an old jalopy we'd impounded, and told Lance to meet him later on tonight and he'd give him money to help get started in another town."

Elizabeth shook her head, horrified. "Siddons wasn't going to help Lance get away. He was going to kill him!"

"I'd have to agree with you on that," Cal said. "I think Lance was suspicious of Siddons's motives, too. He told us that he wasn't sure whether or not he should leave. While he was still thinking about it, Lum came to visit him. Lum told him to get back into his cell, where it was safe.

"And that's when Siddons . . . hit Lum. Lance said that when Lum fell, he hit his head on the corner of the cot and just lay there. Lance started to go to Lum, but Siddons shoved him away and told him to get the hell out of there or he'd charge him with murder. Siddons must have thought Lum was dead.

"So Lance left. But he didn't drive very far because he kept thinking about how much Lum meant to him, and wondering if his friend was alive or dead. Lance abandoned the jalopy and made his way back to the jail. And to avoid being seen, he crawled through the swamp. That's why he was such a mess."

"Poor Lance," Elizabeth said, shaking her head. "And poor Lum, too."

"Yes," Cal agreed. He squeezed her hand. "Thank you for staying here with him tonight. I wish I could have been here, too."

"There's nothing you could have done. And I'm sure Lum would be the first to tell you to attend to your business, do your duty."

He nodded. "He would have told me that, all right, and in no uncertain terms." He closed his eyes. "I don't know what I'll do if . . . if . . ."

"Don't talk that way, Cal! Don't even think it. Lum's going to be okay. I *know* he is."

He opened his eyes and gave her a half smile. "Your intuition's been on target so far. I hope it is this time, too."

"It is. You'll see," Elizabeth said, speaking with far more confidence than she felt. She'd been expecting Lum to be out of surgery long before now. Something must have gone wrong. She'd told Cal not to think about the possibility of Lum dying. Now she tried to tell herself the same thing. But when she remembered how terrible Lum had looked the last time she saw him, and knew how long he'd been in surgery, it was all she *could* think of.

Don't let it happen, she prayed. Lum didn't deserve to die in such a senseless way. And Cal didn't deserve any more pain.

"Would you like some coffee?" Cal asked after they'd sat silently on the sofa for several minutes.

"Yes, let me get it," she said, jumping to her feet. "I know where the coffee shop is, so it won't take me long." She didn't want any more coffee; she'd already drunk so much she felt as if she were about to jump out of her skin. Maybe that was what made her feel she couldn't sit still another instant. Or maybe she was simply trying to escape her morbid thoughts.

By the time she returned to the waiting room with the coffee several minutes later she felt marginally calmer. Until she saw Cal. He was standing in the middle of the room, tears streaming down his cheeks.

No. No. No, something inside her screamed. She tried to place the coffee on a table but missed, and both cups rolled to the floor, splattering hot liquid on her foot. She turned around and ran to Cal, grabbing both his arms. "It's Lum, isn't it?" she asked.

He nodded. *"Tell me!"* she cried.

"He's...he's out of surgery. They think he's going to be all right."

CAL HELD ELIZABETH in his arms for a long time. Then he helped her clean up the mess that the coffee she'd dropped had made on the waiting-room floor. Finally he looked at his watch. "We might as well leave now," he said.

"You don't think at least one of us should stay here?"

"There's nothing we can do at the moment. The doctor said that Lum's sleeping now and probably won't wake up until sometime tomorrow. I'll drive you back to the cabin and..." He stopped, suddenly remembering that he hadn't told her about his plans.

"And what, Cal? Where are *you* going." She waited a moment. "The *meeting!*" she said. "The one Siddons arranged with Lance to give him money. You're going there in place of Lance, aren't you?"

He nodded. "A lot of men will be there—a nice little surprise for Winston Siddons. I wasn't planning to go along unless things were going well for Lum. But since they are, I wouldn't miss it for the world."

"It'll be dangerous," she said slowly, a frown creasing her brow.

"Only for Siddons."

"Will you be careful anyway? Please?"

He started to make some flip comment, but stopped himself when he saw the concern—the *love*—in her eyes as she looked at him. She wasn't making any effort to hide it; she was leaving herself wide open and vulnerable. *And she knew it.* Yet she cared enough about him to reveal her feelings anyway. He knew he didn't deserve her love. He'd even tried to tell himself he didn't want it. But he did.

He swallowed. "I'll be careful," he said. "I promise."

ELIZABETH SLEPT ON the drive back to Planters' Junction from Albany, and Cal was happy she was able to get some rest at last. She'd looked dead on her feet at the hospital. She woke up when they approached Planters' Junction, though, as if some interior alarm had gone off.

"Where are you going first?" she asked, rubbing her eyes.

"I thought I'd drop you off at the cabin and then go to the station from there."

"Would you drive me to my mother's house instead?"

Cal hesitated. "It's awfully late. Won't she be asleep?"

"I have my keys," Elizabeth said, pulling them from the pocket of her slacks. "I found them in the clothes dryer when we washed my things the other day. They must have been in my pocket all along."

"What if your mother's still awake?" he asked, wondering why he was feeling this sudden panic at the thought of Elizabeth going to her mother's house. Was it because he knew she'd never come back to him again once she made the break?

"She probably won't be, just like you suggested."

"But what if she *is?*"

"I'll have to see her sometime. And I really *need* to get some more clothes, Cal. I can't live in what I have on—and what I borrow from you—for the rest of my life. Plus I'd like to get my Jeep Cherokee . . . in case my mother gets so angry with me that she decides to have it towed away."

That made sense, Cal thought, heading for her mother's house. All of it. So why did he still feel so uneasy? "Will you come back to my cabin after you've gotten what you need?" he asked when he pulled up in front of her house and saw the Jeep parked in the same spot she'd left it more than a week ago.

"Yes," she said, getting out of the car. "And please remember your promise to be careful."

"I will. Do you want me to come inside with you?"

"No thanks. It appears that dear old Mom has kept the home fires burning for the prodigal daughter," she said, gesturing toward the house, where every light seemed to be burning. "See you later."

"*Wait!*" he exclaimed before she could walk away. She halted in her tracks. "You don't have a key to the cabin."

"That's right!" she said, sounding surprised. "I'd forgotten about that."

"I keep an extra one beside the porch, on the left side facing the house. It's under the gardenia bush."

"Beside the porch on the left side under the gardenia bush," she repeated. Then she nodded. "Got it."

Cal watched her leave, feeling a terrible desolation. *She has no intention of using the key,* he thought. *Because she's not coming back.* He clenched his hands around the steering wheel and kept them there until he saw her enter her mother's house. He waited a while longer—in case she suddenly came running out—and then he drove to the station.

The place was a beehive of activity, with lawmen everywhere, not only his deputies with the exception of Siddons, but also the state agents who'd come to help. Cal had left George in charge, and his deputy seemed surprised to see him when he walked in.

"Cal," George said. "I thought you were still down in Albany."

"Lum's doing better so I came back. Have Travis and Milo left yet?"

"Not yet. They're in your office now checking their gear."

"Good. I'm going with them." The plan was to send two men into the automobile graveyard where Siddons was supposed to meet Lance. They'd set up a stakeout and try to capture Siddons on the spot, but if they were unsuccessful, the other officers would have roadblocks set up along all the exits into and out of the place.

George grinned. "Planning on getting back some of your own?" he asked, knowing how Cal felt about Lum.

"Maybe." Cal started walking toward his office to join Travis and Milo, but stopped when he felt a hand on his arm. He turned around, and had to suppress a grin of satisfaction when he saw the sweaty face of his old nemesis, Buck Maxwell.

Buck hadn't aged well, he thought, in spite of having succeeded in being elected to the spot he'd always coveted. He was now mayor of Planters' Junction, a respected man, revered by some, hated and feared by many more. And Buck's only daughter was married to Winston Siddons, which no doubt was the reason he was here now.

"Hello, Buck," Cal said, trying to keep his voice smooth as silk, the same way Buck would have done if their circumstances had been reversed. "What can I do for you?"

"You know damn well..." Buck broke off in midsentence, obviously trying to control the impulse to strangle Cal on the spot.

He probably wishes he'd finished doing the job on me all those years ago when he had the chance, Cal thought. "No. I don't know," he said. "Tell me."

"My daughter's husband, Winston. Your trusted deputy—"

"I wouldn't go so far as to say that about him."

"Your own deputy then, dammit! You're getting ready to go after him."

"That's true. But even if he is my deputy—or was—he's still a wanted criminal."

Buck took out his handkerchief and wiped his face. "My daughter pleaded with me to come here. I told her it wouldn't do any good, but she insisted."

"Why wouldn't it do any good, Buck? What did your daughter want?" Cal watched the mayor struggle with himself again...and finally come through the struggle with his best, most sincere face firmly in place.

"Go easy on him, won't you, Cal?"

Cal clenched his fists, and forced himself to wait several moments before answering. "Sure, Buck," he said. "I'll handle him with kid gloves. The same way you did me when you and Elizabeth's father shipped me off to the Army Rangers seventeen years ago."

Buck blanched, but stood his ground. "He's just a youngster."

"He's older than I was," Cal replied. Then he turned and walked away.

IT'S NOT RAINING tonight, so don't panic, Cal told himself as he crouched behind the remains of a car in the automobile graveyard where he and Elizabeth had both been terrified by rats. They wouldn't be out tonight when it was clear and dry, he told himself. Or at least they wouldn't be out in such great numbers, he corrected when he saw a large rat scurry between the tires of the car next to the one he was behind.

And there was only one rat he was going to concentrate on tonight—a very large one named Winston Siddons.

You wouldn't really kill him, would you? he could imagine Elizabeth saying.

Maybe not, he would reply. *But whether I do or not, it gave me a lot of satisfaction making old Buck think I would.*

He wiped the sweat off his forehead with the sleeve of his shirt and wondered whether it was unusually hot tonight or if he was sweating more because he was nervous. *Probably a combination of both,* he decided. And he hadn't been outside in the weather a lot lately, either. He and Elizabeth were usually in bed in the air-conditioned cabin by this time. They might be asleep…or they might not. But they'd be in bed.

He closed his eyes for a moment, aching for her already, even though he'd only realized tonight that he'd lost her. It didn't have to be. He was almost sure of that. If he'd tell her that he loved her and beg her to come back . . . But he couldn't do that to her. His shame belonged to him alone. He wouldn't ask her to share it.

But what had she said to Lance? *Choosing to survive doesn't make you a coward. It means you're a sensible human being.* And then she'd said, *I'm proud of you for that.*

Had she really meant it? Knowing Elizabeth, she probably had. But even if she'd meant what she said to Lance, how would she feel when she found out what the man she loved had done?

He heard a noise, saw a sudden movement, and all his senses came alive. Cal knew it was Siddons. He felt it in his bones. He held his breath, waiting... waiting. Siddons finally came into view and Cal slowly, silently raised his automatic rifle.

Don't kill him, Cal, he could imagine Elizabeth saying.

Why not? he would say. *He's an animal. Anybody who'd do what he did to Lum—and then leave him there to die— deserves to be hunted down and shot like the mad dog he is.*

Cal had Siddons in his sights now.

He's a human being, Elizabeth would say. *And if you kill him in cold blood, you're no better than he is.*

Siddons stopped, and Cal had a clear shot. It would only take one shot, straight to the heart. He tightened his finger on the trigger.

Chapter Sixteen

Cal wearily turned the car onto the dirt road leading to his cabin. He'd been going downhill fast since the adrenaline stopped pumping, feeling older by the moment. He must be about a hundred and two by now, he figured. But he'd soon be home, able to climb into his own bed and sleep for days.

Except he couldn't do that, he remembered. He'd need to get up again in a few hours and drive to Albany to see Lum. And he would. He grinned, thinking about it, looking forward to it. He rounded the last curve to his cabin and saw something he'd thought never to see again—Elizabeth's Jeep parked in front of his house. His grin vanished, and his tiredness along with it.

He parked beside her, crossed the yard in record speed, and took the steps to his porch two at a time. He opened the front door—which she hadn't locked, he noticed—and saw her sitting in a chair, not doing anything, just sitting. She got up as soon as he came into the room.

"I... I didn't expect to find you here," he admitted.

"I didn't expect to be here," she admitted.

"I'm glad you are. Here, I mean."

"I'm not going to stay, Cal. I only came back because I told you I would and I didn't want to lie to you, not now, after what you did for me the past week."

"I didn't—"

"Oh, yes, you did. You gave me back my self-confidence, my ability to believe in myself again. I'll never forget that." She gave a short laugh. "But you did too good a job on me. Now I feel that I have to go out on my own and prove your confidence in me was justified."

"Do you have to go so soon? Can't you stay even a little while longer?"

She shook her head. "It's not a good idea. I think you and I both know that. The longer I stay, the harder it'll be for me to leave."

Don't leave! Ever, he wanted to say.

"I came back for another reason, too," Elizabeth said. "I wanted to make sure you'd kept your promise to me, and that you were all right. Are you?"

He swallowed. "Yes. Tired, but otherwise okay."

"Did you catch Siddons?"

"Yes, we caught him."

"Did . . . did you kill him?"

"I had a chance to kill him. I thought about doing it. And then I thought about what you'd say, and I didn't. It's a good thing, too. The auto theft and chop-shop operation he worked for is huge, spread out all over South Georgia, and Siddons is safely in jail telling all about it right now, talking his head off. You might be interested to know that your friend Peyton Shipp at the savings and loan is heavily involved.

Elizabeth's eyes widened. "No!"

Cal nodded. "It seems that Planters' Junction Savings and Loan was in deep financial trouble, as I'd suspected some time ago . . . and as you very well know, too. Isn't that right?"

He saw her cheeks grow red. "Yes," she said.

"So Peyton decided that crime would be a handy way to bail the savings and loan out of trouble and make himself a hero in the process. He's the one who recruited Siddons into the car-theft operation, when Winston came to him for a loan."

"And that's why Siddons became involved—for money?" Elizabeth asked.

"Partly. He also enjoyed the thrill of it, and enjoyed making me look bad even more."

"I don't understand."

"He wanted the sheriff's job. He figured it should have been his, since he was Buck Maxwell's son-in-law. Didn't you know he ran against me for sheriff when I was elected?"

"No, I didn't know that," she said. "But when I first met him—the time I came into the station to report my car was stolen—I thought something was going on between the two of you."

"I wasn't out to get him because he'd run against me, if that's what you're saying."

"I didn't mean it that way. I thought he was rude and incompetent, and that you might be building up a dossier on him in order to fire him."

"That's true. I should have fired him when I first took office—the way Buck Maxwell would have done—but I decided to give him a chance. And he thanked me by doing everything he could to undermine me. Incidentally, he admitted that he's the one who vandalized your mother's house, too."

"You're kidding! Was it because he suspected there was . . . something between you and me?"

"Maybe. But his main reason was to scare you off Lance Strickland's case. He was afraid Lance might tell you something that would incriminate him."

"But that's crazy. Lance could have told *any* lawyer who represented him."

"You're forgetting that the only other defense lawyer in town is old Pulliam, and he's a total incompetent, so Siddons would have no need to worry about him. Also, Winston probably *is* a bit crazy."

Elizabeth sighed. "So that's that?"

Cal nodded. "That's that." He willed her to look at him. She did for a brief moment. Then she looked away.

"Well," she said. "I guess I'd better be going now."

"Are you sure? I mean, where will you go at this time of night?"

"I made a reservation at a motel down in Albany. I thought I'd stay there for a few days. I plan to visit Lum. And maybe talk to some law firms, too. Sort of test the waters."

"I . . . hate to see you leave, Elizabeth. I'm going to miss you."

"Thank you," she said quietly. "I'll miss you, too. But at least you'll have your clothes back now. And you'll be able to enjoy your privacy again."

Cal clenched his fists at his side. Was this the way it was going to end? After all the years, all the pain, all the heart-break, was he simply going to let her walk out of his life forever, without lifting a hand to stop her?

Don't let her go! he heard a voice screaming inside him say. *Tell her! And let her make the decision. That way, you'll at least have tried.*

"Elizabeth," he said. "Before you go . . . could I tell you something?" He saw her hesitate.

"Certainly," she finally said.

"Maybe we'd better sit down. This might take a while." They walked to the sofa, where she sat at one end, he at the other.

He took a deep breath. "What I'm going to tell you is not something I'm proud of. In fact, I've never told it to another living soul before. And you'll probably hate me after you hear it. But you won't hate me any more than I've hated myself, for years."

"Cal, why don't you stop apologizing?" she said, leaning across the sofa to touch his hand briefly. "Why don't you just tell me, and let me decide whether I hate you or not afterward?"

He nodded. "It happened when I was in the army, not long after I'd completed my ranger training and was shipped down to Central America. Our job was to keep supply and communication lines open, but enemy forces kept breaking through, so we sent out patrols all the time to try to protect the lines, day and night.

"One night when I was on patrol, my squad was spotted by a large group of enemy troops. They opened fire. We were outnumbered, so we all ran like hell. In the confusion, a couple of buddies and I became separated from the others. We ran as far as we could—until we were exhausted—and then held a hurried conference. We decided that the three of us would spread out some yards from each other and hide in the underbrush. Since there were only three of us, there was a good chance the soldiers would miss us."

Cal paused a moment to take out his handkerchief and wipe his face. The story was just as hard to tell as he'd thought it would be. But he had to do it. He put his handkerchief back in his pocket.

"The night was dark and misty. We'd had rain earlier, but it wasn't raining then. There was only a lot of mist, maybe some fog. I clearly remember hearing the sound of the enemy soldiers making their way through the heavy undergrowth. The sound seemed far away at first, but then it kept getting closer. And closer. I noticed I was holding my breath. I squinted my eyes, trying to see what was out there. And then...then I saw two beady eyes, not far away, looking directly back at me."

Cal closed his eyes, remembering the scene as vividly as if it had happened yesterday. "It was a huge rat," he said quietly.

"Oh, dear Lord!" Elizabeth exclaimed.

"Rats were everywhere in the jungle," Cal continued after a moment. "We'd heard horror stories of men being attacked by them, of having their fingers or toes chewed off. And now here I was, face to face with one. I knew I shouldn't move. If I did, the soldiers would find me and shoot me for sure. I remember starting to sweat even more than I was before.

"Then I heard a muffled sound. And a little after that, a single gunshot. I knew it must be one of my buddies, either shooting or being shot at. I didn't know what to do. I was frantic. And then I felt something brush against my hand that I had clutched around the rifle. I looked, and saw the rat. It was sitting on the rifle, right next to my hand. *Touching* my hand. I felt sick to my stomach. I blinked my eyes. Then I passed out.''

Cal looked at Elizabeth and saw her watching him with a horrified expression. ''I fainted,'' he said. ''I don't know how long it was before I came to, but the sky had already cleared and the moon was out. I looked around and didn't see the rat anymore. Then I lifted my head a fraction and saw several enemy troops in a clearing a short distance away. At first I wasn't sure what they were doing...but then I understood, and it made me sick all over again. They were going through the pockets of my buddies—my buddies that they'd shot while I was passed out from fear.

''Something inside me snapped. And I went berserk. I jumped to my feet and started firing my automatic rifle...not aiming at anything in particular, just firing the damned gun. When it was over—when I finally stopped shooting and the smoke cleared—I walked over to check. The enemy soldiers were dead. So was one of my buddies. The other one was still alive but his leg was a mess and his pulse was weak. I threw away my gun, hoisted him over my shoulder, and crawled back to camp. I tried to explain what had really happened, but nobody would listen. They gave me a medal. *A damned medal!*''

He looked at Elizabeth again and their glances met. What was she thinking? Was she horrified? Repulsed? ''I deserved to be shot as a coward,'' he said. ''Not rewarded with a medal.''

ELIZABETH SAW CAL'S uncertainty—heard his defiance—and wished she could tell him how very much she loved him at this moment, and how her heart was breaking into tiny pieces because she could almost feel his pain. But she couldn't say any of that, not yet. He wasn't ready to hear it. She knew she had to be careful what she said. Both their futures—and her only chance for happiness—might depend on it.

"And that's what you've been living with all these years?" she asked quietly.

"The knowledge that I'm a coward? Yes."

"No! I'm talking about *guilt*...because you thought you were a coward when you really weren't."

"Come on, Elizabeth."

"That's why you were so angry at me and my family. Because we were the cause of it all. It's why you reacted to Lance the way you did. You saw something of yourself in him, and you didn't like him because you didn't like yourself. It's why you've felt the need to prove yourself, over and over again, first in the army, then the special forces...and even now."

"That's true," he said. "All of it."

"But when are you going to *stop* trying to prove yourself, Cal? When are you going to stop punishing yourself for something that happened when you were still a kid, barely twenty years old?"

"It's not as simple as that."

"And what exactly *are* you trying to prove, Cal?" she asked, ignoring his comment although she knew it was true. She was fighting for her life here, though, and they could deal with other things together later...if she could win this battle.

"Are you trying to prove your life is worth something? It is. Tonight you were instrumental in exposing a huge, widespread, well-organized criminal operation. *You.* This town and the whole area owes you a gigantic debt of gratitude.

"Are you trying to prove that you're worth loving? You are. Lum loves you. And I love you. Don't we count for something?"

She could see him wavering, but knew the battle wasn't won yet.

"The thing is, Elizabeth, I don't see *how* you could love me, knowing—"

"Didn't you hear a word I said? I love you because I *do* know you. I always have, sometimes better than you know yourself. That's why I can see what there is to love, even if you can't."

"Still..."

"But there's one thing we *haven't* talked about, Cal." She swallowed the lump in her throat. *Now.* "The subject has never been brought up—not by me, and not by you— not once in all the times we've made love the last week, not once in all the times I've told you I loved you...and would have told you more often if you'd let me.

"That subject is—the question is—do *you* love *me?*"

He blinked. "Elizabeth."

"Well?"

"You must know.... You have to know...."

"*No!* I *don't* know! Not unless you tell me."

She held her breath, and for all she knew her heart stopped beating, too.

Then he was across the sofa, holding her in his arms, squeezing her so tight she still couldn't breathe. "I love you," he said. "I love you! Love you. Love you. Love you."

He was kissing her all the time he was telling her he loved her, and she was kissing him back, starting to cry with sheer happiness. She touched his cheek and felt that it was wet, too, but she didn't know whether it was wet from her tears or his. It didn't matter.

"YOU LOOK GREAT, Lum," Cal said, lying through his teeth. The old man looked awful, with both eyes blackened, a huge white turban around his head, and wires attached to almost every limb of his body.

"Damn it all, Cal!" Lum said.

"What?"

"I look like death warmed over, and you know it. Won't you ever learn how to lie properly?" Lum wasn't supposed to move his head, but he shifted his eyes to Elizabeth. "I've tried to teach him, but he won't listen to me. Can you do anything with him?"

"Not much," she said. "How are you feeling?"

"About like I look. But what I want to know is... what happened to Lance?"

"He's okay," Cal said, hurrying to reassure him on that score. "How much do you remember?"

"Well..." Lum squinted his eyes. "I remember going to visit Lance, and seeing that crooked deputy of yours trying to talk him into making a run for it... probably so's he could shoot him down later. I told Lance not to listen to the scoundrel, and then he hit me."

"Lance?" Cal asked, surprised.

"Not Lance. The scoundrel. And that's all I remember. What happened after that?"

"Lance left... got away clean. But he turned around and came back a short while later. He said he was worried about you, although I can't imagine why he would be."

"Ah," Lum said, closing his eyes and smiling.

"We found out that Lance is innocent of the car theft charges, too," Cal said.

Lum opened his eyes. "I coulda told you that a long time ago. That boy reminds me a lot of you, Cal, when you were his age. There's a lot of good in him, just like there was in you."

Cal looked at Elizabeth and saw there were tears in her eyes, along with a certain "I told you so" expression.

"I always said you were a good 'un," Lum continued. "Even when folks kept trying to tell me otherwise. And you've proved me right, Cal, time and again."

"I love you, Lum," Cal said, finding it surprisingly easy to say the words now that Elizabeth had finally gotten him started expressing his feelings. He blinked back the tears that were trying to form in his eyes, though, knowing they'd only embarrass his friend.

He looked on in amazement when he saw tears well up in Lum's eyes, too, before they finally overflowed and ran down the old man's cheeks. Cal turned to Elizabeth, but she was no help at all. She was crying openly, without bothering to hide the fact. She didn't even seem to mind!

"LET'S TRY TO KEEP things on a more even keel this time," Cal said to Elizabeth before they entered Lum's room on their next visit. Lum was doing much better, but the hospital still insisted the visits be kept short.

"What do you mean?" she asked innocently.

"You know—not be so emotional."

"Cal," she said sternly. "*I* wasn't the one who finally told my best friend on earth that I loved him. *I* wasn't the one who caused an old man to cry." She grinned wickedly then, and kissed him on the lips. "But I'm glad that *you* were."

Lum had obviously been expecting them. "What kept you so long?" he asked as soon as they walked into the room.

"Well, uh..." Cal said, hedging.

"We were in bed, Lum," Elizabeth said firmly. "But not asleep. If you know what I mean."

Lum cackled with delight. "I'm not so old I can't remember *that,*" he said.

Elizabeth walked over and kissed Lum on the cheek. After a moment, slightly embarrassed, Cal did the same. He was surprised when Lum didn't seem to mind. It was almost as if he expected it. "So what's new?" Cal asked Lum.

"Glad you asked. I've been thinking about my finances."

Cal was surprised again. He'd thought Lum was well-fixed, but maybe there'd been some reversals he hadn't heard about. "Don't worry about your hospital bill. I—"

"I'm not worried. I got plenty of money. Good insurance, too. But as the beneficiary of my will, you ought to know something."

Cal blinked. He hadn't even known he was the beneficiary of Lum's will. "What?"

"I was thinking I might dip into what I was going to leave you—not a whole lot, just a few thousand. The same amount I was going to loan you to go to college, remember?"

Cal remembered, all right, and remembered how deeply moved he'd been by the gesture. He also had a sneaking idea what Lum intended to do with the money now. "Are you thinking about making some other, uh, worthy student the same kind of deal you offered me? Lance, for instance?"

Lum grinned. "You hit the nail on the head."

Cal took Lum's hand and squeezed it. "I approve," he said. "Wholeheartedly. Not that you need my approval."

"The hell you say. It's your money . . . or will be."

"What on earth are you two talking about?" Elizabeth asked.

"I thought it was perfectly clear," Cal said, still holding Lum's hand. "Lum is going to send Lance to college."

"He is?" Elizabeth said. "That's wonderful!"

"I thought I might ask him to move in with me, too," Lum said. "Just for the summers and all, so's he'd have a permanent mailing address."

"He might prefer to live with you full-time," Cal said. "That way, he and Jacinda could commute to school together. I know for a fact that she has the use of Miss Maudie's car to drive them."

"That so?" Lum asked, obviously pleased with the prospect. Then he frowned. "If Lance moved in with me, I might not be able to cook your supper as often as I do now."

"Well, uh, I have a bit of news for you, too, Lum. I mean, Elizabeth and I do."

"You've gone and done it!" Lum exclaimed.

Cal looked at him with bewilderment, not having the foggiest idea what the old man was talking about. He turned to Elizabeth and she shrugged, obviously as much at sea as he was.

"Not *that*," Lum said. "I know you two been doing *that*, at least for the last week or so. I mean you've finally asked Elizabeth to marry you. And she's said yes, if she has as much sense as I think she does."

Elizabeth laughed. "You're right, Lum, on both counts. On *all* counts," she amended.

"Hot damn!" Lum said. "So when can I expect some grandkids? Or maybe one's already on the way."

"No," Elizabeth said emphatically.

"But we'll work on it," Cal said, looking at her, trying to tell her with his eyes how very much he loved her.

"Conscientiously," she said, promising him her love, too.

"As often as possible," he said.

Elizabeth and Cal both laughed with sheer happiness at the same time, and after a moment Lum joined them.

HARLEQUIN

Season's Greetings

Christmas cards from relatives and friends
wishing you love and happiness. Twinkling lights
in the nighttime sky. Christmas—the time for
magic, dreams...and possibly destiny?

Harlequin American Romance brings you
SEASON'S GREETINGS. When a magical, red-
cheeked, white-haired postman delivers long-lost
letters, the lives of four unsuspecting couples will
change forever.

Don't miss the chance to experience the magic of
Christmas with these special books, coming to
you from American Romance in December.

> #417 UNDER THE MISTLETOE
> by Rebecca Flanders
> #418 CHRISTMAS IN TOYLAND
> by Julie Kistler
> #419 AN ANGEL IN TIME
> by Stella Cameron
> #420 FOR AULD LANG SYNE
> by Pamela Browning

Christmas—the season when wishes *do* come true....

American Romance®

HISTORICAL

CHRISTMAS

STORIES·1991

Bring back heartwarming memories of Christmas past
with HISTORICAL CHRISTMAS STORIES 1991,
a collection of romantic stories
by three popular authors.
The perfect Christmas gift!

Don't miss these heartwarming stories,
available in November
wherever Harlequin books are sold:

CHRISTMAS YET TO COME
by Lynda Trent
A SEASON OF JOY
by Caryn Cameron
FORTUNE'S GIFT
by DeLoras Scott

**Best Wishes and Season's Greetings
from Harlequin!**

XM-91R

"INDULGE A LITTLE" SWEEPSTAKES

HERE'S HOW THE SWEEPSTAKES WORKS

NO PURCHASE NECESSARY

To enter each drawing, complete the appropriate Official Entry Form or a 3" by 5" index card by hand-printing your name, address and phone number and the trip destination that the entry is being submitted for (i.e., Walt Disney World Vacation Drawing, etc.) and mailing it to: Indulge '91 Subscribers-Only Sweepstakes, P.O. Box 1397, Buffalo, New York 14269-1397.

No responsibility is assumed for lost, late or misdirected mail. Entries must be sent separately with first class postage affixed, and be received by: 9/30/91 for the Walt Disney World Vacation Drawing, 10/31/91 for the Alaskan Cruise Drawing and 11/30/91 for the Hawaiian Vacation Drawing. Sweepstakes is open to residents of the U.S. and Canada, 21 years of age or older as of 11/7/91.

For complete rules, send a self-addressed, stamped (WA residents need not affix return postage) envelope to: Indulge '91 Subscribers-Only Sweepstakes Rules, P.O. Box 4005, Blair, NE 68009.

© 1991 HARLEQUIN ENTERPRISES LTD.   DIR-RL

"INDULGE A LITTLE" SWEEPSTAKES

HERE'S HOW THE SWEEPSTAKES WORKS

NO PURCHASE NECESSARY

To enter each drawing, complete the appropriate Official Entry Form or a 3" by 5" index card by hand-printing your name, address and phone number and the trip destination that the entry is being submitted for (i.e., Walt Disney World Vacation Drawing, etc.) and mailing it to: Indulge '91 Subscribers-Only Sweepstakes, P.O. Box 1397, Buffalo, New York 14269-1397.

No responsibility is assumed for lost, late or misdirected mail. Entries must be sent separately with first class postage affixed, and be received by: 9/30/91 for the Walt Disney World Vacation Drawing, 10/31/91 for the Alaskan Cruise Drawing and 11/30/91 for the Hawaiian Vacation Drawing. Sweepstakes is open to residents of the U.S. and Canada, 21 years of age or older as of 11/7/91.

For complete rules, send a self-addressed, stamped (WA residents need not affix return postage) envelope to: Indulge '91 Subscribers-Only Sweepstakes Rules, P.O. Box 4005, Blair, NE 68009.

© 1991 HARLEQUIN ENTERPRISES LTD.   DIR-RL

INDULGE A LITTLE—WIN A LOT!

Summer of '91 Subscribers-Only Sweepstakes

OFFICIAL ENTRY FORM

This entry must be received by: Nov. 30, 1991
This month's winner will be notified by: Dec. 7, 1991
Trip must be taken between: Jan. 7, 1992—Jan. 7, 1993

YES, I want to win the 3-Island Hawaiian vacation for two. I understand the prize includes round-trip airfare, first-class hotels and pocket money as revealed on the "wallet" scratch-off card.

Name _____

Address _____ Apt. _____

City _____

State/Prov. _____ Zip/Postal Code _____

Daytime phone number _____
(Area Code)

Return entries with invoice in envelope provided. Each book in this shipment has two entry coupons—and the more coupons you enter, the better your chances of winning!

© 1991 HARLEQUIN ENTERPRISES LTD.   3R-CPS

INDULGE A LITTLE—WIN A LOT!

Summer of '91 Subscribers-Only Sweepstakes

OFFICIAL ENTRY FORM

This entry must be received by: Nov. 30, 1991
This month's winner will be notified by: Dec. 7, 1991
Trip must be taken between: Jan. 7, 1992—Jan. 7, 1993

YES, I want to win the 3-Island Hawaiian vacation for two. I understand the prize includes round-trip airfare, first-class hotels and pocket money as revealed on the "wallet" scratch-off card.

Name _____

Address _____ Apt. _____

City _____

State/Prov. _____ Zip/Postal Code _____

Daytime phone number _____
(Area Code)

Return entries with invoice in envelope provided. Each book in this shipment has two entry coupons—and the more coupons you enter, the better your chances of winning!

© 1991 HARLEQUIN ENTERPRISES LTD.   3R-CPS